DEMON

Recent Titles by Christopher Nicole from Severn House

The Russian Sagas
THE SEEDS OF POWER
THE MASTERS
THE RED TIDE
THE RED GODS
THE SCARLET GENERATION
DEATH OF A TYRANT

The Arms of War Series
THE TRADE
SHADOWS IN THE SUN
GUNS IN THE DESERT
PRELUDE TO WAR

TO ALL ETERNITY
THE QUEST
BE NOT AFRAID
THE SEARCH
RANSOM ISLAND
POOR DARLING
THE PURSUIT
THE VOYAGE

DEMON

Christopher Nicole

This first world edition published in Great Britain 2003 by
SEVERN HOUSE PUBLISHERS LTD of
9–15 High Street, Sutton, Surrey SM1 1DF.
This first world edition published in the USA 2004 by
SEVERN HOUSE PUBLISHERS INC of
595 Madison Avenue, New York, N.Y. 10022.

Copyright © 2003 by Christopher Nicole.

All rights reserved.
The moral right of the author has been asserted.

British Library Cataloguing in Publication Data

Nicole, Christopher, 1930-
  Demon
  1. Hypnotism - Fiction
  2. Suspense fiction
  I. Title
  823.9'14 [F]

ISBN 0-7278-5887-4

Except where actual historical events and characters are being described for the storyline of this novel, all situations in this publication are fictitious and any resemblance to living persons is purely coincidental.

Typeset by Hewer Text Ltd.,
Edinburgh, Scotland.
Printed and bound in Great Britain by
MPG Books Ltd., Bodmin, Cornwall.

'What seest thou else
In the dark backward and abysm of time?'
William Shakespeare

The Court

'Please tell the court what you saw,' invited Sir Barton Travers. 'Beginning when you were called off the beat.'

A somewhat tall, stout man, the famous Defence Counsel intimidated most witnesses by merely looking at them. Certainly the police constable in the witness box was nervous; his evidence for the Prosecution had been merely that of finding the body – he had not anticipated a grilling. 'Well, sir, I was called by the night porter, who felt that something was wrong. It seems that the cleaning lady couldn't get into Sir Roderick's office, because the door was locked on the inside, although the light was on. She could see this under the door. It seems it wasn't like Sir Roderick to work all night, and she thought he might have been taken poorly. So I went upstairs with her to the directors' floor. Well, sir, the door was definitely locked, on the inside. And the light was definitely on. I tried knocking and calling, but there was no reply. So I called the station on my mobile, and Sergeant Broom said I should force the door.'

'Just one moment,' Sir Barton said. 'You and this cleaning lady' – he glanced at his notes – 'Mrs Gresham, were still alone in the building. Apart from Sir Roderick Webster, presumably. And the night porter. But he did not go up with you?'

'No, sir. He stayed at the street door. No one else had come in yet. It was only seven in the morning.'

'Very good. So you forced the office door. By yourself?'

'Well, sir . . .' PC Trewitt flushed. 'The Sergeant did say he was sending a car, but I had a go anyway. It wasn't difficult.' PC Trewitt was a large young man.

1

'So you forced the door, and . . . ?'

'Well, sir, there he was.'

'Sir Roderick. Where was he?'

'He was on the floor in front of his desk, half on his face.'

'What was he wearing?'

'Well, sir . . .' Another flush. 'Nothing. He was naked. Save for a medallion round his neck. One of those St Christopher things. Gold it was. So was the chain.'

'He was lying half on his face on the floor, naked save for a gold medallion. Now, you have testified that you saw no sign of a struggle or disturbance. What about the desk? Was anything disarranged? Any drawers open?'

'No, sir. It looked normal to me.'

'And did you form any impression as to how Sir Roderick might have died?'

'No, sir.'

'There were no bruises on the body?'

'None that I could see, sir. I didn't touch the body. As soon as I saw what had happened, I telephoned the station again. They told me that a doctor would be along in minutes.'

'You did not report that the death might be murder?'

'Well, no, sir. I thought Sir Roderick might have had a heart attack.'

'Quite so. So, to recapitulate, we have a man lying dead on the floor of his office, the door of which is locked on the inside. The man has no external signs of injury. Thus, very properly, you assumed he had died of natural causes. Do you have any idea when, or indeed how, it was concluded that he had been murdered?'

This was pure rhetoric. Sir Barton knew the answer to that, as he knew the answer PC Trewitt would give. He was out to impress the facts on the jury.

'No, sir. I have no idea,' PC Trewitt said.

'Thank you.' Sir Barton sat down.

Mr Wilcox, second for the Crown, was on his feet. 'I think we need to clear up this matter of the door, Constable.

You broke it open with a shoulder charge. One shoulder charge?'

'Well, sir, two.'

'But still, it was not a very difficult task for a strong young man. This is because, am I not right, the door was on a latch?'

'Yes, sir.'

'So, actually, you did not have to break down the door. You merely had to apply sufficient force to tear the latch out of the inside wall. So therefore, anyone inside the room, wishing to leave, with the door locked behind him, or her, would simply close it.'

'Yes, sir.'

'Thank you, Constable. I have no further questions.'

I felt the Prosecution had scored a point. But they still had a lot to prove. If it hadn't been for that letter . . .

One

The Locket

The surf was the biggest I have ever seen; I've never been to the Bahamas. These waves were ten, fifteen feet high, topped by curling white water, and came crashing down on the sand with a rumble of thunder. The locals called it a 'rage', and it had something to do with a storm out in the Atlantic; apart from the size of the swell there was no suggestion of bad weather in the Bahamas.

The boys of course were all for going in; we were full of the pina coladas we had had with our lunch. We didn't have boards, so we belly-surfed, wading or swimming out no more than thirty feet from the beach to be picked up and sent flying forward. It was great fun, although a bit awe-inspiring, and needless to say I was the first to come a cropper. I was picked up ass over tits and sent straight down to the bottom. The thud on my head made me suppose I had broken my spine, but a moment later I was on my feet, and being knocked down by the next roller; luckily this was in shallow water. 'You all right?' Eric, bending over me, big handsome face contorted.

I had known Eric long enough to be sure he was less concerned about me as a person than about my ability to perform in bed. But what the hell? It had been his idea to holiday in Eleuthera in the first place. 'I'm all right,' I said. 'Oh, hell!'

I had instinctively put my hand up to my throat to find the gold locket my parents had given me on my eighteenth birthday, and which had never left my neck in four years . . .

and it was gone. 'It'll be around,' Eric assured me. 'Mind you, I like you better without it.'

I realized the bra of my two-piece had also come off. But there didn't seem much point in attempting a cover-up; the six of us hadn't exactly been chaste on this holiday. On the other hand, there were two other people further along the beach, young men of indeterminate nationality, who were certainly watching us.

'They don't go for topless bathing in the Bahamas,' Maureen said. 'Not on public beaches, anyway.'

'You could drape your hair in front,' Bruce suggested.

'That's right,' Veronica agreed. 'You remember that film, *The Blue Max*?'

'For God's sake,' Tom said, 'that was made before you were born. Any of us.'

'They had it on the box recently,' Veronica said. 'Ursula Andress. She was in bed with George Peppard, and no matter what they did, her hair stayed in front of her boobs. I think they must have used glue.'

'Well,' Bruce said, 'Frankie's boobs are bigger than Ursula Andress's. But her hair is the same length, and the same colour . . . Trouble is we don't have any glue.'

'Look, just find the damn thing,' I said. 'It's the locket I'm worried about.'

'There it is,' Eric said, dashing into the surf.

But he was talking about the bra, floating about. I regained some decency. 'It'll have sunk to the bottom,' I said, utterly miserable.

Bruce surveyed the tumbling water. 'Then it's gone. I'm sorry, Frankie.'

'It was insured, wasn't it?' Veronica asked.

'I think so.' I tried to remember. As if it mattered. How could a cheque from an insurance company replace something of so much sentimental value?

'They probably won't pay up anyway,' Eric said, as unhelpfully as ever. 'They'll say you shouldn't have worn something like that to go surfing.' I felt like kicking him, but I didn't; he'd probably have kicked me back.

5

'Trouble?' asked one of the watching men, who had approached us unnoticed.

I looked up. It is very difficult to convey exactly how I felt at that moment, and I have done a great deal of thinking about it over the past six years. But I do know I was very powerfully affected. My immediate reaction was that I was embarrassed because he had obviously seen my naked breasts, but I also instantly knew it was more than that. Certainly he had a commanding physical presence. About six foot tall, he was a perfect mass of muscle – he was wearing only trunks – and wasn't lacking anywhere, although again that may have been the sight of me without a bra. His hair was black, and lank, his complexion a shade too swarthy for just sunburn. I reckoned he might have African blood in his background, although there was certainly not enough to describe him as a black man. His features were startlingly handsome, at once strong and decisive, and they were dominated by his eyes, which were dark and seemed fathomless, as if all the experience in the world lay behind their liquid force. For a moment I couldn't speak.

His companion was very definitely white, just as he was even more definitely Bahamian, with sun-bleached yellow hair and a placid expression.

'No trouble,' Bruce said, bristling; he could tell that all three of us girls were at the least interested.

I pulled myself together. 'I've lost my locket.'

'Valuable?' the dark man asked.

'Sentimental.'

'Then we'll see if we can find it for you.'

'In that surf?' Eric scoffed.

'You never know. Where are you staying?'

'The Ocean Lights.'

'I know it. And your name?'

'Frances Ogilvie.'

'Isn't that Irish?'

'Scottish. Once upon a time.'

'I will bring you your locket,' he said.

* * *

I felt that my day should be quite ruined, but it wasn't, even if I didn't believe for a moment that he and his friend – I didn't even know their names – could possibly find the locket. We straggled back into the old town, the boys predictably furious. 'Telling him your name, and where we're staying,' Bruce grumbled. 'You can see they're setting up to be nuisances.'

'On the make,' Eric suggested.

'Or just stalkers,' Tom put it.

'And if they do find the locket, you can bet they'll want a reward,' Bruce said.

'Oh, get knotted,' I snapped, and strode out in front of them.

The resort was known as Harbour Island, and was situated about half a mile off the much larger island of Eleuthera, in the very north-eastern part of the Bahamas. It was a place of some historical importance, as it was here that the Eleutheran Adventurers, on being expelled from Bermuda, some six hundred miles to the north, had apparently first come ashore, to bring, in the course of time, some order to the hitherto lawless communities of places like New Providence and its capital town of Nassau. Low-lying, like all the islands, it was frequently swept by hurricanes – in fact, it had been hit only a couple of years before and a lot of damage caused – but we had been assured that there was no risk of any of these in May, and in fact the weather couldn't have been better, with blue skies and a light north-westerly breeze, although there had to be something out there to have put up the 'rage'.

Our hotel was typical for the islands; our rooms were in one of several chalets surrounding a central building in which were situated the dining room and bar. As each chalet had only two bedrooms, Eric and I had one to ourselves, so when I got there first I locked the door. Then I had a shower and rinsed my hair to get rid of the salt. Predictably, I hadn't finished when he started banging on the door. 'Use the other one,' I shouted.

'For God's sake,' he complained. 'My clothes are in there.'

'You can come in when I'm ready to leave.'
'You really are a bitch.'
'Then you can sleep in the other room as well,' I said.
I knew I was being pretty bitchy – I wasn't really sure why – so I got dressed as quickly as possible, putting on a dress – again I didn't know why, as we always wore jeans or shorts – tied up my still wet hair, and unlocked the door. Eric was sitting on the step, looking at once morose and apologetic. 'You expecting company?' he asked.
'You never know.'
'Look, I'm sorry I called you a bitch. What came over you, anyway?'
'I'm upset about losing the locket,' I said.
'Oh. Right.' He seemed surprised that I should be. 'I'll make it up to you, tonight.'
The best reply I could think of was a snort, as I left him to it and walked across to the main building where I could have a glass of iced tea and sit on the verandah and look out at the view, which from here was mainly ocean, although there was a big ship on the horizon, heading for Fort Lauderdale after presumably having cruised the Caribbean. I remember thinking I'd enjoy a cruise, if they weren't so damned expensive.
'Hi!' I sat up and pulled down my dress; I had been sitting with my feet on the verandah rail and my skirt draped across my thighs; I had only a thong underneath. 'I didn't mean to startle you.'
His name was Roger Gaillard, and he had been a steward on our flight out. Then he had apparently had some time off, and had come to stay at the Ocean Lights. He was quite good-looking in a chunky fashion, and quite interesting to talk to, because he was a Bahamian born and bred. 'You didn't startle me,' I lied.
He sat on the rail facing me. 'Some surf this afternoon.'
'Did you try it?'
'Not me. I was watching from up here, saw you being thrown around.'

Another effing voyeur, I thought. But before I could choose some adequate put-down I saw two unmistakable figures coming up the path from the beach. I stood up. 'Hi!' the dark one called.

'I didn't expect to see you again.'

'Don't you want your locket back?'

I couldn't believe my ears – until he held it up, the chain draped around his fingers. It was definitely my locket, made of heavy gold and just under an inch in height. It opened, but I had never put a photo inside. 'However did you find it?'

'We found it.' He came to the foot of the steps.

I met him half way. 'I don't know how I can ever thank you.'

He stepped up to me, and put the chain around my neck. To fasten the clasp he had to touch me, all the while staring at me, from a distance of no more than a few inches; I felt positively weak. 'You can have dinner with me. Us.'

'Dinner? Here?'

'At our place.'

'You mean, you live in Harbour Island?' Somehow I hadn't supposed that.

'Sometimes. Let's go.'

Am I inviting rape? I wondered. But I couldn't be sure it would be – rape, that is. 'Just a moment.' I looked back at Roger. 'Will you tell my friends I'll see them later?'

'You sure you want to do that?' he asked. 'How're you doing, Damon?'

'I'm doing fine,' the dark man said.

'You two know each other?' I asked, stupidly.

'Everyone knows Damon,' Roger said.

'Oh!' I had a distinct feeling that the two men did not like each other. But I have never been into letting other people choose my friends for me. 'Roger, give the gang that message, will you.'

'They won't like it.'

'That's their business.' I picked up my shoulder bag, went down the steps. 'Is your name really Damon?'

'Sure. He's Roddy.'
'Doesn't he speak?'
'When he has something to say. Speak to Frances, Roddy.'
'I think you must be the most lovely girl in the world,' Roddy said.
'Oh, yes?' I knew I was blushing. 'Flattery will get you nowhere.'
'Roddy always tells the truth,' Damon said.
'I've always thought my nose was too long,' I suggested.
'Yeah, but the shape is fantastic. Makes one think of a ski jump.'
We turned up the path between the hotel and the next property, which led into the town proper. 'You haven't told me your other name,' I said.
'Smith.'
'I beg your pardon?'
'It's a fact. That was the name of my father. He was English.'
'Was?'
Damon shrugged. 'Could be. I haven't seen him in years. To tell the truth, I've never seen him. Not so I remember.'
'I'm sorry.'
'Why? He left me some good things. Like British nationality.'
'Yes, I can see that would be useful.' I had never really thought about the problems of *not* having British nationality. 'Certainly if you ever mean to go there,' I added.
'Sure I do. Do you work?'
'Of course. I work in a real estate office.'
'Say, that's great. So when I come over, you can find me some place to live.'
'Possibly,' I agreed, doubtfully. Even supposing he ever did come, our properties were way upmarket of his appearance. We had now crossed the couple of streets that made up the little town and were heading towards the yacht dock. 'Are we eating at the marina?' I asked.
'Too damned expensive. That's us, out there.' It was

getting dark now, and I looked across the water at a somewhat shabby sailing yacht anchored perhaps a hundred yards from the dock. It was about thirty feet long, and had two masts, with a raised cabin roof amidships.

'Gosh. How do we get to it?'

'The dinghy's right here.' He led me along the dock to the end, where there were several open boats tied.

'I should've changed into pants,' I said.

'You don't want to cover up those legs,' Roddy remarked. 'Ever!' I wondered if they both intended to have a go at me, and nearly turned and ran. But having come this far . . . and they *had* found my locket for me. Besides, thus far they had both been perfect gentlemen.

Damon had already descended the steps, and was standing on the pontoon, waiting for me. I followed him down, acutely conscious that my skirt was flaring in the breeze, but I needed to hold on to the rail. When I reached him he handed me into the boat, which rocked slightly. I hadn't had too much to do with boats. 'Sit,' he commanded. 'Amidships.'

I sat on the middle bench, and he got into the stern, where there was an outboard engine. Roddy got into the bow, behind me, and cast off, pushing the dinghy away from the other boats as he did so. Damon started the engine with a single tug on the cord and steered us away from the dock, while I realized that I had put myself entirely at their mercy. I couldn't even get back to dry land until they decided to take me; I'm quite a strong swimmer, but there was no way I was going into this water in the dark.

It took only a few minutes to reach the yacht. Damon cut the engine and we glided alongside. Roddy tied up. 'Up you go,' Damon said. 'Grab that stanchion and step over the rail.' In for a penny, in for a pound, I supposed, and besides, out here it was dark. I took off my flip-flops and threw them into the cockpit, stood up, grasped the stanchion, got one foot on to the toe rail, and swung my other leg over, then dropped down on to the grating that covered the cockpit deck. 'Well done.' Damon and Roddy followed. 'I think we could have a drink,' Damon said.

Roddy unlocked the hatch, pushed it back, and slid down the ladder into darkness. A moment later a light flared. 'Do you have electricity?' I asked.

'Sure. But that's an oil lamp. Anchored off we have no way of charging the batteries.'

'May I have a look?'

'Sure. Mind your head.'

Cautiously I stepped into the hatchway and went down the ladder into the saloon. I expected Damon to follow me, but he didn't. Roddy was mixing up some kind of a cocktail, standing at the table; the lantern hung from a hook in the cabin roof, which was so low the light brushed his shoulder every time the ship gave a slight roll. I had to sit on the settee berth on the other side to get round the table. 'You looking for the loo?' he asked. 'It's through that door, on the starboard side.'

'I'm just looking.' I sidled forward, stood up when I reached the end of the table, and opened the door in the bulkhead. The light from the lantern only just reached in here, but I made out a hanging locker on my left, a closed door on my right, and forward, a cabin which narrowed towards the bows, and which contained two bunks. Forward of that was another half door, above the bunks, which I assumed gave access to a sail locker.

'Looks very comfortable,' I said, and turned – into Roddy's arms, which immediately went round me while his hands slipped down to raise my skirt so that he could get at my bottom. 'Cut that out.' I pushed him away.

'That's right, cut that out.' Damon was sitting in the hatch. 'That's no way to treat a lady.'

Roddy stepped away from me, looking embarrassed. 'She's so sexy.'

'So we're lucky to have her company,' Damon pointed out. 'Try this.' Roddy had filled three plastic mugs, and he held one out. I sat on the settee and accepted the drink. I was only slightly ruffled; I felt that in his own way Roddy had paid me a compliment.

I tasted the drink, and gulped. It had a lot of rum in it. 'You wouldn't be trying to make me tight,' I suggested.

'Could be an idea,' Damon agreed. 'Let's go on deck. Roddy will make dinner.' I followed him up the ladder, aware that Roddy was staring at my legs, and Damon gestured me to a seat on the locker lid beside him. 'Isn't that romantic?'

Here we go, I thought. But it was an attractive sight, the lights glowing in the town, the stars gleaming in the sky, the moon just coming up out of the ocean, the gentle swish of the water past the hull . . . 'And not a bug in sight,' I remarked.

'That's the beauty of being on the water. They don't come out here.'

He put his arm round my shoulders, and I turned my head to look at him; in the darkness his gaze was less disturbing. 'I didn't come out here for . . . well . . . I'm very grateful, really, for your returning my locket. It really is important to me.'

'But not that important, right? You married to that fat guy?'

I supposed, on reflection, that Eric was a bit overweight. 'Hell, no. We have a relationship.'

'You live together?'

I couldn't imagine why I was answering all these very personal questions. 'I prefer to live alone. We spend most weekends together.'

'If I had you,' Damon said, 'I wouldn't let you out of my sight for a moment.'

'I'm sure you'd be bored stiff. Let's talk about you. You said your father was an Englishman. Your mother . . .'

'Was Haitian.'

'Haitian?'

'She had a Frenchman some way back in her family tree.'

'How romantic. But . . . you're living in the Bahamas.'

'Well, things ain't too good in Haiti right now. They were even worse twenty years ago, when Baby Doc was running things. So my mother left. Lots of people were doing that. They came up here in small boats. It was hairy. I just remember it.'

'How old were you?'

'Five.'

'Good lord! But the Bahamas took you in.'

He grinned. 'Not fucking likely. We were illegal immigrants. I still would be, if I hadn't got hold of a British passport. Thanks to Daddy. He ran off years ago. When I was two. I told you I don't even know what he looked like. But Mummy told me about him, and after she died, I got a smart-ass lawyer down in Nassau to check things out for me. So he did, and got me British citizenship. I'm still an immigrant as regards the Bahamas, but he got me a work permit too.'

'That must have cost a lot of money.'

'It did,' he agreed.

'But coming across the sea in a small boat . . . Suppose there'd been a storm?'

'There was. One of the other boats sank, and a lot of people were drowned. But we were all right. My Mummy knew we'd be all right. She was a mamaloi. A voodoo priestess.'

Two

The Spell

I didn't know whether to be scared, or laugh. 'You mean your mother practises voodoo, here in the Bahamas?'

'My mother is dead. She died just after Christmas.'

'Oh. I'm so sorry.' I really was, but mainly for making fun of her.

'She led a good life. But now she's gone is why I can think of going away,' Damon explained. 'I couldn't while she lived, and she didn't wish to travel again. I don't think there is any voodoo in the Bahamas. But it is very important in Haiti.'

'You don't mean you believe in it?'

He did not reply for a few moments, and now I did begin to feel scared; even by the time I was twenty-two I had learned that it is not a good thing to poke fun at someone's religion. Was voodoo a religion? 'Believe in what?' he asked.

'Well . . . you know. Sacrificing cockerels. Dancing naked to the tom-toms. Cutting off a man's head and then replacing it so that he comes back to life. Being able to kill someone by putting a spell on them. I've read about it.'

'And you regard that as nonsense.'

'Well, isn't it?'

'Oh, certainly. Most of it.' A wave of relief swept over me. 'But its power cannot be denied,' he went on.

'Surely that only applies to essentially simple people,' I argued.

'All people are essentially simple, in one direction or another. Tell me, are you a Christian?'

'Of course.'

'You mean you go to church.'

'Well, not very often, I'm afraid. But I believe in God.'

'You believe in Jesus Christ?'

'Of course.'

'What as? Do you believe he is God? Or God in another form? Or the Son of God? Or just a supernatural being? Or perhaps even just a human being, a great prophet.'

'I have to confess that I've never thought very deeply about it.'

'Yet you believe in it.' There was a slightly cynical lift of one eyebrow, a twist in the corner of his soft, sensuous lips.

'Well . . .' I began to feel like another drink.

'You believe in it,' Damon said, 'because your parents brought you up to believe in it, as their parents had before them and so on back maybe two thousand years. Do you believe in the miracles Christ is supposed to have performed?'

'I've always felt there was a rational explanation for them.'

'But you have no doubt they happened.'

'Well, there were witnesses.'

'There you have it. Ten, twenty, a hundred, even a thousand people say *this* happened, and everyone believes that it did, for the rest of time. But no one knows for certain what those people actually saw, what they were *made* to see.'

'It's a matter of faith,' I said. 'All religion is based on faith.'

'Exactly. But what is faith? Mass hypnotism. Brainwashing, if you like.'

'Oh, come now. How do you hypnotize several hundred people at a time?'

'Just as easily as you can hypnotize one person. Perhaps even more easily, because belief, or faith, is contagious. Where I believe strongly enough, and you are sceptical, unless your scepticism is greater than my belief, you will eventually, perhaps quite soon, come to believe also.'

This was getting altogether too serious. 'You'll be attempting to convert me to voodooism next,' I said, shivering.

Demon

The soft Bahamian night was warm, but suddenly I felt distinctly chilly.

He gave me another of those penetrating stares, and I was grateful for the darkness. Even more was I grateful to hear Roddy calling, 'Grub's up.'

We ate in the cabin, and the food, some kind of stir fry, was surprisingly tasty, washed down as it was with some more of the rum punch. I began to feel quite light-headed, but it wasn't only the punch; I had a feeling that a lot more was going to happen this evening. Did I want that? I couldn't be sure. I found Damon a most attractive as well as fascinating man, not least because he was also slightly sinister. But I didn't want to sleep with him. This was certainly partly because of AIDS, but equally I do not believe in letting any man into my bed until I have known him far longer than a few hours; perhaps, and more importantly than either of the other reasons, it was because I feared the power of his personality, and that if I gave in to him I might find myself totally taken over. During supper, however, the conversation was easy enough, and it was I who, perhaps stupidly – but I was quite tight after my third rum punch – returned to the subject. 'Do you believe in this voodoo thing?' I asked Roddy.

He flicked his long blond hair back off his face and looked at Damon before replying. 'Sure thing. It's the best.'

'Frances thinks it's all rubbish,' Damon said, grinning.

'You agreed with me,' I reminded him.

'Sure. Everything that is supposed to happen is nonsense. But if enough people *believe* it is happening, then it becomes true. That is the power of mass hypnosis. It operates on several levels. At the top level it has to be very powerful indeed. Thus at a voodoo ceremony, the acolytes first of all have a great deal to drink. This inflames their senses, at the same time as those senses are being numbed and obsessed by the cadence of the drums. The sacrifice of a fowl cock is real, and necessary. Blood flies, and the senses are further aroused and distorted. Then it is easy for the mamaloi and the hougan

– the male priest – all the while invoking Damballa and our other gods, to convince the worshippers that a man's head is actually cut off and replaced, while a little bit of sleight of hand has more blood flying. Then the orgiastic dancing follows, and the power of the hypnosis is gradually decreased by the loss of energy. But it is never entirely dispelled. Those people believe in what they saw for the rest of their lives.'

'You mean it is all a charade. If one person were to stand up and say, this is nonsense, the whole ceremony would collapse.'

'Anyone who tried to stop a voodoo ceremony would be torn to pieces by the worshippers,' he replied seriously. Ominously.

I gulped, but still wanted to argue the point. 'But you have never seen any of this happen.'

'No I haven't. But I have been told about it by my mother. She gave me all her knowledge. If I was still living in Haiti I'd be a famous hougan by now.'

I smiled at him. 'I believe you. Thousands wouldn't.'

'Would you like a demonstration of my power?'

The alarm bells returned. 'I said, I believe you. But I do think I should be getting back. Otherwise my friends will be turning out the police to find me.'

'It will not take five minutes; then I will take you home. I promise.'

'Well . . . all right. What exactly are you going to do?'

'I am going to hypnotize you.'

'You'll be lucky. I've had professionals try that, at parties, and it hasn't worked.'

'I am a hougan,' he said simply.

'But you don't have any bongo drums, or chickens.'

'I am not intending to send you into a frenzy,' he laughed.

'Thank God for that. I do mean to resist you.'

'Of course. You should. Roddy.' Roddy started clapping his hands together, very rhythmically, at the same time humming. It was not a tune I had ever heard before, but it had a definitely soporific cadence to it. 'Look at me,' Damon said. I obeyed, and was enveloped in his gaze. None of the professional party hypnotists I could remember had ever looked at me like that; they had relied on the movement of some compelling object. I realized that Damon was moving his hands – exactly to what purpose I couldn't tell – as I continued to stare into his eyes. I was not aware of feeling anything, except perhaps a sense of total relaxation, as if my entire being was in someone else's keeping. Well, it was. 'Now,' he said, 'I wish you to understand that whatever I ask you to do, you will do, entirely of your own free will, because you wish to please me.'

'Yes,' I said, and was surprised. I hadn't intended to reply.

'Very well. Take off your dress.' And why not, I wondered? Hadn't I known it was going to come to this, even before I accepted his invitation? The ceiling wasn't high enough for me to stand straight, so I unbuckled my cloth belt, raised myself from the seat, and lifted the dress over my head. I wasn't wearing a bra – I never did, except for work – but unlike this afternoon on the beach I didn't feel the least embarrassed. 'Now the thong.' I slid it down to my thighs, then again raised myself to slip it right off. 'You are a very lovely creature,' he said. 'Now, if I were one of your professional entertainers, I would tell you to forget everything that has happened. But I am not going to do that. I want you to remember everything that has happened, and remember too that you did it of your own free will, to please me. Now.' He did not snap his fingers, but instead passed his hand over my eyes, without touching me, while Roddy fell silent.

For a moment I did not realize what had happened, then I looked down at myself. 'Oh, my God!' I gasped.

'You wanted to,' Damon reminded me. I realized I *had* wanted to. In a moment of total madness! And neither of them had touched me! Embarrassment was tinged with a feeling of total humiliation, which increased as I instinctively, and quite inadequately, tried to cover my breasts and my pubes at the same time – I would have needed at least three pairs of hands. 'Why don't you get dressed?' Damon suggested. 'Then I can take you home.'

I dragged up my thong, knelt on the bunk, my back turned to them both, while I dropped my dress over my head, smoothed it on my thighs, and fastened the belt. I could feel the tremendous heat in my cheeks, but there seemed to be heat everywhere. Damon went up to the cockpit to pick up my shoes. Then he waited for me. I turned round, put my feet on the deck, and glanced at Roddy, who seemed entirely unaffected by what had happened. 'I'll say goodnight. It was a lovely meal.'

'Glad you liked it. I'll see you again.'

Not bloody likely, I thought, but I got a smile going. 'Sounds like fun.'

Damon handed me down into the dinghy, and I sat amidships, clutching my flip-flops against my chest while he started the outboard and headed for the shore. I felt I should say something, but I couldn't think what, and in any event it was difficult to talk over the noise of the engine. But eventually he cut it and we glided into the steps at the end of the marina dock. Damon stepped out, made the painter fast, and turned to offer me his hand. His grip was cool. 'Thank you for a most interesting evening,' I said.

'I'll walk you home.'

'I can manage.'

'It's after eleven. Not a good time for a pretty young woman to walk the streets alone.'

I didn't really have an answer to that, so I walked beside him up the street. Yet I couldn't leave things the way they were. I couldn't believe I had sat naked between two men and neither had made the slightest attempt to touch me. There could only be one explanation, however disappointing that might be. 'I guess you're not into women,' I remarked.

'What makes you say that?'

'Well . . .' I flushed again, although presumably he couldn't see it in the darkness.

'We're not gay,' he said. 'Unless we feel like it.'

'And you felt like it tonight.'

'Not in the least. I will make love to you, when the time is right.'

'You're very confident.' I gave a short, sharp laugh. 'When do you suppose the time will be right? We go home the day after tomorrow.'

'I will come to see you, in England. To have tried it tonight, on board my yacht, would have been to take advantage of you. I know you will be there, when I am ready.'

His total, arrogant confidence quite took my breath away. I had to riposte. 'And you think I'll wait for you to turn up? What about Eric?'

'You will get rid of him as soon as you return home. As for waiting for me, why yes, that *is* what you will do. And until I come to you, you will not have sex with anyone else. Even if you wish to, and try to, you won't. You must understand, Frances.' He smiled down at me. 'I have put my mark on you, in your brain. It is there for ever. It does not matter that we are going to be separated for a while. You will still be mine.'

We had reached the hotel. I didn't want to end what had been certainly an interesting evening by telling him that he had to be as mad as a March hare. 'Perhaps you'd like to come in for a drink,' I said. The lights were still on in the bar.

'No.' The whites of his eyes and his big, even teeth were gleaming in the surrounding darkness.

'Oh, right. Well, thanks again for returning my locket. I suppose you will claim that it was magic that helped you find it.'

'Magic,' he laughed. 'Magic is an illusion.' But there was no humour in his laughter.

'I hope you're not trying to tell me that the locket is an illusion?' I closed my hand over it. It felt real enough.

'As long as you believe it is real, then it is real.'

Another conversation stopper. 'Well . . . then it's goodbye. Do voodoo worshippers kiss when they part?'

'You should not make fun of things you do not yet understand,' he admonished. 'I will not kiss you, tonight.'

'Oh. Right then.' I held out my hand, and he gave it a gentle squeeze.

'It will not be long,' he said, and disappeared into the darkness.

It took me several minutes to pluck up the courage to go into the bar. I do not remember ever having been so confused in my life. Clearly I had, for all my certainty that it could not happen, been hypnotized for several minutes, without actually being aware of it. And I had done something I would never have dreamed possible either: that I should calmly strip myself naked before two utter strangers.

But as much as I was ashamed of myself for what I had done, I could not deny that I had wanted to do it – because I had been told that was how I should feel? And then, not to be touched, when I had been expecting it, perhaps even anticipating it! My brain, and my body, had been taken over by an alien force, one so confident in its power it could put me aside for another, and perhaps better, occasion. *I have put my mark on you, in your brain. It is there for ever.* That was of course the most utter nonsense. I would awaken tomorrow morning and the whole thing would have been a stupid nightmare. Would it have been a nightmare? I climbed the steps and walked across the verandah. The bar was still quite full, including the gang. 'Well, hey!' Bruce called. 'Look who's back!'

'We were just about to turn out the national guard, or whatever it is they have around here,' Tom said.

Veronica got up, and peered at me. 'You look as if you've seen a ghost.'

'Just tired.'

'So where have you been?' Eric demanded, also getting up. 'I think you owe us an explanation.'

'I don't owe you anything at all,' I told him.

He glared at me, but Veronica had been more observant than any of the others. 'You're wearing your locket!' she cried.

'I always do.'

'But . . . it was lost in the surf.'

'Now I have it back.'

Eric pointed. 'Those fellows. That darkie. You've been with that darkie.'

'I'm going to bed,' I said. 'Alone. You can sleep next door. I'll put your things out.'

It apparently took him several minutes to get his act together. I was actually in the room and throwing his clothes and toiletries on to the little porch when he arrived, panting. 'Just what the hell do you think you're playing at?'

'I think you and I have come to an end.'

'You bitch!' he said. 'That darkie . . . he's had you!'

'No one has had me. And no one is going to, either.' I turned away from him and went through the doorway, but before I could close the door he launched himself at me. I saw him coming and got my hands up. We were roughly the same height, but he was much the heavier, and his weight propelled me across the room so that I fell over the first bed, Eric on top.

'Bitch,' he said again. 'You're my girl. *Mine*, do you hear?'

'Get off,' I gasped, thumping him on the back. For reply he began pulling my dress up to my waist and snatching at my thong, all the while nuzzling my neck and sucking at my flesh. I was really angry by now. Hitting him on the back wasn't doing any good. I tried pulling his hair, but that didn't have any effect either. But then he pushed himself up to release his pants. As my thong was now just above my knees I had to use both legs together, but I got them up, between his own, as hard as I could. He gave a little scream, and fell off me, on to the bed and then the floor, clutching his dick in both hands and moaning. I pulled up my thong and stood above him. 'Move your hands and I'll stamp on him,' I threatened.

Veronica appeared in the doorway. 'You all right?' She peered at Eric. 'My God! Is *he* all right?'

'Why don't you ask him?' I kicked him in the thigh. 'Get out.'

He crawled to the doorway, still groaning. The others had arrived by now. 'This looks like the end of a perfect friendship,' Bruce remarked.

'It was never perfect,' I told them, and locked the door.

That certainly put the kibosh on our holiday, at least as far as I was concerned. I was clearly considered the guilty party. Nobody spoke to me at breakfast, and after the meal they all went off together, making it clear that I was not welcome. I wouldn't have gone anyway. Instead I went down to the marina, but the little yacht was no longer there; they must have sailed at first light. Had they ever *been* there? I clasped my locket. Had it ever been lost? And if it had, how had they found it? I was as confused today as I had been last night.

It was impossible to avoid the others. There was lunch. Then there was a long afternoon, which I spent in bed reading a book. Then there was supper, then early to bed and my book, leaving them in the bar. But the next day there was the boat trip across to the landing on Eleuthera, then the taxi drive to the airport, and then the flight in a small plane to Miami – I was seated next to Veronica, but as she studiously ignored me, I spent my time looking out of the window. We landed at Miami in time for lunch, and then had the afternoon to kill, as the London flight didn't leave until six. The others got a taxi and went off to Marine World. They didn't invite me, and again I wouldn't have gone anyway. I tucked myself away in a corner of the huge concourse and finished my book. Then I made sure I got a separate seat for the long overnight flight home.

I couldn't have been more relieved to regain the privacy of my flat. It was very small, with a single bedroom, a lounge/diner/kitchen, and a bathroom. But it was in a quiet square off King Street, Hammersmith, and once I had locked the door behind myself I felt utterly secure.

This was all mine, as long as I paid the rent. I had furnished it entirely to my taste. A sofa and two matching armchairs before the twenty-seven-inch TV screen, with a VCR and a stack of videos underneath, a drinks cabinet covered in family photos, and pale, fake parquet flooring with scatter rugs, a full bookcase, and a couple of sub-Picasso-blues on the wall. Very sub; I couldn't even decipher the artist's name. But they suited my present mood. The kitchenette was all mod con, but the bedroom was my pièce de résistance. It was a small room, ten feet square, and eighty per cent of the area was taken up by the king-size bed. To get to the chest of drawers on the far side of the room you had to crawl across the duvet. I was very fond of that bed, for a variety of reasons. There was a TV in here as well, somewhat smaller than the one in the lounge, and I liked nothing better after a day at the office or showing people houses than to get in here and relax, mostly alone; as I had told Damon, Eric only came in on weekends, and even that was now history.

I telephoned Mummy to let her know I was back – they lived in Hastings. 'Oh, darling,' she said. 'Did you have a good time?'

'Different.'

'You must tell us all about it. When are we going to see you?'

For the first time in my life I didn't actually want to see them, right then. 'It'll have to be next weekend. I'm due at the office tomorrow morning.' This was a lie; I had deliberately left myself an extra day's holiday to sort myself out before going back to work. But I felt I needed the rest of the week before facing my parents. Not that I had any intention of telling them about Damon. But I would have to tell them that Eric and I had split, and although I knew they had never actually gone for Eric, there would inevitably be questions asked and I wasn't in the mood for that. I would, in any event, have to answer questions as to the holiday at work. But for the next forty-eight hours I just wanted to be alone, and remember, and think. As it was still only just past ten, I went out to buy some groceries, then returned home, locked the door, and went to bed. At some time during the next couple of hours the phone rang, but I ignored it. When I got up I called 1471, and discovered it had been Veronica. Bugger her, I thought.

Had it really happened? Had I really stripped off in front of those guys? Suppose Damon did turn up in London, claiming what he apparently considered his rights? I belonged to him, in his eyes. Well, bugger *that*. But if he did turn up . . .

Of course he wouldn't. That had been pie in the sky. He didn't even have my address. But the very thought gave me goose pimples.

Getting back to work helped. There had been an interest rate cut while I was away, and although it had only been a quarter point it had, as always, stimulated the market and there was a constant stream of would-be clients wishing to look at properties. As it was company policy never to let the female agents go out on their own, I always had someone with me, and more often than not it was a young man named Jeremy Nichols. Jeremy was actually older than myself, by a couple of years, but I had been with the firm longer than him, and so had seniority. I knew he was interested in me, but he wasn't the only one. I wouldn't care to comment on Roddy's remark that I was the most beautiful woman he had ever seen, but I knew that with my long straight blonde hair, my equally long legs, my good boobs, and my well-shaped features, I was certainly worth a second look. Not that I had ever thrown it about. And as for the past year, Eric and I had been an item; I had hardly looked at another man.

But now Eric and I were no longer an item, and I had something to prove, at least to myself. And Jeremy was a good-looking man. On the Friday we showed this couple a house they were interested in, in south London. The vendors were away – they had another house in Spain, and were contemplating moving down there altogether – and they had left the house in complete working order, as it were, sheets on the bed . . . One almost expected to find a joint in the oven. The would-be purchasers were impressed, and said they would let us know the following week. They had come in their own car, and we stood on the front porch and watched them drive away, chattering to each other. ' I think we may have a sale,' Jeremy said.

'Hope springs eternal.' I looked at my watch. 'No point in going back to the office until this afternoon. I'm for an early lunch. Dutch?'

'Why not.' We found a neat little trattoria quite close to the property, studied each other's methods of eating spaghetti. 'Rumour has it you and that Glossop fellow have split,' Jeremy remarked.

'Rumour gets around.'

'So you're footloose and fancy-free.'

'And enjoying it.'

'Don't you ever get lonely?'

'Not yet.' But I smiled at him as I spoke. This was necessary for my peace of mind. *And until I come to you, you will not have sex with anyone else.* Well, I didn't think I any longer had any desire to sleep with Eric. But no other man? I couldn't wait the rest of my life.

Jeremy was sufficiently quick on the uptake. 'You know,' he said, 'I don't think we got the measurements of that house absolutely right. I think we should go back and check them out. We don't want any slip-ups with this sale.'

I finished my coffee. 'Good point.' We paid the bill, both of us I suspect feeling the adrenalin starting to flow, then got back into the company car and returned to the property. Jeremy unlocked the front door, and then locked it again behind us. Then we stood against each other for a long, deep kiss. 'This is terribly unethical,' I said.

'Having it off with a fellow member of staff?'

'That too, I suppose. But having it off in a client's house!'

'We'll use the spare room,' he decided.

We went up the stairs, holding hands, just like two young lovers. Well, that is what we were – or at least, what we were intending to be. I was quite excited. When one has a fairly long-standing affair one gets used to your partner's habits, how he likes to do things, where he likes to touch, how long it takes him to get off . . . and then it's done and one has to start all over again with someone else, a new set of rhythms.

I was wearing my usual working gear of navy blue trouser suit with a white shirt, and faced him to undress, so that I could watch him and he could look at me. When I took off my shirt he commented, 'That's a whopper.'

I unfastened my bra. 'I have a matching pair.'

'I was talking about that locket. Do you wear it . . . well . . .'

'It never leaves my neck.'

'Ah.' He was obviously wondering if he would lose any teeth if I started bouncing up and down on top of him. But when I was naked, he said, 'Has anyone ever told you that—'

'Please don't say it.'

He raised his eyebrows. 'Don't you like compliments?'

'Not that one.'

'Ah! You mean someone has.' That killed it stone dead. I didn't mean it to happen. We lay on the bed together, and kissed passionately, rubbing our bodies against each other. He stroked my bottom and my breasts and my pubes, put his hand between, and there was nothing. I tried holding him, but that didn't have any result either, on me at least. He got the message, suddenly released me and rolled away. 'No turn-on.'

I rose on my elbow. 'I'm sorry.'

'So am I.' He got out of bed. 'I had no idea Glossop could possibly have that effect on a woman.'

'It has nothing to do with Eric,' I said without thinking.

'So it is me.'

'No!' I pulled up my knees and hugged them. 'I *am* sorry. Sorry, sorry, sorry. More sorry than I can possibly convey. Maybe some other time.'

'I'll keep it in mind. You'd better get dressed. We should be getting back.'

I obeyed, checked that my hair wasn't too untidy, and followed him down to the car. When we stopped in our parking bay, I put my hand on his arm. 'Still friends?'

'Anything you say,' he agreed. But he freed his arm and got out.

I tried to rationalize what had happened, sitting alone in my flat that evening, drinking a glass of wine. *And until I come to you, you will not have sex with anyone else.* That had to be absurd. But it was just possible that Jeremy's attempt to describe me in the same words Damon had used had turned me off. Only Damon hadn't actually used those words – it had been Roddy. Well, then, delayed reaction from Eric? But every time I thought of Eric I was merely glad it was over. How had I ever gone for him in the first place?

So, then, Jeremy had been a turn-off after all. But I knew that wasn't true either. Up to the moment of those fatal words he had been a distinct turn-*on*. Those words had reminded me of Damon – and what he had said – with an immediate and inhibiting result. So what? I could *not* be a victim of a continuing hypnosis at a distance of four thousand miles. Not, not, not! But how to prove it? Go out and pick some man off the street? What sort of a turn-on would that be? I giggled at the very idea.

Next morning I took the train down to Hastings, which was shrouded in a heat haze far warmer than it had been in Harbour Island. Ma and Pa's flat overlooked the crowded beach and the English Channel, lazily calm. 'You've had some sun,' Pa remarked, giving me a hug and a kiss.

One never knew with Pa how much he knew, or remembered what he had been told; he enjoyed his reputation for absent-mindedness. 'I've been in the Bahamas,' I reminded him.

'Is that a fact? Whatever for?'

'To have some sun.' I turned my attention to Ma, who had come bustling out of the kitchen.

'You must try this cake I bought at the church bazaar,' she said. 'It looks rather good.' But Ma had far more nous than she pretended, and after tea, when Pa was settled in front of the box watching a cricket match, she remarked, 'Now tell me what happened.'

'What makes you think something happened?'

'You look different.'

I got up and peered at myself in the mirror, as if I didn't do this several times a day anyway. 'In what way?'

'Your eyes.'

Another peer. Then I sat down again. 'I really can't see anything different about my eyes.'

'Because they're *your* eyes,' she pointed out, with devastating logic. 'Something happened out there.' She waited.

'I split with Eric.'

'Oh, dear. Mind you, I always knew he wasn't right for you. You were on different sides of the social divide.' Ma was a bit of a snob. But then, most mothers are, when it comes to their children. 'But in the middle of a holiday.' She frowned. 'He hadn't paid for it, had he?'

'We each paid our own way. And it wasn't in the middle. It was two nights before we were due to leave.'

'But even so . . . Was it a quarrel? Or a mutual thing?'

'He tried to rape me.'

'Oh! But I thought . . .'

'We did, regularly. But there are times when a girl doesn't feel like it, and then she expects her partner to understand.'

'Oh . . . yes. I quite see that.' I wasn't at all sure she did. Ma had been my age in the late sixties, and although she had never talked about it, from what I had read it had been a time when anything could happen, and one simply got on with it. Of course out of that had come the totally liberated nineties and what was promising to be an even more liberated new century, so I had no right to complain. But there was a bit of a generation gap. 'So what is the plan now?' she asked.

'A little bit of R and R.'
'I'm sure you haven't told me everything.'
'Because of my eyes?'
'Well, they are different,' she insisted. 'As if you had looked at something, well . . . unpleasant. Or perhaps frightening.'
'Have you ever been raped?'
'Of course I haven't.'
'Well, I can tell you that as an experience it is both unpleasant and frightening.'
'You mean he actually . . .'
'No he didn't.' I said. 'I kicked him in the whatsit. But it was still both unpleasant and frightening.'

I lay awake in bed that night. Because although I hadn't actually been raped, I felt as if I had, twice. Once by Eric and the other time . . . But neither of them had actually touched me. What was I to do? Be rational! Damon himself had said that all the supernatural aspects of voodooism were fake; they only appeared real to the people who believed in them. Thus any idea that he had put some kind of an evil eye on me to stop me having sex had equally to be unreal; it only existed because I believed it did. Step number one was therefore to cure myself of that belief.

But how did I do that? Or to be precise, how did I know I had done that, until I actually found myself in bed with another man? And with what man? I felt I needed someone whom I knew very, very well, and I didn't know any men particularly well, except for Eric. I almost contemplated calling him and making it up. I didn't doubt he would go for it. But the idea was simply repulsive, not to mention the fact that when he found out I was just experimenting, as he almost certainly would, there would be a blazing row, and I didn't think I could handle another one of those right now.

By morning I had come to a decision. I had always had a total contempt for shrinks, or for those who thought they needed them. But I needed someone to talk to, someone who would have to listen without getting emotionally involved and who should be able to give me some rational advice. It was not something I dared ask anyone about, so when I got back up to town on Sunday afternoon I hunted through the yellow pages. The trouble with the yellow pages is that they don't carry photographs, so one is choosing blind. And there were an awful lot of psychiatrists listed, some of them with distinctly odd names. I wanted someone who was absolutely British, and hopefully down to earth, and finally settled on JRE Smith-Lucas, with a string of initials after his name.

I telephoned from the office the next morning, and got an appointment for three o'clock on Wednesday afternoon. Mr Randell quite happily gave me an hour off; I had always had the notion that but for his dragon of a wife he would have sunk his teeth into me himself. I was very nervous as I took a taxi right across town to Hampstead. I was really breaking the mould. But I suspected my mould had been broken for me.

The house was old and reassuringly ordinary, but there was a brass plate. I wondered if the taxi-driver had known what it was. But he drove off without a word, while I remained on the pavement, pretending I was looking for the right address. Having made sure there was nobody about, I climbed the steps and rang the bell, and after a few moments the door was opened by a very pleasant-looking middle-aged woman who, to my great relief, was not wearing uniform. 'I have an appointment with Dr Smith-Lucas,' I explained.

'You'll be Miss Ogilvie,' she remarked. 'Or is it Mrs?' She allowed me into a neatly furnished front hall.

'It's miss.'

'Of course. Will you wait in here?'

Again, a pleasantly furnished room, with the usual centre table and a collection of magazines. I turned these over, and was pleased to find there was no *Psychiatrist's Journal* or whatever. I picked up a *House & Gardens*, sat down, but had only turned the first page when an inner door opened. 'Miss Ogilvie?'

I stood up. This was another woman, only in her mid-thirties, I estimated, handsome in a strong fashion, not very tall, with a solid figure and jet black hair cut short, wearing a dress and low-heeled shoes and looking perfectly ordinary. I felt enormously relieved; I was wearing my blue suit. 'Will you come in, please?' I stepped past her into an office, which had all the trappings I would have expected, that is, a large desk on which there was a PC, a standing lamp, several filing cabinets, thick carpet on the floor . . . and a chaise longue.

'I'm to see Dr Smith-Lucas,' I explained.

'I am Jetta Smith-Lucas,' she said. 'And I'm Mrs, not Dr.'

'Oh,' I said, all my apprehensions rushing back.

'You didn't know I was a woman. Wasn't I recommended by someone?'

'As a matter of fact, I picked your name from the yellow pages.'

She smiled. 'Original. Although, as you have discovered, possibly disconcerting. Would you like to leave?'

'Eh?'

'Well, you see, psychiatric treatment only works if there is complete trust between doctor and patient. We cannot possibly create a complete trust if you are the slightest bit uneasy about dealing with a woman.'

'No, no,' I said. 'I'm rather glad you're a woman.' It would certainly be less embarrassing.

'Well, then, have a seat.' She indicated the chaise longue.

'Do you wish me to lie down?'

'Only if you feel like it.' I sat down. 'What I need you to do,' she said, 'is relax. Most people find this easier to do lying down. But let's get some facts down first.' She sat behind her desk, and laid a pad of paper in front of her.

'You mean I don't talk into a tape recorder?' I asked.

'I'll load these notes into the computer later, and perhaps add some of my own. Now let's see. Your full name is Frances . . .' She paused.

'Anne.'

'Frances Anne Ogilvie. Date of birth?'
'11 December 1974.'
'A Sagittarian.'
'Do you believe in that?'
'As regards foretelling the future, no. As regards various characteristics, it can provide an insight.'
'If you mean, am I wildly romantic and inconsequent, I'm afraid that's probably true.'
'It's always valuable to be able to observe oneself objectively,' she remarked. 'Now status. Presently single. Divorced?'
'No.'
'Partner?'
'No.' She glanced at me, and raised her eyebrows. 'I'm in between,' I explained.
She made a note. 'How long?'
'Oh, about ten days.'
'M or F?'
'Oh, M.'
'You don't go in for F?'
'I've never tried. I've never even thought about it.'
'Okay. So let's talk. About your partner?'
I decided to lie down, so I kicked off my shoes and stretched out. 'We went to the Bahamas on holiday. Six of us.'
'Both sexes?'
'Three of each.'
'And something happened.'
'Well, yes. I met this guy.'
'Good-looking?'
'You could say, wow.'
'So you went for him instead of current. That's not altogether unique. You don't share too much, do you? I mean, joint mortgage, something like that?'
'Our lives were completely separate, except for bed.'
'Then I don't see the problem. Or is he making threats?'
'No, no. He's not that sort of bloke. It's the other one.'

She waited, pencil poised. 'He hypnotized me.' I felt a complete fool.

'Say again?'

'He hypnotized me. He told me he was going to do it, and I laughed at him. People have tried that before, people at parties and things like that. Not one succeeded. One told me that I was not good material, too strong-minded.'

'Which is a compliment. But this guy succeeded. Because you'd gone for him?'

'I . . . I don't think so, really.'

'Tell me what happened. You say he hypnotized you, so presumably you can't remember anything he made you do while under the influence.'

'That's the point. He told me I would, and I do.'

'Then how do you know you were hypnotized?'

'He told me to do something I would never have considered in ordinary circumstances. He told me I would want to do it, and I did.'

She frowned. 'He didn't make you commit a crime?'

'No. He made me strip.'

'Everything?'

'I wasn't wearing that much.'

'And then you had sex. I would say you have a rape case. Even if you wanted it at the time, if you can prove that you were under hypnosis . . .'

'It wasn't like that at all. He never touched me. He just told me to get dressed again. I was totally embarrassed.'

'You mean he brought you back, but you could remember what had happened. He does sound a bit of a weirdo.'

'That's the point,' I said. 'I don't think he brought me back. He didn't snap his fingers, or anything like that. He just told me to get dressed.'

'But when he did that, you were ashamed of what had happened. Therefore you must have recovered your normal senses.'

'I thought so at the time. But when he took me back to the hotel, he told me that he would have sex with me one day, when he came to England, and that until that day, I would not be able to have sex with any other man.'

'Definitely an MCP. No doubt you gave him two fingers.'

'Well, the fact is, I was still a bit shook up by what had happened. And then, that same night, I quarrelled with Eric. That's my boyfriend. My ex-boyfriend. Well, I don't suppose that was very exceptional. I was supposed to be on holiday with him, and I'd been out to dinner with another man.'

'Did you tell him about having to strip?'

'No, I didn't. I just didn't want to have sex with him anymore, and when he tried to push the point, I slugged him.'

'Atta girl! But as you say, this seems to have been a fairly normal course of events. What makes you feel you were still hypnotized?'

'Well . . .' I knew I was flushing. 'When we got back, I sort of got together with an old friend who I'd always had a thing for, vaguely, and we, well, had a go. And the moment I was in bed with him I was turned right off.'

'So what happened?'

'Nothing. Jeremy is a perfect gentleman. He realized there was nothing doing, so we went home.'

'And you say that up to that moment you were attracted to him.'

'I still find him attractive.'

'Why don't you try again?'

'No way. When something like that happens, it kind of puts you off.'

'You don't think this is just a blip? I mean' – she glanced at her notes – 'you broke up with your boyfriend only ten days ago, in a fairly unsavoury fashion. That's a very short period of time. Maybe you tried to, shall we say, exorcize him just a shade too quickly. That's the most likely explanation.'

'And if it isn't *the* explanation?'

'You really think you were hypnotized? Still are hypnotized? Have you noticed anything different about yourself?'

'Not a thing. Except for that afternoon with Jeremy. And that wasn't different, in the sense that you mean. I really did want to do it, until it came to the crunch. And then, zilch.'

Jetta Smith-Lucas considered her notes. 'I need to ask you one or two intimate questions.'

'That's why I'm here.'

'Do you masturbate? *Can* you masturbate?'

'Yes.'

'So there is nothing the matter with your physical responses. You say you've never had any physical relations with a woman. Have you ever wanted to?'

'Well . . . perhaps at school, briefly. Not recently. You're not suggesting I have a go? I wouldn't know how to start.'

'I'm trying to find reasons. One could be that you have, without realizing it, changed your sexuality.'

'Well, I haven't.'

She smiled. 'Don't protest too vehemently; it could indicate a subconscious feeling of guilt. All right, Frances. If we accept that you genuinely feel that you are still hypnotized, we could have a problem. Are you in touch with this man?'

'No.'

'But you can get in touch with him?'

'I don't think so. I don't have an address or anything. He took me out to his boat, but I don't remember the name. It was dark.'

'Just tell me again. This man had you alone on board a boat, at night, and made you strip off, and never attempted to have sex with you?'

'Yes. Actually, we weren't alone. He had a friend with him.'

'And the friend didn't attempt to interfere with you either?'

'Actually, he did. But Damon – that's the one who hypnotized me – wouldn't let him.'

'As the White Rabbit might have said, this gets curiouser and curiouser. Please don't take offence, Frances, but I have got to ask you this: are you absolutely sure all of this happened? I mean, given the situation, out in the Bahamas, an idyllic holiday being spoiled because you could see the end of your relationship with your boyfriend looming, moonlight, a gentle breeze, surf and sand . . . No one could possibly blame you for dreaming.'

'Is that what you think happened?'

'I'm trying to find out what happened. But I have to explore every possibility.'

'It wasn't a dream,' I muttered, and instinctively began to finger my locket. 'It was . . . voodoo.' I hadn't meant to tell her, but it just came out. 'Black magic.'

Three

The Visitor

Having said it, I bit my lip in embarrassment as Jetta regarded me for several seconds, somewhat quizzically. But then she was disturbed by the buzz of an alarm. 'Damn,' she remarked. 'Our chat has been so interesting I've quite forgotten the time. I've another appointment now. But I would like to continue this talk. Would you like that?'

'Yes,' I said. 'If you would.' I was realizing that it was extremely doubtful she would be able to help me, but it was such a relief to be able to share it with someone.

'I have said I would. Janet will make an appointment.'

I sat up and put on my shoes. 'How much do I owe you?'

'We'll send you an account. When we've made a little more progress.'

'And in the meantime?'

'Live as normal a life as you can. If you feel like having a go at anyone else, do so. But also try to remember everything you can about this Damon. When we meet again, I wish you to tell me everything you have been able to remember. If you go out of that door' – she pointed at one opposite to that by which I had entered – 'you will see no one except Janet.'

'Thank you.' I went to the door, and there paused and looked back. 'Do you believe anything that I have told you?'

'Whether I believe you or not is quite immaterial,' she said. 'You have a problem. It is my business to get to the root of that problem, and see if I can get rid of it. With your cooperation, of course. Together, I'm sure we'll have you as right as rain in no time at all.' She gave a bright smile, and I was dismissed.

Janet was waiting for me, and we went to her little office, where it turned out that Jetta, who seemed to be very popular, didn't have another free date for a fortnight. I found this a little odd, as I had got this first appointment with no delay. However, I made the date. 'Now I'll just see you out.' Janet escorted me down a passage to a door opening on to a back garden, through which there was a path to a gate. 'The street is just down that alley. I hope you don't mind this charade, but we find that many patients do not like it to be known they come here.'

'Oh, quite.' I felt the same way. 'I work in the West End. Can you tell me how I get back from here?'

'Turn right, and you'll come to the main road. It's only a hundred yards. There are usually taxis about. It's also on a bus route, if you prefer.'

It was only just four, and I felt obliged to return to the office, although what I really wanted to do was think. But it was a fairly long taxi drive back. Was I any further ahead? I felt I was, or I had been up to that disastrous blooper. Had it been disastrous? Presumably, if one went to a psychiatrist at all, one should bare one's breast and anything else that came to mind. But I felt that while in the beginning Jetta had accepted that I did have a problem, the mention of voodoo had got her thinking that I might be a little nuts, or certainly suffering from too much imagination. Well, there was going to be another session, and I could put things right then. Or would she merely suppose that having gone away and thought about it, I would decide that I had to put forward some reasonable explanation for it? At that moment I felt that if Damon were in the taxi with me, I'd wring his effing neck.

But what *about* Damon? I had deliberately tried to stop myself thinking about him since returning from the Bahamas.

A figure like that belonged in the heat and on the beach, wearing shorts and a sweatshirt. I simply could not imagine him on Shaftesbury Avenue wearing a pinstripe suit. So, could Jetta have been right in her hint that it had all been a dream? I touched my locket. It couldn't have been a dream, unless losing the locket had also been a dream. I almost felt like contacting Veronica to make sure that that afternoon had actually happened. But that would be both humiliating and absurd; of course it had happened. Thus Damon was real; he had hypnotized me, and he had left me in that state. It was up to me to break the spell. If Jetta could help, well and good. But it was still up to me.

How to do it? Make myself have sex with someone? But I really didn't want to get the reputation of an easy lay – I just couldn't imagine what Jeremy had told his mates about me, and could only pray that he was as much of a gentleman all of the time as he appeared in the office – or in that bedroom. I pride myself that I was brought up to old-fashioned principles, those espoused by Grannie rather than Mummy, perhaps. It was my intention to get married in the course of time and have a family. Okay, so a girl was entitled to sow a few wild oats before undertaking that responsibility, and I had a long way to go – but I needed genuinely to like the guy and be turned on by him.

Then what about Jetta's hint about trying a woman? I don't really have any hang-ups about sex. I believe that every man, and every woman, should get on with whatever suits them best, without any outside interference. But the idea frightened me. Firstly because it was totally unknown territory, and secondly, and more importantly, because I had observed that lesbian lovers usually projected an intensity in their relationships that far transcended anything conceivable with a man. I wasn't sure I was ready for that, or ever would be. I valued my privacy, mental more than physical, too much. There had never been any intenseness between Eric and me. We had just enjoyed sex together, and even that had begun to fade long before the bust-up.

Yet such was my mental state I decided to have a go, while understanding that I was being entirely irrational in my panic. It was not yet a fortnight since I had broken with Eric. I have never considered myself a particularly sensual animal. Sex is great when it is there and is mutual, but it has never been the be-all and end-all of life for me. Even with Eric, what with his rugby commitments during the winter, we had sometimes gone weeks without actually getting together, and it had never bothered me in the least. Yet here I was, slavering for it – simply because I was afraid I might never have it again, save with Damon, and I had no guarantee I would ever see *him* again. I wasn't even sure I wanted to. I had more than a suspicion that would cause far more problems than I was prepared to cope with.

'So how's your mouth?' Daphne asked. She was a redhead with a short and somewhat stocky figure but good legs and pertly pretty features.

I had told everyone I was going to the dentist. 'Not too bad. The real work starts in a fortnight's time.'

'Dentists give me the shits.'

'It's all painless nowadays,' I pointed out, and watched Jeremy come into the office from showing a client a property. He gave us his usual bright smile as he went to his desk.

'Do you know,' Daphne said, 'I could have sworn he had something going for you, certainly when he found out you and that Glossop bloke were through. But he hasn't spoken to you once in the past few days.'

'They come and they go,' I said.

She shook her head. 'Not good, sitting all alone in that little flat of yours . . .'

'If you must know, I'm enjoying the peace and quiet.' If one is going to tell a lie, one may as well make it a whopper. Then I drew a deep breath. 'But I don't object to company. Why don't you come and visit some time.'

She raised her eyebrows. I had never invited her, or any of the girls in the office, to my flat before. 'What a lovely idea. When?'

'What's wrong with tonight?'

'Oh, I can't tonight. I'm going to a party. I know, why don't you come with me. We'll have a good time, and then, if you like, I could come back to your place after.'

'Oh . . . but I'm not invited.'

'No one will even notice. It's a bit of a rave. The more the merrier.'

'Sounds like fun,' I said.

Daphne arrived at seven, and I asked her up. She looked around herself with some envy, much to my gratification. 'Cool,' she commented.

'It's a bit small.'

'Big enough for one.' She winked. 'Or even two. Do you own, or rent?'

'Own, on my salary? You have got to be joking. But I have three years to run on my lease, so it's as permanent as possible.'

'Unless your landlord sends round a big bloke with an Alsatian to persuade you to move.'

'No chance. My landlord is a sweet little old lady. As long as I don't make myself a nuisance to the other tenants, there are no problems.'

'Sounds like heaven. I share a flat with Phoebe Luscombe. You know her?'

'We've met.'

'And our landlord is a Greek gentleman, who keeps dropping in when he reckons we might be in the shower.'

'You should keep your door locked.'

'He has his own key. We'd better be moving on.'

'Am I all right?' I spun round.

She surveyed me. I was wearing a dress which had little more hem than a pussy pelmet. She was wearing jeans and a T-shirt into both of which she might have been poured, drop by drop.

'Always live dangerously,' she remarked.

I gathered she was referring to me rather than herself, and

braced myself for a rough evening, while reflecting that it might help with my problem.

For the first half of the night my every fear was realized. The music was loud enough to give a deaf person a headache. There was a good deal of fumbling, on and off the dance floor, to cope with – my short skirt was a distinct liability. Ecstasy and various other substances, hard and soft, were passed around, and I did my popularity no good at all by refusing them; I actually had tried ecstasy before and made myself sick, but in any event, in my present uncertain state of mind as to whether or not I was still under hypnosis, I couldn't imagine what might be the result if I added drugs to the problem, and I wasn't about to risk it. So there I was, having undoubtedly accumulated several bruises and feeling as asexual as it was possible to feel, when suddenly someone said, 'Hi, there!'

I nearly jumped out of my skin, because the voice was both familiar and West Indian. I swung round . . . and found myself looking at Roger Gaillard. 'What on earth are you doing here?'

'I was going to ask you the same question.'

'I came with a friend.'

'So did I.'

'I meant, what are you doing in London? In England?'

'I fly with British Airways, remember? Now I'm back on duty, but with a couple of nights off. Would you care to dance?'

I didn't, actually, but I reflected that if I had to be felt up I'd enjoy it more with someone I at least knew, if only slightly. Besides, I was getting an idea. 'I'd love to,' I said.

He was of the holding close and massaging variety, which was a welcome change, and as we were pressed against each other so that my mouth was against his ear, I was able to get started immediately. But he beat me to it. 'Seems a long time since last we met,' he remarked, into *my* ear.

'Not that long. A couple of weeks.'

'The night you split with your boyfriend.'

I pulled my head back. 'How in the name of God did you know that?'

'It was all over the hotel.'

'Shit,' I muttered, and then remembered that I wouldn't be going back to Eleuthera, unless . . . 'He lost his rag because I went out to dinner with that guy Damon Smith.'

'I remember.'

I got my mouth back beside his ear. 'I had the idea you didn't approve. I really would like to know why you didn't go for him.'

'Did you have a good time?'

'He was a very interesting companion,' I said, trying to stick to the truth. 'He told me he was half Haitian. Is that right?'

'I believe so. A whole lot of them came up during the seventies and eighties when times down there were very bad.'

'And he had an English father? Who ran off and left his mother when he was very small? Is that why you didn't like the idea of my having dinner with him?'

He grinned into my ear. 'A pretty chick like you. You know they say Haiti is riddled with AIDS.'

'But he left there when he was five.'

'He could've inherited it.'

'Well . . . if it relieves your mind, there was no bodily contact between us.'

'That's good. Although surprising.'

'Why? Does he have a reputation for knocking up women?'

'Some. But any man lucky enough to take you out to dinner must have high hopes.'

'Would you like to take me out to dinner?'

'And how.'

'Then let's go. I'll pay my way.'

'Just like that?'

'It's difficult to hear yourself think in here. I really would like to talk to you.'

'About Damon?'

'Yes.' He made a face, but dinner with a good-looking

woman was not something he wanted to pass up. 'Just hang in there while I square things with the friend I came with.' I found Daphne involved in hectic dance-floor gyrations with a shaven-headed, multi-earringed bloke, and managed to convey my intention of leaving by way of hand signals. She smiled, shrugged, and carried on dancing.

'I thought you said you and Damon never actually got together,' Roger remarked as we ate hot curry.

'We didn't. But he suggested he might look me up when he came to England, so I'd like to know what I might be getting into. Do you think he'll come to England?'

'Probably. If he wants to.'

'It's not exactly cheap, and he won't have a job . . .'

'He has lots of money.'

'Damon? He gave the impression of being a beach bum who happens to own a boat.'

'Don't you believe it. That's how he likes to appear.'

'So where'd he get this money from? His mother was a Haitian emigrant. He never knew his father . . .'

'He inherited a fortune. Just over a year ago.'

'Who left him this fortune? Some uncle in Australia?'

'A rich guy, right there in the Bahamas. The story won't make you very happy. The old guy, an Englishman, was gay. And Damon was one of his stable.'

'Shit,' I muttered. But hadn't I hinted at that on board the yacht? And he had never actually denied it.

'And then this English guy suddenly dropped dead, and left everything to Damon. A big bank account, the house, a swish car, and that little sailboat.'

'You mean there were no other relatives?'

'Oh, sure. A whole clutch of them. There was a hell of a stink. They tried to get the will put aside on grounds of diminished responsibility. But that didn't work. The old chap was behaving, conducting business, doing what he always did, with perfect lucidity, up to the moment he died. They then tried to claim that Damon had influenced him into changing his will; this had been done only six months before, soon after he took Damon on as his boyfriend. But there again, they could produce no proof, save for the fact that the will *had* been changed. Everyone who knew them, and saw them together, while there could be no doubt that the guy was besotted with Damon, could find no evidence that Damon was influencing him in any way. As a matter of fact most people had the opinion that Damon was embarrassed by the whole thing, by the way this guy lavished attention on him in public. And besides, the guy was in perfect health. He was only in his early fifties, had every reason to expect he'd live another forty years. That's a long time to wait for an inheritance, especially as this guy had had several partners in the past and no one really expected his relationship with Damon to last more than a year or two.'

'So Damon inherited.'

'Oh, they had another go. They actually suggested that Damon had murdered his lover, having got him to change the will. Well, that didn't work either. As the guy had dropped dead so suddenly, with no record of ill health, there had to be an autopsy. Everyone supposed he died of AIDS. But they could find no trace of it. His heart had just stopped beating. It was certainly odd, and there was quite a fuss. But the fact is that there was no sign of violence, nothing the least toxic in his stomach, nothing. Like I said, his heart just stopped beating while he was sitting in his armchair having an after-dinner drink.'

'Was Damon there?'

'Sure. Sitting on the other side of the room. It was him that called the doctor when he realized Clermont – that was the guy's name – was dead.'

I found I was clutching my throat. 'Do you think he did it?'

'There's no way he could have done it.'

'But you don't like him.'

'Well, I don't go for gays. And then, to have one inherit all that bread . . .' He grinned. 'Maybe I'm just jealous.'

'Do you think he has AIDS?'

'There's no indication of it.'

I didn't know all that much about it, although I suppose like most women my age I was terrified of the very idea. But being one man's partner for more than a year had done a whole lot for my confidence that I at least wouldn't ever be a victim. As for that moment of madness with Jeremy, I was still young enough, and stupid enough, to feel sure that a man who looked so healthy could not possibly be carrying any dreaded disease.

There was so much of what Roger had told me that needed serious thinking about, but I had had several drinks at the party and my brain wasn't working that well. So I asked my next question without thinking. 'Did you know that Damon's mother was a mamaloi? A voodoo priestess?'

'He tell you that?'

'Well . . . yes he did.'

He snorted. 'And you believed him? It's a come-on.'

For some reason that annoyed me. 'Then who was she?'

'Some harmless little old woman who didn't have two pennies to rub together.'

I was frowning. 'Wait a minute. You said this case, about Damon's inheritance, came up more than a year ago. And he told me that his mother died less than a year ago. Or do you reckon that was a lie, too.'

'No, I think that's true.'

'So she certainly had more than two pennies to rub together before she died.'

'Supposing he shared any of it.'

'You really have it in for him, haven't you?'

'You asked, Frances. I've been trying to answer.'

'Thank you. Now would you like to call for the bill? I'm going home to bed. Alone.'

'I thought we had something going.'

'You were wrong,' I told him.

How not to make friends, I thought, as I got between

the sheets. Presumably Daphne would also feel she had been stood up. But I did need to think. As it happened, I didn't, because what with the alcohol and the dancing, I was exhausted and fell asleep in seconds. But a cold shower in the morning cleared the cobwebs.

If Damon had indeed hypnotized me in such a way that I was continuing to obey him, even if I didn't want to, while at the same time remembering everything that had happened, it was at least possible that he had tried the same trick on his friend Clermont. Of course he couldn't possibly have known that Clermont was going to suddenly drop dead, but if he could keep the old fellow in a perpetual state of hypnotism, as he seemed to be keeping me, he had at least taken care of his future.

I couldn't believe that he hadn't shared at least some of his wealth with his mother; he had come across as genuinely fond of her, and grateful for the knowledge she had imparted to him, particularly this sinister ability to impose his personality on others. It seemed likely that sudden wealth coming on top of a lifetime of poverty had been too much for the old lady. And left him free to pursue his life in his own way. With his gay lover; it seemed obvious that Roddy Webster was currently filling that role.

Then why on earth had he come after me? Just to amuse himself? I felt genuinely angry about that. The bastard! Now it seemed certain I would never see him again anyway, and so I was left with . . . nothing? For the rest of my life?

That was both unacceptable and absurd. I had always prided myself on my will-power. Until Damon no one had ever had the least success in either bullying me or cajoling me into doing anything I did not wish to do. My parents had discovered that when I was very small. All I had to do was exert that will-power to break the spell, surely. But it would not be accomplished by running around like a chicken with its head cut off. I needed to think things through, and plan my course very carefully.

Was Jetta Smith-Lucas a possible answer? The more I

thought about it, the less I felt she was. Obviously she had never come across a case like mine before. Until the mention of voodoo she had been inclining towards feeling that I was making too much of what was a very short time between splitting with Eric and becoming anxious about my sexuality. Now she probably thought I was a nut. And what final advice could she give me? Go out and get laid. I had worked that out for myself. Anyway, I didn't have to keep my next appointment.

So, go out and get laid. Or bring someone in to get laid. Maybe I should've kept going with Roger; he had certainly been keen. But he was not in any way a turn-on. Well, then, gone back to the party and found someone else? Ugh! Put my tail firmly between my legs and offer to make it up with Eric? At least I knew I *could* have sex with him. But quite apart from my pride, I didn't *want* to have sex with him anymore. That I was sure had nothing to do with any curse Damon might have placed on me. It was just that, having split, I was for the first time seeing him as he really was: an overweight, chauvinistic slob. I couldn't imagine how I had ever found him attractive.

What was required was a patient, confident approach to the problem. I knew I was attractive. All I had to do was swan along in my usual fashion, and soon enough the right guy would turn up, and I would discover that I had imagined the whole nightmare.

That settled, I felt a whole lot better. I even smiled at Daphne when I got to the office; she didn't smile back.

I began to pick up the threads of my life, went down to Hastings on the weekends, resumed going to my keep fit classes, showed clients various houses, often with Jeremy, with whom I kept a cool distance . . . and spent the evenings quietly at home in my little flat, reading and watching television. I even had a pleasant chat on the phone with Veronica. I spent an entirely peaceful fortnight. Of course I realized that the only way I was going to meet a turn-on was by getting out, going at least to the pub on the corner, but that wasn't a terribly exciting prospect. I even toyed with the idea of giving a party, but there were quite a few reasons against it. One was that it wasn't practical to squeeze more than a dozen people into my flat at the same time. Another was that the dozen would be people I already knew, none of whom caused me the least desire to leap into their arms. A third, more important, was that Mrs Thurgold and I got on so well because I had never been, or caused, the slightest trouble. I didn't want to break that relationship in any way, as would inevitably happen if one of my neighbours complained about noise.

But the most important reason of all was that I just didn't feel like it. Could that be Damon again? But I wasn't going to believe in that any more. When I was ready to emerge from hibernation I would do so.

Feeling more content than I had for a long time, I was in bed early, as usual nowadays, with a book and a glass of wine, watching the TV with one eye and reading with the other, when the street bell rang. I looked at my watch; it was just after nine. I had no idea who it could be. I swung my legs out of bed, pulled on a dressing gown – I never wore a nightdress or pyjamas – and went to the phone. 'Yes?'

'Frances Ogilvie?' A woman's voice, vaguely familiar.

'Yes.'

'Will you let me up?'

'I might,' I said. 'If you tell me who you are.'

'Jetta Smith-Lucas.' She seemed surprised that I hadn't recognized her voice. But she wasn't half as surprised as I was.

I released the latch. 'Come up.' I opened the door and waited for her. It seemed to be raining outside, for she was wearing a mack and a hat. 'What a pleasant surprise,' I lied.

'May I come in?' I stepped aside and allowed her into the flat. 'How very nice,' she remarked, taking off her hat and coat and handing them to me; underneath was a well-cut trouser suit and boots. I hung the raincoat and hat on the hook inside the front door. 'And so warm,' she added. 'It really is a miserable night.'

'So I can see. Would you like tea, coffee, or alcohol?'

'Do you know, I think a little drink would be very nice. Warming.'

'I have some dubious brandy, some quite good scotch, and some off-the-shelf gin.'

'May I have a brandy?' I charged a balloon and gave it to her. She took it in both hands and sat on the settee. 'Aren't you going to join me?'

'I'm in bed. I *was* in bed.'

'Oh, I am sorry. Would you like to go back there? We can talk with you in bed. Actually, you might find it more comfortable.'

It did occur to me that this woman might be on the hunt for some mutual therapy, but I kept my cool. 'Do you mean you came here at nine o'clock at night to analyse me?' Which was one way of putting it.

'I can give you a session if you'd like me to. I actually came to find out if you are all right. You never kept your appointment.'

'Ah. Well, something came up, and—'

'You are a terrible liar,' she remarked. 'You got cold feet.'

'Maybe.'

'Well, if you wish to terminate our relationship, that is up to you.' She opened her handbag. 'I have your account. I'm afraid I had to charge you for the second appointment, because it was half an hour of my time wasted, waiting for you.'

I took the envelope, slit it, glanced at the account. It was considerably more than I had expected, but at that moment my finances were in quite good shape, as I wasn't spending money on anything save groceries. 'Will you take a card?'

'I'm afraid not. However, I could forget the whole thing.'

'Why should you do that?'

'Well, I should like to think that you and I are friends. I never charge my friends for my services.'

'I'll just write you a cheque.' I went to the little desk in the corner of the room.

'I see. Well, then, I'd prefer cash.'

'I'm sorry, I don't keep this much cash in the flat. So it's a cheque or nothing.'

'You could get the money tomorrow. And bring it round to my place. Or I could come here to collect it.'

'Sorry. I am busy all day tomorrow, and tomorrow night. I'll write down the card number.'

'I'm beginning to feel that you don't like me.' I decided against answering that, sat at the desk and wrote the cheque. I then held it out. 'Well,' she said. 'If I must.' She put it into her handbag.

'I would appreciate a receipt.'

She raised her eyebrows, then went to the desk herself and receipted the account. 'You are a very hard-headed young woman. All that nonsense about being hypnotized. I would like to know why you really came to me.'

'I'm researching a book on psychiatrists.'

'And as I have said, you really are a very poor liar, although you do seem to have the imagination necessary to be a writer.' She finished her drink, placed the glass on the coffee table. 'Well, it's been nice knowing you, briefly.'

'I found it very interesting.'

'I may say that I won't deposit this cheque until Friday. If you change your mind about resuming our relationship, I'll be happy to tear it up.'

'I am bound to say, Mrs Smith-Lucas, that you are a most determined woman. But changing my mind isn't really my scene.'

She shrugged, went to the door and put on her hat and coat . . . and the street phone rang again. 'Well,' she commented. By now she had deduced that I was wearing nothing beneath my dressing gown. 'You seem to have solved your problem by yourself. Would that be M or F?'

'I have absolutely no idea,' I snapped, and picked up the phone. 'Yes?'

'Well, hi, baby,' Damon said.

The Court

'*Professor Prendergast,*' Sir Barton said, '*my learned friend has just described you as the leading forensic scientist in Britain, perhaps in the world. Would you agree with that assessment?*'

'*It is hardly my place to do so.*' Professor Prendergast was a small man, precise in his dress and movements, and in his speech.

'*That is very modest of you. I can assure you that it is a widely held view. That is why I find it so very strange that you should have lent your name and reputation to such a remarkable and, I may say, untenable charge as that made by the Prosecution.*'

Professor Prendergast remained gazing at the barrister, face expressionless; he had crossed swords with Sir Barton before.

'*I would thus like to run through your evidence for the Prosecution,*' Sir Barton went on, '*in order that I, and I am sure the jury, may be certain that we did not miss something that might lend both credence and substance to the Prosecution case. Professor, you carried out the post-mortem examination on Sir Roderick Webster.*'

'*That is correct.*'

'*I have a copy of your report here.*' Sir Barton waved the sheet of paper. '*Let me see what you have written. Heart, sound. Lungs, sound. Liver, sound. Kidneys, sound. Stomach, sound. Gall bladder and spleen, sound. Intestines, sound. No evidence of any internal injuries or bleeding. No evidence of any external injuries or bleeding. Brain condition, excellent.*

I am bound to say, sir, that this must be the healthiest corpse in existence.' Sir Barton paused, waiting for the laughter, but there was none. His penchant for making macabre jokes in the worst possible taste was well known. *'Yet,'* he went on, *'you have given as your professional opinion that Sir Roderick died as a result of an external influence by, I quote, the person who was responsible for his death.'*

'That is correct,' Professor Prendergast agreed.

'You will forgive me, Professor, if I, and I am sure the jury, are a little confused by this. There is absolutely no evidence, apart from this remarkable letter in which Sir Roderick seeks to name his murderer before he even died, that when he did die it was from anything but natural causes, yet in effect you have stated that he was murdered. I do feel that you need to enlarge upon that opinion. We do have the evidence of the policeman who found the body that it was naked. I hope you are not suggesting that he, ah, fornicated himself to death?'

'No, sir,' Professor Prendergast said. *'That is very difficult to do, unless one has a weak heart.'* That did raise a titter. *'In any event,'* the professor went on, *'there was no evidence of any actual sexual activity immediately before death. However, with respect, Sir Barton, you are incorrect in assuming that, because there is no evidence of bruising, either internally or externally, or of injury or a malfunction of any of his vital organs, Sir Roderick necessarily died a natural death.'*

Sir Roderick glared at him; he was not used to being told he was wrong, and certainly not in court. *'In fact,'* Professor Prendergast went on, *'the fact that there is no evident cause of death goes to prove that he did not die of natural causes. When we speak of death by natural causes, we mean death due to a malfunctioning of some vital organ, whether by disease or old age. However this happens, the evidence is there to be determined by an autopsy. The vital failure may have been long foreseen by the patient's doctor, or it may be the result of a sudden catastrophe, but I repeat, the evidence of the failed organ, whether it be heart or lungs or kidneys, will be there to be found. In the case of Sir Roderick Webster, no disease or failed organ can be discovered, therefore it cannot be said he died of natural causes.'*

'Are you suggesting some kind of odourless and undetectable gas?'

'No, I am not. Such a gas might be odourless and undetectable, but its effect on the heart and lungs would certainly be detectable.'

'Then what are you suggesting? Or have suggested to the police, for this case to be brought at all?'

'It is my opinion that Sir Roderick died because he was told to die.'

'Would you mind saying that again, Professor?'

'Death by suggestion has been around for a very long time, Sir Barton.'

'You are talking of some kind of witchcraft?'

'Call it what you will.'

'Are you trying to tell this court that you, a highly qualified and respected scientist, believe in witchcraft?'

'No, sir, I do not believe in witchcraft. You used the word. I have, however, in the course of my experience, and the experiences of other medical men, come across quite a few similar occurrences, and in fact there have been several in the past few years.'

'So,' Sir Barton said. 'Someone told Sir Roderick Webster, head of a large and growing business, that it was time he died, and Sir Roderick happily obliged.'

'You can put it that way. I would suggest that the death was linked to some external event. If such and such a thing happens, you will die.'

'Do you mind, Professor, if I remark that such a theory is preposterous?'

'You may call it what you wish, Sir Barton. But Sir Roderick Webster is dead and he did not die of natural causes.'

Four

The Confrontation

I was so surprised I was for a moment paralysed; I was also terrified out of my wits, and stared at Jetta with my mouth open. She was certainly quick on the uptake. 'You don't mean . . . Well, let him up, please. I want to meet this guy.'

I took a deep breath. 'Damon? I'm opening the door.' I leaned against my door, panting.

'You mean this character actually exists?' Jetta asked. 'Then I apologize.'

'What am I going to do?'

'You wanted to see him again, didn't you? You want him to release you from this hypnosis, don't you?' I was not at all sure what I wanted, at that moment. 'Just leave it to me,' she said.

For the first time I was actually glad she was there. 'I must get some clothes on,' I said. But before I could move, Damon was at the door, and Jetta was opening it to let him in.

'Hello,' he said, looking her up and down, taking in the hat and coat. 'You coming, or going?'

'At the moment, I'm staying. You must be Damon Smith. I'm Jetta Smith-Lucas.'

She held out her hand, but Damon ignored it, looking past her at me. 'You look good enough to eat. You always did. Did you miss me, baby? I sure as hell missed you.'

He came towards me, while I stood there like a ninny. At that moment I was a ninny. He put his arms round me, and for the first time it registered that he was wearing only shirt and pants and shoes, no coat, and that he was soaked through.

'Do you think she wants you to do that?' Jetta asked.

Damon turned his head to look at her, and Jetta frowned. 'Who is this dame?' he asked.

'A friend,' Jetta said, before I could speak.

'You two been having it off?' Damon inquired.

'Of course not,' I snapped, pulling myself together. 'Jetta just happened to stop by.'

'Yeah?' He used both hands to pull my dressing gown open. 'Still got your locket, eh? You think I was born yesterday?'

'That is a criminal assault,' Jetta pointed out.

Damon looked at her again. 'Bugger off. Just close the door behind you, before you make me angry.'

'You cannot frighten me,' Jetta told him. 'If you lay a finger on me, I will have you in prison.'

'Lady, I wouldn't touch you with a ten-foot pole.'

'That is very sensible of you.' Jetta took off her raincoat and hat, rehung them on the door. 'I would like to speak with you.'

Damon looked at me. 'Just what is this dame to you?'

'I am Frances's psychiatrist,' Jetta announced, re-entering the lounge, sitting down, and crossing her knees. From her handbag she took a notebook and pen.

'You been telling her about us?' Damon asked.

'Well . . .' I knew I was flushing. 'You left me in a bit of a spot. Didn't you?'

He grinned. 'So you've been a good girl. That's great. But I told you I was coming.'

'You told me a lot of things,' I said defensively. 'I didn't know how many of them were true.'

'Why don't you sit down,' Jetta invited, as if it were her flat.

'Sure.' Damon sat opposite her. 'You got anything to drink, baby? This is one hell of a climate.'

'Give the man some brandy, Frances,' Jetta said.

My initial alarm was beginning to give way to irritation: I was being treated like a skivvy in my own flat! But I poured the brandy and gave it to him. He ran his hand up and down my arm. 'So you went to this dame and told her all about us. Right?'

A sudden jerk on my wrist and I was sitting beside him. 'I had to do something,' I said.

'Frances has the idea that you have somehow hypnotized her, and forgot to break, shall we say, the spell,' Jetta said.

'I didn't forget.'

'You realize you are confessing to an offence?'

'What offence? She agreed to it.'

'She was under the impression that it was a party game, which would be ended when the party was over.' She paused, expectantly.

'I don't play party games.'

'You mean you genuinely believe that you hypnotized her.'

'You said that she does. I know she does. That's what matters.'

'That's an interesting point of view. Very well, now I would like you to unhypnotize her. Bring her out of it.'

'Why should I do that? I like her the way she is.'

'I'm sure you do. However, to keep someone hypnotized is against the law. If you do not release her, I am going to go to the police, and they will lock you up and then deport you.'

'They can't do that. I have a British passport.'

'That is no longer a guarantee of the right to residence in this country,' Jetta pointed out. 'And they can certainly lock you up. At the very least you are infringing her civil liberties.'

'You sure are an aggressive woman,' Damon observed. 'I'm going to have to do something about you.'

'You touch me—'

'Here we go again. I have said that I wouldn't touch you with a ten-foot pole. Say, Frances, you got any music?'

'I have a CD player.'

'Let's have a look at it.' I showed him my deck, while Jetta watched us, frowning. 'That's great,' Damon said. 'Some gadget.' He flicked through my disks. '*Bolero*. That's just what we want.'

'You want me to play that? Now?'

'That's what I want.'

'Just what is going on?' Jetta asked.

'We're going to listen to some music. Don't you like listening to music?'

Jetta looked at me, and the penny suddenly dropped. 'Damon,' I said, 'you can't do it.'

'Can't do what?' Jetta asked.

'He means to hypnotize you.'

Jetta laughed. 'I'd like to see him try.'

'See?' Damon asked. 'She doesn't object.'

I looked from one to the other, totally uncertain what to do.

'I'm not some silly little girl, you know,' Jetta remarked.

Clearly she was referring to me. And that just about settled it. If she felt she could take Damon on, that was up to her. And if she couldn't, and he put some kind of a hex on her, which might interfere with *her* love life, then she had it coming.

The music was slowly becoming louder, and as *Bolero* does, was filling the mind with its cadence. Jetta and Damon were staring at each other. I couldn't imagine what they were thinking. When Damon had been hypnotizing me, I don't remember thinking of anything – my mind had gone a complete blank. 'I think you want to go into the other room, sweetheart,' Damon said, never taking his eyes from Jetta's. 'I'll call you when we're finished.'

'Yes,' Jetta said. 'Do it, and close the door.'

I went into the bedroom. I did reflect that I could be in a spot of bother if Jetta woke up and discovered that she had been raped in my flat . . . but she had joined in the command to leave them, and I was feeling pretty fed up with both of them.

I sat on the bed, and toyed with the idea of switching on

the TV, and then remembered that I had nothing on, well, virtually. There didn't seem much point in getting dressed if he was intending to stay the night. Did I want him to stay the night, with everything that would involve? I didn't really know how I was going to get rid of him, and besides, if we had sex together I might be released. Even more, the thought of having sex with Damon had me quite excited.

'You can come in now,' Jetta called. So who had won in the battle of the wills? I went into the lounge. They both seemed in the best of humours. 'That was fun,' Jetta said. 'Well, I must be getting along. I know you and Damon have a lot to talk about.'

'How did you get here?' I asked. I was so relieved that they hadn't actually come to blows.

'I came by taxi.'

'Then I'd better call you one; you won't pick one up out here.'

'No, no,' Jetta said. 'I'll walk.'

'You intend to walk from Hammersmith to Hampstead?'

'It's only about five miles. The exercise will do me good.'

'But it's pouring with rain.'

'A little water never did anyone any harm.' I looked at Damon, who shrugged. Jetta stood up. 'I'll say goodnight. Oops, I almost forgot; there's something I have to do.'

I raised my eyebrows – and they would have gone even higher had that been possible – as she proceeded to undress. 'Oh, no,' I said. 'Damon . . .'

'She wants to,' Damon said. 'Ask her.'

'I've always wanted to take off my clothes in front of people.' Jetta was down to her tights.

'Listen,' I said, 'don't you understand? He's hypnotized you, just as he hypnotized me.'

'Oh, nonsense,' Jetta said. 'He's made me feel free.' Now completely naked, she did a pirouette in the middle of the room.

'Go, girl, go,' Damon said.

'Yes, of course. I must be off. I'll say goodnight, Frances.'

'I think you should put on your raincoat and hat,' Damon suggested. 'That way you won't be arrested.'

'Good idea.' Jetta obeyed.

'Don't forget your key,' Damon said.

'Oh, yes.' She opened her handbag and took out her latchkey, closed the bag again, and placed it on the settee. She had reached the door before I came to my senses.

'Jetta,' I shouted. 'You can't go out like that. In the rain!'

'Nonsense. I have my coat.' She opened the door.

I turned to Damon, who was still sitting on the settee. 'You must stop her.'

'How can I do that, save by physical force? And I promised I wouldn't touch her. Let her get on with it, if it's something she wants to do. But you remember what I told you to do as soon as you get home,' he added.

'Oh, I'll remember,' Jetta promised, and stepped outside, closing the door behind her.

'Damon,' I said, 'that was diabolical.'

He grinned. 'I think she had it coming. She was trying to take over your life.'

I couldn't deny that he might have a point. 'But to leave her like that . . .'

'I haven't. I gave her a specific instruction. If she does what I told her to, and she will, she'll snap out of it.'

'And what do you think she'll feel like then?'

'I have no idea. But I don't think she'll trouble you again.' Which would be a relief. 'Now,' he said, 'I'm soaked through. What I would like is a hot shower and then something to eat.'

'Oh. Right. The bathroom's through there. I'll just put something on, then—'

'I don't want you to put something on.' He got up. 'I'd prefer it if you took that thing off.'

'We need to talk.' While his presence, and what he had

done to Jetta, still excited me, I wasn't going to let him get the idea that all he had to do was snap his fingers and I'd lie on my back with my legs apart. Even if I knew that was next to inevitable.

'Sure,' he said. 'I want to talk, too. But after I've had my shower.'

'I'll just get you a towel.'

'I can use yours.' He went into the bathroom. 'Eggs,' he called over his shoulder. 'Poached eggs.'

'Oh. Right.' As soon as the bathroom door was closed I nipped into the bedroom and pulled on a pair of knickers and a T-shirt, added the dressing gown again, and went into the kitchen. He emerged a few minutes later, starkers. I have to say that if I had found him a come-on in trunks, he was a lot more of a come-on without them. The thought of that thing inside me gave me the shakes. I began breaking eggs.

'You got a washing machine?' he asked.

'No. I use the laundrette.'

'Shit. Well, I can put them on the radiator to dry out.'

'Don't you have a change of clothes?'

'Not here. They're with Roddy.'

'You mean he's in England as well?'

'Where I am, Roddy is,' he said.

'Right. And where is he right now?'

'In a hotel. I left him there while I came to see you.'

'Just how did you find out where I live, anyway?'

'You're in the phone book, darling.'

I'd never thought of anything so simple. But . . . 'You're not going to tell me I'm the only Frances Ogilvie in the phone book.'

'No, there are some others. You're the third I've tried.'

I served the eggs, and he sat at my little dining table. 'You not eating?'

'I already did. Ten-thirty is a bit late for me. Wouldn't you like to put something on?'

'Don't you like looking at me?'

Well, I did, but I didn't think it would be a good idea to admit it. 'Won't you feel cold?'

'If I do, I have you to warm me up, eh?'

I sat opposite him, found myself looking at Jetta's clothes. 'Oh, my God! What about those?'

'She'll come back for them. Or send for them.'

'She could accuse us of stealing them.'

'How? She took them off of her own free will. They're not torn or damaged in any way to suggest we took them off her.'

I sighed. 'Like I said, we need to talk.'

'Sure. What about?'

'Well, us. I don't know how you did it, but you put me in one hell of a position. That's why I went to Jetta. She's a psychiatrist.'

'So she said. How many other people have you told about us?'

'No one.'

He raised his head to gaze at me for several seconds. Then he was apparently satisfied. 'Then there's no problem.'

'Yes, there is a problem. Me.'

'Tell me about it.'

'Oh, for God's sake. I just told you about it. I want to live a normal life. I want you to release me.'

'How do you know I haven't released you? I could've done it that night on the boat.'

'You didn't. I know you didn't.'

'Aha,' he said. 'You've been trying.'

'Well . . .' I knew I was flushing.

'With that fat guy you had out in the Bahamas with you?'

'No. We quarrelled. That . . .' I bit my lip.

'That same night, eh? You did the right thing. But you've been trying to have a go since coming back, eh? How many?'

'Well . . . just one.'

'And what happened?'

I didn't know why I was baring my all to this man – and not for the first time – but I knew I was going to. 'Nothing happened.'
'He missed out?'
'He never had the chance. I went right off the boil.'
'You mean he didn't get inside you?'
'No he did not.'
'But he messed you about a bit.'
'A bit.'
'And that didn't turn you on? I mean, you liked this guy, right?'
'Yes, I did like him. But he didn't turn me on.'
'But I reckon getting hold of you turned him on. What happened when you said no dice?'
'I said, nothing happened.'
'He didn't beat you up? I sure would have.'
'Well, he didn't. He's a perfect gentleman.'
'Is that a fact? Let's go to bed. You're getting me all randy.'
Well, I could see *that* the moment he stood up.
'Just hold on a minute,' I said.
'Baby doll, I came four thousand miles to fuck you. You should take that as a compliment.'
'I want to know what happens next. Supposing I allow you.'
'Yeah, we have a lot to talk about. From here on, with your help, it's all up.'
'Will you release me?'
'After.'
'First.'
'Frances,' he said, very reasonably, 'you can't fight me. You have to understand that.' I knew he was right, even if I hated myself for knowing it, and allowing it to happen. But then, wowee. Like I said, sex for me, good sex, has to be the time and the place, the ambience and the turn-on, added to my own mood. Well, I certainly had the mood. Perhaps Jetta had started it, and then Damon sitting there naked . . .
We were in bed before I really knew what was happening.

But I knew what I wanted, after all the emotional trauma of the past month – and I sure got it.

It took an hour, which was about twice as long as it had ever taken any other man I had ever been acquainted with. Not that I have much to go on; if you discount poor Jeremy, there had only been two, and the first had been a one-night stand when I had first discovered I was an adult. Eric had been my only regular and he had been a five-minute man, huff, puff and bang. He had regarded even 'brace yourself, sheila' as excessive foreplay. Damon actually seemed to feel that getting me off was more important than doing anything for himself, and he had amazingly gentle hands and fingers. Halfway through I had a start of alarm as I remembered that this guy was supposed to be gay, but by then it was obvious that he had practised on a lot of women. So what the hell? He might even have AIDS, but by then I was past caring.

We did all this cavorting with the light on, another new experience, and when he was finally done I was lying on my face feeling as if I had been run over by a herd of buffalo. Very amorous buffalo.

It may be gathered that this was the fuck of my life, certainly to that point. This is no excuse for my behaviour, or for my surrender, although of course that is retrospective. Up front was the fact that I felt sexy, that I had been waiting for this to happen for several weeks . . . and that I still had the idea that by having sex with him I would be released from the spell. When he finally rolled off me, I merely felt, as I have said, trampled. If I had a sensation of mental release, it was because of the enormous physical release that had just happened to me. I lay still for several minutes, my face still buried in my pillow, but he also seemed sated for the moment, and so eventually I looked at my watch. Eleven-thirty. I wasn't at all sure what time Jetta had left, but it had to have been getting on for two hours ago.

I got out of bed. I had left my mobile in the lounge together with the flat phone, so I went in there and called her number.

And got the ansaphone. Surely she had got home by now? 'Jetta,' I said, 'this is Frances Ogilvie. Please call me back the moment you get in. I really am worried about you.'

I switched off the phone, returned to the bedroom. Damon had his eyes open. 'Another confession? Who to? Mum?'

'I was calling Jetta, just to make sure she got home.'

'And has she?'

'There was just the ansaphone.'

'So what the hell? She probably went straight to bed.'

'I'm worried about her. You did a dreadful thing, sending her out like that.'

'Listen,' he said. 'She's history. Come back to bed.'

Five

The Psychiatrist

That I obeyed him was proof that I was still hypnotized. On the other hand, it was still possible to find reasons, excuses, like I was still randy as hell, etc., etc.

When my alarm went off I automatically tumbled out of bed, wondering how much of what had happened was a dream/nightmare, and realizing, as I saw him still lying there, that it had all been real. And the phone had never rung. But I had been sleeping very deeply. I ran into the lounge, tried my own ansaphone: not a dicky bird. I called Jetta again, and got hers again. 'Where are you?' I shouted, banged the phone down, and fled to the bathroom. When I emerged, feeling a whole lot better for having showered and the face I'd put on, I folded Jetta's clothes in a neat pile on the settee. Damon was up, naked as always, poking around the kitchen. 'What's for breakfast?' he inquired.

'Orange juice and coffee. That's all I ever have. If you want something else, you'll have to cook it yourself. I'm in a rush.'

I put the kettle on, went into the bedroom and started to dress. He followed. 'You always off this early?'

'That's a working girl's life, in London.' I put on my blue suit with a white shirt, brushed out my hair.

'You said you wanted to talk.'

'You bet I do. But it'll have to keep. Where did you say you were staying?'

'Some crummy hotel. You were going to find us a place to rent or buy.'

'I might be able to do that.' I poured fruit juice, swallowed it. 'Come and see me in the office.'

'Where's that?' I gave him one of my business cards. 'There's also the matter of a job.'

I drank coffee. 'I thought you had lots of money?'

'No one ever has enough.'

'Good point. What qualifications do you have?'

'I can sail a boat.'

'I'm not sure that's going to get you very far. We'll talk about it later. But listen, both for house-hunting and certainly for getting a job, you need some decent clothes. A suit and tie. Something quiet.'

'Anything you say.'

'What I really need to say is, I want to be released.'

'There's time.'

'I should brain you.'

He grinned. 'You're not going to do that. You love me.'

'Because you say so?'

'Can you think of a better reason?'

Arguing with him was a waste of time, especially when I didn't have the time. I told myself I would just have to be patient – knowing that I was totally stuck. 'I have to go.'

'Right. I'll see you later.'

'But you're still here.'

'So leave me the key.'

'I only have one key.'

'Okay. When I leave, I'll make sure the front door is shut behind me.'

I sucked my lower lip in between my teeth. It was totally against everything I had ever stood for to leave anyone alone in my flat, much less an itinerant Bahamian beach bum. Yet I knew I was going to; he was giving me one of those stares. 'Well, please leave the place exactly as it is.'

'Sure. I'm just going to have a shower. Tell you what though, I don't have a razor or a toothbrush.'

'Oh, use mine.' Whatever he had in his mouth had long been deposited in mine.

I reasoned that once I was away from him I would be able to look at things more rationally. And I was right, although it didn't help much. The fact was that I had had a whale of a night. Damon was everything I could have wished as a lover: handsome and virile, gentle and generous, and so knowledgeable . . . He could have had me any time, entirely without the use of hypnotism or voodoo rites.

But it was the presence of those things that left me in a state of tension, and equally because of that streak of sadism he had revealed in dealing with Jetta. So maybe he had been jealous, but as soon as I got to my desk I telephoned her. At least the ansaphone didn't cut in, and after a couple of rings the phone was picked up – by a man. 'Hello?'

He had a low, somewhat caressing voice, and it immediately occurred to me that all of my suspicions about Jetta's sexuality had been unfounded. 'May I speak with Mrs Smith-Lucas please?'

'I'm afraid she's not available right now.'

'Oh.' But that suggested she was there, so I had nothing more to worry about. 'I'll call back.'

'Excuse me,' he said. 'Would you be Miss Ogilvie?'

'Why?'

'I'd like to speak with you. Where can we meet?'

'Forget it.' I hung up. Obviously he had been listening to her ansaphone. But I had no intention of getting mixed up with any of Jetta's friends. That she was at home was all I needed to know.

I got busy. There were three appointments for this morning, apart from Damon, who didn't actually have one. As I was going out early with Jeremy to meet a client, I had to tell Daphne to keep her eye out for him. 'He didn't name a time,' I said, 'but I know he's keen. If he comes in, tell him I'll be back in an hour.'

'How will I know him?'

'He's tall, dark and very handsome, and speaks with a West Indian accent.'

'Oh, yes,' she remarked.

I left her to it, but when I got back to the office he hadn't been in, although something had very definitely happened in my absence. 'The boss wants a word,' Daphne said, breathlessly.

I couldn't imagine what she was on about; it couldn't possibly be anything to do with Damon – Randell didn't know he existed. I made my way upstairs to the inner sanctum, and smiled at his secretary, Louise. 'Trouble?'

'I don't know,' she said, but she too was breathless. 'He said you're to go right in.'

I tapped on the glass door, opened it, and stepped into the office . . . and checked. Randell, who was short and stout and always breathless, was not alone. And the man seated beside his desk, and now getting up, was very evidently a policeman of some sort, from his rather hard face to his well-worn raincoat. My brain went entirely blank. 'You wanted to see me, Mr Randell?'

'Oh, yes, Frances. This is Detective-Sergeant Borrow.'

I smiled at him, but he didn't smile back. 'Tell me what law I've broken,' I invited.

'We spoke on the phone,' he said. His voice was certainly familiar. Of course, he would have found out where I was calling from by using 1471. But what had a policeman been doing in Jetta's house? My heart started to bump. 'You are a patient of Mrs Smith-Lucas, the psychiatrist.'

'Yes.' I looked apologetically at Randell. 'A small emotional problem.'

'Oh, my dear,' he said.

'You telephoned Mrs Smith-Lucas,' Borrow went on, 'three times, last night and this morning. May I ask why?'

'If it's any business of yours, I wanted to make sure she had got home all right.'

'You had seen her earlier last evening?'

'She came to see me. I hadn't kept my appointment with

her.' I looked at Randell again. 'I had decided I didn't really need her after all.'

'Good for you,' he said.

Borrow was looking somewhat impatient at these asides. 'When did Mrs Smith-Lucas come to see you?'

'About a quarter to nine.'

'And when did she leave you?'

'Oh . . . about half past nine. Look, what is this all about?'

'Can you tell me what she was wearing?'

Oh, Lord, I thought. Damon had promised that once she got home she would be released from the spell. What hadn't occurred to him, or to me, was that she might go to the police! What was I to say, that wouldn't get us into trouble? 'I don't really remember.'

'It was raining, just about all of last night.'

'Well, she had a raincoat, of course. I remember that. And a hat.'

'I see. Now you say she left you at half past nine. According to the address on your entry in her computer, you live in Hammersmith. That is some five miles from Hampstead. So I assume when she left you she took a taxi. She doesn't drive a car, does she?'

'I don't know.' I felt sure he was busy laying traps for me, which I somehow had to navigate. 'She didn't take a taxi. She wanted to walk. I tried to persuade her against it, but she insisted. That's why I kept telephoning. I wanted to make sure she'd got home safely. I was so worried.' All of which was the truth.

'I can understand that,' Borrow agreed. 'How well did you know Mrs Smith-Lucas?'

'Well, I only met her twice. Once when I went for a session in her office, and then last night.'

'So you didn't really know her at all. But, going on what you did know of her, would you say, last night, that she was perfectly normal?'

'Ah . . . yes. Look, would you please tell me what this is all about? Has Mrs Smith-Lucas made some kind of complaint?'

'Only in a manner of speaking, Miss Ogilvie. Mrs Smith-Lucas is dead.'

'What?!' I think I screamed the word.

'Sit down, Frances. Sit down.' Randell decided to take action before I fell down.

'I'm sorry to have broken it like that, miss,' the police sergeant said. 'But it seems that on getting home, Mrs Smith-Lucas switched on the gas oven in her kitchen, and lay down with her head inside.'

'Oh, my God,' I said. 'My God, my God, my *God*!'

'I think you need a sip of brandy.' Randell opened his deep drawer and took out a bottle and a glass. I accepted it and drank without thinking; my brain was a total mess of conflicting thoughts and emotions.

'I realize this has been a great shock to you,' Borrow said, 'but you see, it would appear that you were the last person to see Mrs Smith-Lucas alive. But if, as you say, you hardly knew her, and she called upon a business matter . . .' He paused, hopefully. My immediate reaction was that I had to keep quiet about both Damon and what had happened in the flat. If Jetta had killed herself because of the hypnosis . . . 'Then I'm afraid you won't be able to help us. It's really rather odd. As far as we have been able to ascertain at this short notice, and according to Mrs Smith-Lucas's secretary, Janet Albright, the lady had absolutely no reason to do such a thing. Her business was doing well, she had no large debts, she was in perfect health – that will be confirmed by the autopsy, I have no doubt – and she appears to have had no emotional entanglements.' Again he paused, hopefully.

'I'm sorry,' was all that I could think of to say.

'There are other things that are very odd. As for example, you say she left your flat about half past nine, to walk five miles. That would have taken her, if she was brisk, about an hour and a half. So let us say she got home at about eleven. Our surgeon has placed the probable time of death at about eleven thirty. In other words, she did it almost immediately after she entered the house.' Another hopeful pause. I could only stare at him; she might still have been alive when I called the first time – with her head in the gas oven! 'And then, as we have agreed, it was raining, fairly heavily, and you say she was wearing a mackintosh and a hat, which is what we would expect. Now, these are in her house, still damp. This indicates that she must have got wet through on her walk. But we cannot find any other damp clothes such as she would have been wearing. We cannot even find her handbag, which, according to the secretary, would have contained her chequebook, her pen, various female things.'

'Wait a moment,' Randell said. 'If she didn't have a handbag, in which presumably she had her key, how did she get into the house?'

'Just one more oddity, Mr Randell. She certainly let herself in. We found the key on the kitchen table. So you see, we have to face the fact that this woman, having elected to walk home five miles through the rain, then stripped herself naked—'

'What did you say?' Randell was one of those middle-aged men to whom words like 'naked' acted as an aphrodisiac.

'The body was naked when it was found, Mr Randell. And as I said, we cannot find any trace of the clothing she was wearing, or of her handbag. It is almost as if she undressed on the way, threw away her bag, and put the key in her raincoat pocket.'

'Perhaps she was attacked,' Randell said, warming to his theme. 'Stripped' – he glanced at me with a flush – 'and raped, and her handbag taken. And she was so upset that when she got home she killed herself. That would fit the facts, Sergeant.'

'Not altogether, sir. As to whether Mrs Smith-Lucas had had, ah . . .' – he also glanced at me – 'sex shortly before her death, we shall have to wait on the autopsy. But women who are raped generally show *some* signs of external injury. Mrs Smith-Lucas was quite unharmed. Equally, the clothing of women who are assaulted is invariably damaged. The raincoat she appears to have been wearing is in perfect condition, apart from still being wet.'

'Hm. What about her husband? You say she was a missus.'

'He died some years ago, sir. There are no children, and as yet we have located no other relatives. I am sure there are some, but obviously they were not particularly close.' The sergeant stood up again. 'I'm sorry to have troubled you, sir, miss. It was just that after your rather agitated telephone calls we thought you might be able to shed some light on the tragedy. I'll bid you good day. Oh . . . you may be called at the inquest, but it will only be a formality.' He closed the door behind himself.

'You look quite done up, my dear,' Randell said. 'Would you like to take the rest of the day off? Or perhaps lie down for a while? You can use that settee.'

Which was against the far wall. But I had no desire to stretch out under Randell's prying eye. Besides, I had to be downstairs for when Damon came in. 'I'll be all right, really, Mr Randell,' I said. 'I'll just get back to my desk.'

I hurried out. 'What a business,' Louise said. Which meant that she had heard every word – which equally meant that the whole office would know about it as soon as she could get downstairs for a gossip. 'I had an aunt who topped herself. Everyone thought she was nuts.'

'That's always the verdict,' I assured her, and went down the stairs.

'What did he want?' Daphne asked. 'The copper.'

'Seems I didn't pay my last parking ticket,' I said. She made a face. Everyone knew I didn't have a car, and if it had been one of the company cars the entire office would have known about it.

It was a long morning. I passed my second appointment entirely on to Jeremy, and he took one of the other girls with him. While I waited. But it was past eleven before Damon appeared, and I didn't recognize him for a moment. He was not wearing a suit – presumably he hadn't been able to find a perfect fit off the peg. But in a blazer and jeans, a smart tie and new Docksiders, he looked good enough to eat. All the female heads turned, especially as he had Roddy with him, similarly attired. He checked with reception, and a moment later the two of them were coming across the office towards me. 'Wowee!' Daphne muttered.

'Miss Ogilvie?' Damon asked. 'Damon Smith. I hope you remember me.' He held out his hand.

'How could I forget, Mr Smith,' I said, squeezing his fingers. 'And . . . ?'

'My associate, Mr Webster.'

Again I shook hands. 'Do take a seat.'

There was only one chair in front of my desk, but Daphne hurried over with another, and hovered, clearly waiting for an invitation. 'Thank you, Miss Yardley,' I said. She pulled one of her faces, but withdrew. 'Now let me see.' I laid out the various specifications I had already selected, although I had no idea of his actual financial position. 'It was a flat you were after.'

'I think to begin with.'

'I have several here. Shall we go and look at them?'

'Give me the specifications, and I'll look over them and come back to you.'

'There is one I would like to show you today. In fact, right now.'

We gazed at each other, then he shrugged. 'You're the boss lady.'

We used a company car, ignoring the raised eyebrows that I should be going out, by myself, with not one but two male clients. Damon sat in front beside me. 'Where is this place?' he asked.

'I have no idea. Does he know about last night?'

'I don't have secrets from Roddy.'

'I'm talking about Jetta Smith-Lucas.'

'Who?'

'Oh, for God's sake. My psychiatrist. The one you sent home starkers in the rain.'

'Oh, her. I didn't send her anywhere. She wanted to go.'
'After you were finished with her. What did you tell her to do when she got home?'
'Ah . . .' He appeared to think. 'I told her to have a hot bath and go to bed.'
I glanced at him. 'Honest?'
'Why should I lie about it?'
'You told her if she did that she'd wake up?'
'That's right.'
'And she would remember everything, or not?'
'I told her she'd remember.'
'Didn't you reckon she'd be terribly ashamed?'
'Sure. I was trying to get her off your back. Remember?'
'Well, she's dead.'
'Come again?' Roddy whistled.
'Apparently when she woke up, which seems to have been the moment she got into the house, and found herself naked, and remembered that she had stripped off in front of us and then walked home like that, she flipped her lid and stuck her head in the gas oven.'
'Well, shit! Who'd have supposed that?'
'Damon, you and I killed that woman.'
'Oh, don't be daft. How did we do that?'
'By hypnotizing her. Making her feel so utterly ashamed.'
'Nuts. She had some other reason. You said you and she had nothing going. Was that the truth?'
'Of course it was.'
'Well, most likely some other dyke stood her up. Or she had money troubles.'
'According to the police, she didn't. As for another lover, I suppose it's possible. But what are we going to do?'
'What should we do? It's nothing to do with us.'
'Oh . . .' But losing my temper with Damon was a waste of time. 'It is to do with us, on two counts. Firstly, her clothes and handbag.'
He nodded. 'I took a look through those. Not a lot. Save for a cheque of yours. I burned it.'

'Suppose the police search my flat?'

'Why should they do that? You didn't tell them about me?'

'Of course I didn't.'

'So why should they search your flat?'

'I don't know. But they might.'

'So we'll get rid of the stuff. You said there was something else on your mind.'

'The police say I will almost certainly be called at the inquest.'

'Why?'

'I'm the last person to see Jetta alive. Apart from you, and they don't know about you.'

'So you go to the inquest. Where's the problem? If you satisfied the police, surely you can satisfy a coroner.'

'You don't understand. I lied to the police.'

'So lie to the coroner. Just make sure they're the same lies.'

'I'll be under oath. Right now I've committed no crime. The police asked me if Jetta had acted strangely before leaving my flat, and I said no. They didn't pursue the matter. If the coroner does, and asks me the same question, and if I know of anything that might have triggered the suicide, and I say no, I'll be committing perjury. I could go to gaol for fifteen years. But if I tell the truth, I'll be involving you.'

'And we don't want that,' he said. 'You just keep on lying. There's no way anyone can ever find out what happened in your flat last night, because your psychiatrist is dead and the only other people who know anything about it are us three. Right?'

I bit my lip. 'If . . . if I lie on oath, I'll be in your power.'

He squeezed my thigh. 'Darling, you already are.'

I had never expected him to put it quite so bluntly. It left me feeling as if I'd been kicked in the stomach. And yet, not only was there nothing I could do, there was nothing I wanted to do, certainly when anywhere near Damon. I began to wonder if I had been hypnotized all over again. And not being near Damon was a difficult business.

That afternoon we house-hunted in earnest, and finally settled on a very nice two-bedroom flat. It was a rental but as it was in Mayfair it seemed to me that he was virtually buying a much cheaper place every quarter. 'I like it,' he said. 'When are you moving in?'

'Me? I have a place, with three years to run.'

'I want you with me.'

'It only has two bedrooms,' I argued faintly.

'So? Roddy has one, and we have the other.'

'We might as well be married,' I grumbled.

'I have that in mind,' he said.

I could hardly consider that a proposal of marriage, if that is what it actually was. I had never had a proposal before – Eric had always made it perfectly plain that he did not have marriage in mind, and even if he had, I wouldn't have gone for it, not with Eric. But Damon was a dream around the house. He was scrupulously clean, scrupulously tidy, and once he got the idea that in London clothes made the man, always impeccably turned out. And then there was bed! From which it will be gathered that I did as I was told, and moved in. What else?

But I didn't cancel my lease. I felt I needed to retain that bolt-hole, as I didn't know how the future was going to turn out. Because this was the oddest thing about our relationship, and an aspect that made it the more difficult to resolve. Apart from where he had given me a direct instruction, I was entirely my own person. In the Bahamas, the only instruction he had given me was not to have sex with any other man, and this had been less an instruction than a kind of prophecy. Since arriving on my doorstep he had only told me two things; one was to have sex with him and then move in with him, neither of which was a hardship, and the other was to perjure myself at the inquest into Jetta's death. Well, that wasn't difficult either, although I was very nervous about it. But everyone was very sympathetic, and no one seemed to have the slightest doubt that I was telling the truth.

But marriage? To a man to whom I was little more than a slave? Of course I understood that if he said we were going to get married tomorrow I would do it, but as with the inquest, I didn't really like the idea. What made the situation worse was that the next time I went down to Hastings, both Ma and Pa commented on how well I was looking, and how I seemed to have entirely gotten over the break-up with Eric. 'So who's the lucky new one?' Pa asked.

'What makes you think there is one?'

'It's as plain as the nose on your face. You have a permanent beam.'

'Do tell us about him,' Ma invited. 'When do we get to meet him?'

There was temptation. Except that I had no idea how it might turn out. Suppose he hypnotized *them*? But even if there was no abnormality at all in our relationship, I wasn't sure how Ma and Pa might react to Damon. They would both have denied strenuously that they were the least bit racist, but the ethnic difference between them and Damon was considerable. So I said, 'Give me a break. I've only known this guy a couple of weeks. When we get to know each other better I'll bring him down.'

'He's all right, is he?' Ma asked. I knew she was talking about things like AIDS.

'Oh, yes,' I said. 'Definitely.' And I couldn't even be certain about that.

The entrance of Damon into my life meant a considerable social difference. Not in terms of friends. I didn't have that many anyway, and over the past couple of months I had become a considerable hermit in any event, while those in the office, such as Daphne and Jeremy, both considered that I had stood them up. I couldn't argue with that. Damon naturally didn't have any friends in England, save for Roddy, and he didn't seem to be in any hurry to make them. But he did like going out in the evenings, whether it be to bars, discos, cinemas, or just strolling the West End. I found this exciting. London at night is no place for a woman unless she is adequately protected. As Roddy always accompanied us, I felt safer than at any previous time in my life, but in fact he wasn't the least bit necessary. One night we were in this pub and he had to go to the men's, leaving Damon and me in the midst of a bunch of large guys who could have been members of a rugby team drowning their sorrows after a particularly heavy defeat. Needless to say they began making advances to me. I told them to get lost, and this one very large guy stepped up to me and hooked his finger in my cleavage. 'I'm going to eat these,' he said.

I looked for Damon, who had been buying drinks. Now he turned back, just as the lout was reaching behind me with his other hand to feel my ass. 'Why don't you drop dead,' Damon said, in a low but penetrating voice.

The lout raised his head to stare at him, which was his big mistake. 'Listen, darkie,' he said, 'I'm going to . . .' Then his voice sort of trailed away, and he backed off to join his pals, who had been watching. They moved down the bar and went into a huddle, muttering at each other.

'I wonder what he had in mind,' Damon said.

'Let's get out of here before there's a punch-up.'

'No way. I like it here. And there's not going to be a punch-up, darling.' He was right. A few minutes later Roddy had rejoined us, and a few minutes after that the rugby team left.

The strange thing about that incident, and others like it, combined with the entire ambience of my new life, was that it made me feel lonelier than ever before. For all the creature comforts with which I was surrounded, the ecstasy of Damon's lovemaking, the feeling of utter security when he was around, I felt like an alien. Now I had absolutely no friends, no one I could confide in, or even indulge in a little girl chat. The idea of trying another psychiatrist did not appeal, even supposing I wasn't afraid of what Damon might do if he found out.

Until the Bahamian holiday there had always been Veronica. We had been friends at school and always since. We had cried on each other's shoulders when necessary, and we had giggled together over what we considered to be amusing. And she had shown that she wouldn't mind making up by telephoning me the day after we got back. And indeed had been perfectly friendly when I had finally called her. But for all our long friendship I had a notion she wouldn't understand. Besides, it had been Veronica who had introduced me to Eric; I had always had the feeling that she was more his friend than mine. That meant Veronica was out. And there was nobody else. I got myself into such a state that I nearly wrote Harriet.

Harriet was my sister. She was six years older than I, and had gone off to Canada when I was only twelve. Before then she had treated me as a sort of toy, so we had never been very close. Since then she had got married, and was three times a mother. Such domestic bliss, added to the fact that she had always been rather jolly hockey sticks in her approach to life, left me in no doubt that she would either write back to say I was an idiot, or write Ma recommending that I be locked up.

So I didn't write. I was on my own.

So what did the future hold? Damon, Damon and more Damon. Our relationship was complete. It even really excluded Roddy. He was there all the time, and yet he wasn't there any of the time. To my surprise, and my relief, he never attempted to muscle in on my relationship with Damon, even though in Damon's flat we simply dripped sex. I couldn't help but wonder if he too was in a permanently hypnotized state.

Damon didn't raise the subject of marriage again, and I certainly wasn't going to. I was still brooding on when would be the right time to take him down to Hastings. He had never enquired after my parents, or any aspect of my family or background; presumably he didn't know, and certainly didn't care, if they existed. He was more interested in getting a job. But here again his approach was unique. As he wouldn't go to any employment agency I brought home a bunch of newspapers crammed with situations vacant, which he scanned without great interest. By now I had got the message that in the first instance the job was for Roddy. But he seemed even less qualified than Damon. Then came the morning when Damon asked, casually, 'How well does your business do?'

It was a Sunday, and so we were having a late breakfast. 'Pretty well,' I said without thinking. 'We're not only in London, you know. We have an office in Birmingham and one in Manchester.'

'Is that a fact? All owned by that guy Randell?'

'I'm not quite sure of the set-up,' I confessed. 'He's the chairman of the company, so I suppose he has a majority shareholding. But it's a family affair. You know, wife, brother, cousins, children, all with a piece of the action.'

'Sounds cosy. I reckon that's where we'd like to work. Roddy, anyway.'

'You have to be joking.' He raised his eyebrows, and I flushed. 'Well, to be a real estate agent you have to take exams, become qualified.'

'Is that a fact? You're qualified?'

'Of course I am. I'm an FNAEA.'

'Which means what?'

'I'm a Fellow of the National Association of Estate Agents.'

'Jesus, I had no idea I was shacked up with a brain. How'd you do that?'

'I went to university.'

'For how long?'

'Two years.'

'That's too long. Roddy'd never stand two years of school.'

I refrained from pointing out that Roddy would never get near a university place, no matter how long he might be prepared to spend at it. 'There must be another way of doing it,' Damon said. 'Why can't he just join the firm and pick it up as he goes along?'

'That's not how we do things,' I said. 'The only way he could get into Randell & Company without proper qualifications is as office boy. We have an office boy.'

'I reckon you could use two.'

'You'd have to persuade Randell of that. And what about a work permit? Roddy's a Bahamian. He can't take a job here without a permit.'

'I'm sure Randell can sort that out. Fix me up an appointment with him.'

We gazed at each other. 'Oh, no,' I said. 'Oh, no, no, no, no, no. Anyway, it wouldn't work. You can't play music or clap your hands in Randell's office.'

'Then I can't do him any harm, right? Just get me the interview.'

I told Randell that Mr Smith was already a client of ours, and that he might be coming up with a big deal. Randell was happy with that. I wish I could explain my own attitude. I suppose the best way would be to say that I was permanently driving a car. It was a very comfortable, even luxurious car, and I just adored sitting behind the wheel as I drove along through the streets of this town. I had various destinations in mind, some quite urgent, and from time to time I could see them. But when I tried to go to them, I found myself up against a 'No Entry' sign and a one-way system. Obviously it occurred to me that this was a nuisance, but it never crossed my mind to drive the wrong way up the street; I took the system. I suppose in many ways all of us living in a modern society are to some extent brainwashed, or hypnotized, into our behavioural patterns, knowing that if we crash a red light because we didn't feel like stopping, or break the speed limit because we feel like going faster than usual, or threaten to shoot the obnoxious next-door neighbour, or indeed possessing the gun to do it with, we are going to be done.

My situation was just more acute than most. But at that time I had no real understanding of how acute it was; my life, my being, my personality, were all mine to command, with the single exception that I could not bring myself to walk out on Damon, despite any doubts I might have about him as a person. If I could not escape the feeling that his party trick had been responsible for Jetta Smith-Lucas's suicide, and that there could be something sinister in his relations with the man Clermont in Nassau and his subsequent inheritance, I had been a party to the one and was at least partly benefiting from the other. I still felt that the whole situation was related to me and me alone, quite illogically, as Damon and I had not even known the other had existed when Clermont had died. I was therefore quite happy to go along with the interview with Randell, even if I knew my own reputation within the firm might suffer after Damon had put forward his preposterous proposal. On the other hand neither Randell nor anyone else yet knew that Damon and I were living together, so I reckoned the risk was not so great after all.

Which is not to say that I wasn't a bundle of nerves on the morning Damon and Roddy, both wearing new suits and looking very posh, were shown into the office. 'Wasn't that your client?' Daphne asked. As usual, when Damon appeared, all the female heads had turned.

'Why, yes,' I agreed, casually. 'He did ask for an interview with the boss.'

'Is he going to complain about the flat you negotiated for him?'

'I hope not. He seemed satisfied.'

'You never can tell with people like him,' she said darkly. 'What other reason can there be? To go to the boss, when he's been dealing with you?'

'Perhaps he wants to buy some more property. He's seems to be loaded.'

'He's too young to be loaded. It's not as if he's a pop star or something.'

'How do we know he's not a pop star?' I countered. 'He

comes from America.' This was stretching the point a bit. But America really covers everything across the Atlantic, not merely the United States.

She didn't appear to agree, but her phone went and she had to buzz off. It was only ten minutes later that Randell came down the circular staircase, followed by Roddy; Damon had apparently remained in the office. 'Mr Harpe,' Randell said.

Harpe, who was the office manager, left his desk and hurried to the steps. 'Mr Harpe,' Randell said, 'this is Mr Roderick Webster. Mr Webster will be joining our staff tomorrow, as an agent. I wonder if you would show him round and introduce him. Thank you.'

Six

The New Boy

I was probably more flabbergasted than anyone else; I was the only one who knew that Roddy had no qualifications whatsoever. Everyone else, in fact, seemed pleased to have him join us; he was a good-looking and personable young man, even if certainly not in the Damon class. Needless to say, I was the one who got stuck with him.

'I believe you've met,' Harpe said. He was a little man, heavy-set and with beetle brows. That he had never cast a lascivious glance in my direction or managed a surreptitious caress of my bottom when I was bending over my desk I put down to the fact that, for all his aggressive appearance and demeanour, he was basically afraid of women – and of being slapped with a harassment suit.

'Yes, we have,' I said. 'Good morning, Mr Webster. Glad to have you with us.'

'My pleasure,' Roddy said.

'So I think it would be a good idea for you to take him under your wing, Frances,' Harpe said. 'You don't know London very well, do you, Webster?'

'I don't know London at all,' Roddy confessed.

'Yes.' Harpe's tone indicated that he was just realizing that he had been sold a pup. 'Frances will instruct you.' He bustled off and went up to the office, which Damon had just vacated. Obviously he wanted to find out what was going on, but equally obviously the answers he got were not satisfactory, for he came back down looking more like a thundercloud than ever.

I realized that things had worked out better than I had dared hope, in that as Roddy's tutor I could disguise from the rest of the office his total ignorance of the real estate business. But I could still hardly wait to get home that evening.

Damon was soaking in the bath. I stood above him, looking, I hoped, like an avenging angel. Or at least an inquiring one. 'Just how did you do it?' I demanded.

'I explained that Roddy would like a job, and that we were both impressed with the office and the people there, and he agreed.'

'Oh, come off it. You hypnotized the old buzzard. But how did you do it?'

'I told him a story.'

'You're going to make me angry,' I warned.

He grinned; he knew I wasn't serious. 'It's the truth. I told him a story, and when I was finished, he gave Roddy the job.'

'Okay. Tell me this story.'

He shook his head. 'There's no need.'

'Because you have me already, is that it?'

He got out of the bath. 'Listen, stop keeping up this angst and start enjoying life. What have you got to worry about?'

'I would like to know,' I said, 'if you reckon you can hypnotize anybody you choose simply by telling them a story or playing them some music.'

'I reckon I can.' He dried himself. 'Given the right circumstances.'

I opened my mouth and then closed it again; there are some things that are better left unsaid. Because if he could do that, surely he could, in time, rule England, or rule the world. But as – for the moment, at any rate – his horizons seemed strictly limited, it might be a serious mistake to point that out to him. But I still had my own axe to grind. 'Are you ever going to release me? Haven't I done everything you wish of me?'

'Sure. But I keep thinking of new things for you to do. Like I said, if you'd just sit back and relax, you'd start enjoying life.'

'Well, tell me this. Will I be released when you die?'

He chucked me under the chin. 'Who's a naughty girl, then. You haven't got the guts, darling.'

Well, of course he was right, even if I could ever contemplate killing somebody. Especially somebody with whom I had shared my all. 'I'm just trying to find out where I stand.'

'Well, you'd better keep praying that I stay alive. If I die, then the spell goes on for ever, until *you* die.' He sure knew how to cheer a girl up.

And yet, when I sat back to think about it, I wondered why *didn't* I just relax and enjoy life, as Damon presented it. I might have been able to do that if I hadn't felt sure that he was actually following a plan, which might not include political power – he simply lacked the imagination for that at this stage – but which certainly was designed to improve the physical well-being and prosperity of Damon Smith. I must admit though, I was in the beginning totally mystified as to how getting Roddy a job at Randell & Company was going to further this determination. Roddy's pay as a new agent was minimal, and he took only a very small share of any commissions we obtained.

The penny dropped when in the mail one morning in October I discovered an invitation to a cocktail party, from Mrs James Randell. For a moment I supposed I had to be back in my dream world. Did modern women really call themselves by their husband's names? Did people in 1997 really have cocktail parties via gilt-edged invitations? Obviously they did, but it was not an aspect of society with which I had ever come into contact.

And to be invited to the boss's house? That had never happened to anyone in the office, to my knowledge. I showed it to Damon. 'What do you think of this?'

'I think we need to buy you a new dress.'

I frowned at him. 'You got one too?'

'Of course. So has Roddy.'

'How?'

'While we were playing golf on Sunday I mentioned to Randell that we needed to do a bit of socializing.'

'You have been playing golf with Randell?' I had spent the weekend in Hastings, with his blessing.

'He took me to his club. Swish place.'

'But . . . can you play golf?'

'Sure. I used to caddy at the Country Club in Nassau when I was a kid. Picked up a lot. And frankly, Randell isn't very good.'

I wondered if he had actually been hypnotized into playing badly. For the first time I actually felt sorry for my boss. But that was lost in the anticipation of the party. Neither Roddy nor I told anyone in the office how we had been honoured, of course, but that Roddy was Randell's blue-eyed boy was obvious to everyone, and raised at least mental eyebrows amongst some. 'If he didn't have three children I'd have supposed he was gay,' Daphne remarked.

'Quite a few men actually become gay after a virtual lifetime perfectly straight,' Jeremy said seriously. 'Or at least realize that they would enjoy a gay experience.'

'So which half of your life are you in?' Daphne demanded.

'I haven't even got through the first half yet,' he pointed out, with a meaningful glance in my direction.

So that's what he had concluded, I thought. That the reason I hadn't been able to go through with it with him was because I was basically gay myself. I supposed it was a more reasonable explanation than the truth.

Damon took me to a small but frightfully expensive boutique off Berkeley Square that he had discovered during his ramblings around London. Here I tried on several very pricey but enchanting party frocks. I would have gone for a pale blue, but he preferred a black, above the knee, low cut and a mass of frills. 'Shows off your hair,' he explained. Perhaps he was thinking of both ends of the spectrum, but he was paying. Then there were matching shoes and bag.

He wanted to buy jewellery as well, but I declined; I had my locket.

The boys also fitted themselves out in new suits – the whole thing must have cost well over a grand – and then we took a taxi to the Randells' town flat, which was a large affair in Eaton Square. Here we found ourselves in the midst of an enormous crowd of the upper crust, and I at least was taken aback to discover that we were amongst the half-dozen youngest in the room, by a long shot. We were, however, immediately rescued by another of the youthful minority. 'I'm Jane Randell,' she said. 'You must be Damon Smith. Daddy has told me so much about you.' She was a small girl, with dark hair and a mass of jewellery. In general she took after her father, except that she was much better-looking. 'And you're Miss Ogilvie,' she said, surveying my dress with contempt; hers was far more modest. 'And Mr Webster. Daddy has told me all about you.'

He hadn't apparently told her anything about me. But I felt better when Jane led us through the throng to meet her mother. 'But my dear,' Mrs Randell said, holding both my hands, 'you are absolutely lovely.' I felt like curtseying. But it seemed quite a few other people thought so too, at least amongst the men. I was the centre of attention; included in my circle of admirers was at least one MP, and someone who was introduced to me as a minister – I didn't catch of what.

In the course of this adulation I met the two Randell sons. Like their sister they took after their father in size, although they were *not* so good-looking. Having been told I was a mere employee of the firm, they were rather supercilious, and wasted no time in telling me that *they* would be joining the firm, at board room level, as soon as they came down from university. I had always known that Randell's was a family firm without possessing any knowledge of how it actually worked, but these two lager louts rapidly managed to inform me that they were shareholders, as were their sister and mother, although the majority holder was of course their father, with seventy-five per cent. This information meant nothing to me at the time, as I could not imagine it possibly ever having anything to do with me, save for the reflection that if old Randell were to drop off his perch I, and all the other staff, would probably be left at the mercy of this pair. Fortunately the old man was neither very old nor appeared to have any health problems.

He had other problems, though. The evening was half over before he caught up with me. Then I found his hand grasping my elbow as he steered me away from the immediate throng. 'I am so glad you could come, Frances.'

'It was very good of you to invite me, Mr Randell.'

'I think, as we are not in the office, and are such good friends, that you could call me James.' I wondered if I should be alarmed or not. But at the moment, with several glasses of champagne inside me, I was merely interested in discovering how far he meant to go. 'One of the reasons I'm glad you came,' he said, 'is because I have something to show you.'

'Oh, yes?'

'I know you'll be interested. It's through here.' Hand still on my elbow, he guided me out of the drawing room and along a corridor. To my right was the dining room, the table laden with trays of canapés while staff hurried to and fro. On our left was a closed door, which he now opened to show me into his study. It was a place of book-lined walls and leather armchairs, extremely cosy. It also contained several glass-fronted display cases, filled with wooden statuettes, mostly females, some of them quite indecent. And I had expected etchings! 'My African collection,' he said, opening one of the cases and taking out a bust of a woman who seemed to be all breast and nose, in very dark wood. 'Feel that.' I took it very carefully, but it was not as heavy as I had feared, and yet was difficult to handle because the wood was so smooth as to be almost slippery. 'Isn't that lovely?' he asked.

I had to agree that it was – the wood rather than the representation. 'Is it very valuable?'

'Priceless.'

'Then you'd better have it back.' Relieved, I looked at the other cases. 'Are they all priceless?'

'Just about.' He followed me about the room. 'Have you ever been sculpted?'

'Good lord, no. Who'd want to?'

'I can think of a lot. You're a very beautiful woman.'

I fell back on my old defence. 'My nose is too big.'

'Your nose is just perfect. Would you like to be sculpted?'

'I don't know. I'm not very good at keeping still for long periods.'

'Oh, he'd work from a photograph to begin with. He'd just need you for the final touches. Would you like me to arrange a sitting for you?'

'How much would it cost?'

'He'd pay you, my dear.'

'You're kidding. And who gets the sculpture when it's finished?'

'It'd be up for sale, officially. But I'd buy it before anyone else could see it.'

'And put it in one of these cases?'

'That depends on its size.'

'You mean it would be bigger than head and shoulders?'

'Oh, yes. It'd have to include your breasts.'

'Which would first of all have to be photographed. By you?'

'I will certainly do it, if you prefer. But I would like a sculpture of all of you. Your legs are at least as attractive as your breasts.'

'You say the nicest things,' I remarked, my brain doing handsprings. This was certainly the most unusual approach I had ever had. 'But I really don't think it's me, James. The idea of me standing permanently in that corner, in the nude, waiting for you to give me a rub whenever you felt the urge, would give the real me the heebie-jeebies.'

'Damon said you wouldn't object.'

'He did, did he?'

'He's your partner, isn't he?'

'I suppose he is. But he's certainly not my pimp.' I bit my lip. 'I'm sorry. I don't mean to offend you, Mr Randell. James. Look, just let's forget the whole thing and rejoin the party.'

'He said you wouldn't object to anything I might say, or propose, or even do,' Randell said. 'And he wouldn't either. He said there'd be no question of harassment charges.'

'He does say these things,' I agreed, and went to the door. But I knew I wasn't going to get there without a struggle. He would have to be slapped down, regardless of the consequences. Both his arms went round my waist and his hands came up to grasp what he was really after, while he was now trying to fit himself into my bottom. 'Please, Mr Randell,' I said, trying to keep it civilized.

'You are so beautiful,' he mumbled into my neck. 'And I am so lonely.'

'You?' I asked, still trying to make up my mind what to do. 'With your wife and children, this house . . .'

'But no sex,' he groaned. 'Alice thinks we are too old for that sort of thing.' Again I almost felt sorry for him, but he was now squeezing, quite hard. There was nothing for it. I took a deep breath and struck behind me with both elbows. 'Oof,' he gasped, but he let me go. I sat down on the nearest chair and panted.

For a moment I was quite anxious. I hadn't really meant to hit him that hard. I bent over him. 'Are you all right?' He went on panting and grunting for several seconds. 'I'm sorry,' I said. 'But it's not me.'

'You said there'd be no harassment business,' he gasped.

'I didn't say that,' I reminded him. 'Damon did. But if you were acting in that belief, I'll go along with it. On condition we both agree this session never happened.'

'Oh, yes,' he said. 'I'll forget all about it, if you will.'

'Done.' I straightened my dress. 'And no more talk about photographs or sculpting.'

'And you'll stay in your job,' he begged. 'You're one of our very best.'

'Certainly I'll stay in my job,' I said. I didn't have anywhere else to go.

I was very angry, but I contained myself until we got home, which wasn't for a while, as Damon was busily chatting up the MP and the minister; at least, I reflected, he couldn't possibly hypnotize them in the middle of a noisy party. But when our own door had closed on us, I cut loose. 'Did you really offer me to Randell?' I demanded while Roddy prepared supper.

'I told him I wouldn't object if he made a pass at you.' He grinned at me. 'I knew you wouldn't be having any of it.'

'Because of your spell?'

'Maybe. But equally because he's a dirty old man.'

I couldn't argue with that. But I was not mollified. 'And how many other men are you going to offer me to?'

'Don't you enjoy it?'

'No, I do not. It's humiliating, and I hate being handled like a sack of potatoes.'

'Point taken. There won't be any more.'

'Promise?'

'Absolutely. I just want to keep Randell sweet. He's our ace in the hole.'

I was intrigued, angry as I was. 'What do you hope to get out of him? He's as mean as can be – you've seen my paycheques. So you got him to give Roddy a job. That's not going to make any of us millionaires.'

'Patience, my love,' he said. 'Roddy has a great future.'

I resisted the temptation to remark that if one believed that, one could believe anything. And I was, as usual, the one left gaping when, the following week, Mr Randell set off on one of his quarterly tours of the regional offices, and elected to take Roddy with him. 'The more he learns of the real estate business the better,' he announced

That really set the tongues wagging; there was even some debate as to whether or not Mrs Randell knew what was going on, and whether or not, if she didn't, she should be informed, but there was no volunteer to do that. I even found myself in the remarkable position of defending the old buzzard. Well, I knew beyond a shadow of a doubt that he was certainly not gay, no matter how frustrating he might be finding his current love life, or lack of one. But I didn't want to let him down even further. He had kept his word and our relationship in the office was as normal as it had ever been; I could hardly do less than keep mine.

Damon of course was as pleased as punch. 'He has made Roddy his protégé,' he explained. 'Every successful man needs a protégé.'

'And you have some vague idea that he will promote Roddy, who doesn't have a clue.'

'That is exactly what he is going to do.'

I gazed at him in a mixture of amazement and consternation. 'Because you have told him to do it? Or was that business of telling him he could feel me up a bribe?'

'I have suggested that Roddy is just the man he needs at his shoulder. The business with you was merely insurance. If the fearsome Alice were to hear of it there'd be hell to pay. He's terrified of her.'

'And what about his sons? Aren't they coming into the business as soon as they leave university?'

'That is the present intention,' Damon said. 'But they're not due down for another couple of years. Long enough.'

'Damon,' I said, as earnestly as I could, 'you cannot just take over people's lives, make them do what you want them to do, regardless of their own ideas, their own ambitions.'

'Why not?' he asked. 'You're happy, aren't you?'

'No, I am not,' I shouted.

'God, but you're hard to please. You have everything any woman can want. And on top of that you have me. Every girl and woman in that office of yours would like to change places with you. So would that Jane Randell. She pants every time she sees me.'

'So how often have you seen her?'

'We meet at the Golf Club,' he said, having the grace to look embarrassed.

'And I suppose you've hypnotized her into bed.'

'No, I have not. I'm a one-woman man.'

'Thank you for those kind words.'

'So tell me why you're unhappy.'

'I'm unhappy because I'm a fucking slave,' I said.

'When last did I tie you up and whip you?'

'Oh, for God's sake. Be serious. I'm your slave because you made me so. I don't enjoy that. I hate it. You had no right to do it. You have even less right to keep me in this state.'

'Let me ask you something. Forget the hypnotism bit. If we had met at a party, and I had asked you out, and then suggested getting into your knickers, would you have turned me down?'

'Well . . .' I knew I was blushing.

'I could've had you on the boat that first night. You know that?'

'Yes, I do,' I muttered. 'You behaved like a perfect gentleman.'

'And don't I behave like a perfect gentleman all the time? With you, anyway?'

I sighed. 'Yes, you do.'

'But you don't enjoy living here with me, making love with me, spending my money.'

'Of course I do. It's just that . . . I'm doing all of these things because *you* want me to, not because *I* do.'

'You just agreed that you did.'

'But I don't know that I would feel that way if I hadn't hypnotized me. Can't you understand that?' I held his hands. 'Listen. Set me free. Then I'll know. I would say nothing will change. I am happy here with you. But I'd be so much happier if I knew I was doing it of my own free will.'

'And suppose I set you free, and you realized you didn't want this after all? You'd walk out, wouldn't you?'

'Would you want me to stay, knowing that it was over?'

'I want you to stay. I don't want ever to know it's over. I told you, you're my woman, and I'm a one-woman man. I like everything about you. I *love* everything about you. I want you here, always. I know women. Especially women like you, real lookers who can have any man in the world. Even if you agreed to stay at this moment, the time would come when you'd get the itch and want to find out if the grass was greener somewhere else.'

All of this was very flattering, of course. But he had overlooked something. 'And what happens when *you* get tired of *me*? In my experience it's much more likely to happen with a guy than with a girl.'

He took my face between his hands and kissed me on the mouth. 'If it ever happens, which it won't, I'll set you free.'

'Promise?'

'I promise. Satisfied?'

'Well . . .' That was something.

'Now,' he said, 'I'd like to come with you to Hastings, and meet your folks.' He kissed me again. 'I have to ask your dad for your hand, right?'

He had this knack of snatching thoughts, ideas, right out of one's head and replacing them with his own. I was delighted, and relieved, that he should want to marry me. But I was also as nervous as hell at what my parents' reaction might be. On the other hand, they had repeatedly asked to meet this new partner of mine, and it had to happen some time. 'You must understand,' I said as the train rumbled south on Saturday morning, 'my folks are very old-fashioned.' That certainly went for Pa. But old-fashioned seemed an odd way to describe Mummy. On the other hand she certainly clung to the ideals of the sixties and seventies, even if total sexual freedom was behind her.

Damon understood immediately. 'You mean they're racist.'

'I don't know that they are. But, well . . .'

'You've told them about me?'

'Not exactly.'

'I see. So they're expecting some yellow-haired kid with blue eyes. We should've had Roddy with us.'

'I'm sure they're going to like you very much,' I said. 'It's just that they may be a little stiff at first. They're very shy,' I added, quite untruthfully.

'But they know I'm coming, right? I heard you on the phone.'

'Yes, they know you're coming. They're quite excited about it.'

'Then it should be all right. I sure would like to be welcomed by your folks.'

'I want that too. But I'd like you to promise me something.'

'Tell me.'

'Well . . .' I licked my lips, unsure of his reaction. 'Should you get the impression that they don't like you, leave it. They'll come round, given time, and when they realize that we're both serious. What I am trying to say is, I don't want them hypnotized into liking you, under any circumstances. Right?'

He considered for a few minutes, then said, 'If that's how you want it.'

'Promise?'

'Of course.'

He clearly intended to make a good impression. When we got off the train he went to the flower stand and bought a large bouquet for Ma, then made me take him to a tobacconist to buy some of Pa's favourite mixture. I couldn't help but remark, 'Beware a Greek bearing gifts.'

'I'm not Greek,' he pointed out.

But I could tell he was nearly as nervous as I was as we took the lift to the fourth floor. I rang the bell. Ma opened the door. 'Frankie! How nice to see you. And this is . . .' She looked past me, and definitely did a double-take. Ma is a trifle short-sighted, and she wasn't wearing her specs, but it was obvious Damon was not what she had expected, although I doubted she immediately realized he had mixed blood.

'Damon Smith, Mrs Ogilvie,' he said. 'This is a great pleasure. These are for you.'

Ma's expression of bemusement grew as she accepted the flowers. 'Come in, do,' she said. 'Harry! Frankie's here. With Mr Smith.'

Pa duly got up, and stood in the lounge doorway. His eyesight was much better than Ma's, and he also did a double-take, although his had nothing to do with Damon's good looks. 'Damon Smith, Mr Ogilvie,' Damon said, holding out his hand.

Pa took it. 'You're Welsh.'

'Not guilty, sir. I'm Bahamian.'

Pa looked at me. 'We met when I was on holiday,' I reminded him. I had already told him this, but he was in one of his can't-remember modes.

'I brought you this, sir,' Damon said, and offered the box of tobacco.

'How very nice,' Pa said.

'Tea's ready,' Ma said.

It went off far better than I had dared hope, although I didn't care to consider what might be said when next I visited them – without Damon. But they couldn't fault him for charm, or personality. 'On a visit, are you?' Pa asked, perhaps optimistically.

'No, I think I'm here to stay. I am British, you know. My father was British.'

'And you've found yourself a job?' Ma asked.

'No, no. I'm in real estate. That's how Frances and I got together. She sells it, and I buy it.'

'Expensive, nowadays,' Pa said. 'Real estate.' He was fishing.

'I have some capital,' Damon said.

'Damon came into some money a couple of years ago,' I said, inadvertently.

He shot me a glance, and too late I remembered that he had never actually told me about Clermont. But immediately he was all smiles again. 'So I thought I should find a home for it. Several homes.'

'Investment trusts,' Pa said. 'That's what you want to be in.'

'I prefer to have complete control over my money,' Damon said.

After tea the two of us went for a walk on the beach; we both reckoned Ma and Pa needed to mull things over. As it was a blustery and quite cold autumnal afternoon, the sand was deserted, which was just as well, as we had to shout at each other to make ourselves heard.

'So who told you about Clermont?' he asked.

'I'm sorry. I should have mentioned it. I ran into that fellow Roger Gaillard at a party, and he told me.'

'You and Gaillard talked about me?'

'Well, if you must know, I asked.'

'Why?'

'For God's sake, Damon, I was just beginning to realize that you had actually hypnotized me, and I had no idea if I'd ever see you again. I was desperate, which is why I went to that shrink, and then I bumped into Roger, and as I knew he knew you, I wanted to find out something about you.'

'And he told you I was gay.'

'Well . . . when you wanted to be. You told me that yourself, in Harbour Island.'

'And who else have you told?'

'No one at all. It's your business. And mine now, I suppose. But you don't behave as if you're gay. Not when you're with me. It must have been a terrible experience.'

'Assing about with that guy?'

'I meant when he dropped dead. Roger said you were actually in the room with him when it happened.'

'Yeah,' he said. 'It's never nice.' As if it happened every

day of the week. 'He have you?' he asked. 'That guy Gaillard?'

'Of course he did not. Even if I had fancied him, which I didn't, he couldn't, or I couldn't. You ought to know that.'

'Yeah,' he said. 'I'd forgotten. Let's get back; this wind is killing me.'

He insisted on taking Ma and Pa out to dinner. He asked them to pick a restaurant, and they came up with a choice of three, but when they wanted to dismiss one of these as too pricey, the decision was instantaneous.

We had a bang-up meal, but Ma had apparently been doing some thinking, and when the two of us went to the ladies' together, she asked, 'You going back up to town tonight?'

'We hadn't thought of it. We'll go up tomorrow.'

'Ah,' she said. 'You know there's only the one spare room.'

'There only ever has been,' I pointed out. 'That was never a problem with Eric.'

'Yes,' she said doubtfully.

'Ma, your racism is showing.'

'Well, when I was a girl, going out with black men was an indication that one wasn't as good as one should be. They were mostly pimps.'

'That was more than thirty years ago. There are three things you need to remember. One, Damon is not a pimp; he doesn't need to be. Two, he is not a black man. His father was English; his mother was half French and half black.' That was probably an exaggeration, but I intended to make my point. 'Three, I am in love with him and intend to marry him.'

'Oh,' she said. 'I hadn't realized.'

By the time we got back to the table, Damon had posed the question to Pa, who was looking even more flabbergasted.

'That's all right,' I said. 'Ma knows, and approves.'

Talk about old-fashioned looks. But the deed was done; they had been outmanoeuvred.

The rest of the weekend was devoted to dates and times and places. I didn't want a winter wedding, so we decided on June. Damon wanted a London wedding, so we decided on St James's Chapel. Then there was the reception, which would have to be at a hotel.

By now Pa was scratching his head. 'This is really a little out of our financial league,' he remarked.

'Not to worry,' Damon said. 'I'll take care of it.'

'Well . . .' Pa looked at Ma; he was obviously warming to Damon by the moment.

'That was really sweet of you,' I told him as we took the train back up to town on Sunday afternoon.

'I enjoyed it. They're nice people.'

When he was in this mood he was so good to be with. If only our relationship could have been normal, I would have been the happiest girl in the world. And always there was this niggling temptation at the back of my mind: why not be the happiest girl in the world. 'Are we going to have children?' I asked.

'You bet. Lots and lots.'

'Does that mean you want me to give up my job?'

'Not right now,' he said. 'I'd like you there for another year or two. There's time.'

'You almost make me feel that you intend to take over Randell & Company.'

He grinned at me. 'That's the idea.'

I could never be sure when to take him seriously, or how seriously to take him. So I changed the subject. 'Are we going to put a notice in the papers?'

'All in good time.'

'Damon,' I said. 'You *are* serious about this?'

'You bet I'm serious. But there's a proper sequence in which things have to happen.'

'You mean you don't want me to tell anyone at work that we're engaged?'

'Not right at this moment.'

'Do I get a ring?'

'When it's time to go public.'

Of course I went along with what he wanted; I was doing that all the time. But I simply could not make up my mind what he was up to. Just as I continued to have no real idea of what he was up to during the day when I was at work. Certainly all his plans seemed to be working out. Roddy returned from his office tour even more Randell's favourite companion, and the rumours grew. So much so that Harpe finally took umbrage and early in the new year resigned. Guess who was promoted office manager in his place, after less than six months in the firm?

Needless to say, we were invited to the Randells' Christmas Eve party. The place was, as usual, packed to the door with bigwigs and politicians with whom Damon seemed on the best of terms; I began to wonder, and worry, if the extent to which he could use his occult powers was beginning to dawn on him. This left me very much on the fringes of the party, as Roddy was being chatted up by most of the younger females, and Jane Randell, and her brothers, pointedly ignored me. I compensated by downing several glasses of champagne, and I suppose I was a sitting duck when someone asked, 'Where have you been all of my life, you gorgeous creature?'

'Being gorgeous,' I replied, turning to face him. He was very well dressed, in a suit with a polo-necked white shirt; his dark hair was cut short, and he had an attractively weather-beaten face, with a tan to match. I put him down as a rugby player or an ocean sailor – he had the build to be either, and towered above me, even at my five eight.

He held my hands, inspecting my fingers. 'And fancy-free.'

'For the moment.' I did not pull away; I had the vague,

champagne-induced idea that if Damon saw me flirting with another guy he might lose some of that arrogant right of possession he maintained towards me.

I also had the idea, undoubtedly champagne-induced, that if I was looking for someone to prove that I was no longer under hypnosis, this was what I would have chosen. 'I'd like to fill that moment,' he said. 'Where do you figure in this mob?'

'I'm one of Mr Randell's employees.'

'You mean you sell real estate?'

'I try to.'

'How about selling me some, like tomorrow. Preferably a vacant house in the country.'

'There are some caveats about that.'

'Tell me, and I'll get rid of them.'

'Number one is that tomorrow is Christmas Day. Shouldn't you be spending it with your wife and family?'

'There's a caveat about that too. I don't have a wife and family.'

'I see. There is also the point that our agents always sell in pairs. For our own protection.'

'And you think you might need protection from me.'

'I'm absolutely certain of it.'

'Well, how about coming out anyway. As you say, it's Christmas Day, so you don't have to go to work. We could take a drive in the country.'

'That's very nice of you,' I said. 'But there are two more caveats.'

'Your list seems endless. What are these?'

'One is that I have a partner. That chap over there, talking to the minister.'

My admirer looked across the room, and wrinkled his nose. 'I'd have thought you could do better than that.'

'Watch it,' I told him, 'or I shall step on your toe. The second is that, as we keep reminding each other, tomorrow is Christmas Day, and I, and my partner, are having lunch with my parents.'

'You're all tied up,' he said. 'At least give me your phone number.'

I gave him the number of my own flat. He could talk to the ansaphone.

I had those three possibilities roaming around my mind, dangerously so. I had no real desire to break with Damon, who, as regards me at any rate, was everything he claimed to be. But I did resent being hypnotized into that state. When one is drowning, one is inclined to clutch at straws, and my only straw was to break the original spell. I felt that if I could do that, I would be a totally happy woman. My continued surrender to him in everything could be put down to the psychological superiority he had established over me, but even that could be resisted and perhaps overcome once I was sure I was free of the hypnosis. There was also the establishment of some independence. And there was the attractiveness of this man . . . I didn't even know his name.

So, would I dare do it? I felt I had given myself some breathing space to come to a decision. How much I didn't know, because he said, 'I will call. But not tomorrow,' and then wandered off into the throng, leaving me quite breathless, and desperately in need of some more champagne.

This was achieved without difficulty, and then I found myself standing next to Jane, somewhat to my surprise, as she had been avoiding me all evening. 'So what did Anthony have to say to you?' she asked.

'Is that his name? He never mentioned it.'

'He seemed very interested.'

'He was.'

'And so were you. I should warn you about him. He is a womanizer and a cad.'

'They go together,' I agreed.

'He has shagged nearly every woman in London.'

'Prodigious,' I said. 'Does that include you?'

She gave me a glare, but then we were interrupted by her father, who was standing on the far side of the room and clapping his hands for quiet. To my surprise, Roddy was standing beside him. 'Ladies and gentlemen,' Randell said. 'Tonight I have both an introduction and an announcement to make. Actually, I am sure that you all know Mr Webster, one of our brightest young men. Tonight I have to tell you that I have decided to make Mr Webster a partner in the firm of Randell & Company.'

The Court

Before opening the case for the Defence, Sir Barton always spent a good five minutes shuffling his papers, stooping to whisper to his seconds, clearing his throat, and adjusting his wig. This had the effect of heightening the tension in the courtroom, even for those acquainted with his methods, such as Lord Justice Mahaig and Mr Buckston, QC, leading for the Crown. It certainly reduced the young woman in the witness box to a shivering wreck, and when Sir Barton finally condescended to address her she gave a convulsive jump.
'Your name is Louise Mazender,' Sir Barton suggested.
'Yes, sir.' Louise's voice was low.
'You will have to speak a little louder,' Sir Barton told her. 'Or the jury will not be able to hear your answers.'
'Yes, sir.' Louise raised her voice.
'Now, Louise . . .' Sir Barton beamed at her as a lion might beam at a gazelle he has just brought down and is preparing to eat. 'You were private secretary to the late Sir Roderick Webster. But you were not always Sir Roderick's secretary, were you? Before his so rapid rise in the company, you were Mr Randell's private secretary. Am I right?'
'Yes, sir.'
'You could say that Sir Roderick inherited you. Ha ha ha.' No one else laughed. 'Did you enjoy working for Sir Roderick? This would have been before his so strange elevation to a knighthood.'
'He was very pleasant, sir.'
'But surely you found his sudden promotion in the company to a partnership surprising?'

'It was unexpected, sir. Sir Roderick had only been with the company a few months when Mr Randell made him a partner.'

'Was it unexpected to the rest of the staff?'

'Oh, yes, sir.'

'Including Mrs Smith? She would have been Miss Ogilvie, then.'

'I think Miss Ogilvie was as surprised as any of us, sir.'

'Did you know Miss Ogilvie well?'

'I only knew her in the office, sir.'

'You weren't friends. Why was this?'

'Well, sir . . . Miss Ogilvie kept very much to herself.'

'But she was friendly with Mr Webster, as he then was?'

'Oh, yes, sir. Well, Mr Webster was a friend of Mr Smith's.'

'They were all friends. Good friends?'

'I would say so, sir. They shared a flat, even after Mr Smith married Miss Ogilvie.'

'Now, Miss Ogilvie actually worked in the same office as Sir Roderick. Mr Smith didn't. But he was a friend of Mr Randell.'

'Oh, yes, sir.'

'Very well. So you worked for Mr Randell, and then for Sir Roderick, for several years. And you found Sir Roderick a pleasant man, and easy to get on with. Now, Miss Mazender, as I am sure you are aware, the Prosecution has determined that Sir Roderick was murdered. That is why we are here today. Unfortunately, they are unable to tell us how he was murdered. There has been some vague talk that he was hypnotized to death, which I am sure you will agree is absurd.' Louise didn't actually look as if she agreed at all, but she kept silent. 'But you actually worked with the deceased for several years. Did you, at any time during those several years, notice anything odd about him?'

'No, sir.'

'He was always unfailingly pleasant. Was he always, or did he appear to be, in full command of all his faculties?'

'Oh, yes, sir.'

'No indication of having been hypnotized?'

'No, sir. Although—'

'Please just answer my questions, Miss Mazender. Now I wish to turn to the fatal night. Was Sir Roderick perfectly normal that day?'

'Yes, sir.'

'What time did you go home?'

'I left the office at six, sir.'

'And Sir Roderick was still there. Did he tell you he was going to work late, or perhaps all night?'

'Yes, sir. He said he would be working late. He often did, recently.'

'Did he give any indication that he might be expecting a visitor later on?'

'No, sir.'

'I see. Now, Randell & Company employs a night watchman, Mr Hatch, who has a desk in the outer office. Now, Mr Hatch has stated that no one entered the building during the night. Equally he has testified that no one left the building. Would you agree that it would have been impossible for anyone to do either of those things without him seeing them?'

'No, sir. I mean, yes, sir. Mr Hatch would have been able to see anyone entering or leaving the building.'

'Therefore we may assume that no one did. Thank you, Miss Mazender. I have no further questions.'

Louise stepped towards the box exit, and was checked by Buckston. *'Just one moment, Miss Mazender.'* Louise gave a little sigh as she turned back to face the Prosecuting Counsel. *'As my learned friend has reminded us, Mr Hatch has testified that no one could enter or leave the building without his seeing them. But this was by the main front entrance. Is there not another way into, and out of, the building?'*

'Well, yes, sir. There is a private entrance at the back. But . . .' She bit her lip.

'Go on, Miss Mazender.'

Louise drew a deep breath. 'That door is strictly for the use of the partners.'

'You mean the partners are the only people who have keys for this door.'

'Yes, sir.'

'So, how many of these keys are there?'

Another deep breath. 'As far as I know, sir, there are only two keys.'

'Held by whom?'

'Well, one was held by Sir Roderick, and the other by Miss Ogilvie.'

'You mean Mrs Smith. Now, Miss Mazender, you have mentioned that before Sir Roderick, as has been suggested, inherited you, you worked for Mr Randell. For how many years?'

'Six years, sir.'

'And may we suppose that you were present on the day Mr Randell—'

Sir Barton stood up. 'Objection. The question is irrelevant, m'lud. What happened to Mr Randell has nothing to do with this case.'

'Mr Buckston?'

'With respect, m'lud, in my opinion it has everything to do with this case.'

Lord Justice Mahaig looked from one barrister to the other. 'This is a matter I will have to take under consideration,' he said. 'I will give my decision this afternoon.'

'Very good, m'lud.' Buckston sat down.

'Are you finished with this witness, Sir Barton?'

'There are just a couple more matters, m'lud.'

'Very well.'

'Miss Mazender, you have said that this private doorway was for the use of the partners only, and that only they possessed keys to it. However, can you swear that the door was always kept locked?'

'Well, sir . . .'

'Can you swear it, Miss Mazender?'

'Well, no, sir.'

'Neither, I assume, can you swear that if Sir Roderick had remained alone at the office after hours, perhaps for the purpose of a private meeting with someone, he might not have left the door unlocked, so that his guest or client could gain access without disturbing Mr Hatch?'

'Well, sir . . .'

'Can you swear to that, Miss Mazender?'

'No, sir, I cannot.'

'Thank you. Now, you have said that you, and all of the staff at Randell's, were totally surprised by Sir Roderick's sudden elevation into the partnership. Can you tell us if Mr Randell's family were similarly surprised?'

Buckston looked as if he might be considering an objection of his own, but decided against it; he was content with the way things were going. 'Yes, sir,' Louise said. 'I understood that they were.'

'You mean that, to the best of your knowledge, Mr Randell had not discussed this surprising decision of his with them.'

Once again Buckston clearly considered an objection, but once again let it go.

'To the best of my knowledge, no, sir.'

'Have you any knowledge of their reaction?'

'I believe they were upset, sir.'

'Quite. Thank you, Miss Mazender.'

Seven

The Attempt

The entire room was silent for a moment. Alice Randell was the first to speak. 'What did you say?' she demanded. She had been standing in the front row of the guests, smiling at her husband in anticipation of what he might be about to say. She was no longer smiling.

'I said that I have decided to take Roddy into partnership, my dear.'

'How can he be a partner? He has no shares in the company.'

'I have just transferred to him ten per cent of the shares.' He beamed at us all. As he held seventy-five per cent, transferring ten would still leave him in overall control, and obviously he would expect Roddy to back him in any decisions.

Now there was a rush of chatter and conversation, and one bold soul went forward to shake Roddy's hand. Thus given the lead, most of the guests followed suit, with the conspicuous absence of any member of the Randell family. I glanced at Jane. 'He's gone mad,' she said. 'Stark, raving mad. He can't give away our shares.'

'I think he's given away his,' I suggested.

'And admitted a total stranger into our firm?' She glared at me. 'You had something to do with this, didn't you?'

'Me?'

'He's your friend, isn't he? This Webster person.'

'Well, of course he is. We share a flat.'

'So you knew what was going to happen.'

'No, I did not. I knew nothing about it. Your father does not confide in his staff.'

'Do you take me for a fool?'

'It does appear as if you are,' I said, wondering if I had just lost my job.

But the Randell family was now firmly split down the middle, and I happened to be on the winning side, at least at that moment. Needless to say, shortly after the old man's announcement, the party broke up. Equally needless to say, I tackled Damon and Roddy the moment we got home. 'Well, of course I suggested it,' Damon said. 'Roddy is the ideal man for the job. I mean to say, think of those two ghastly brothers. They'd make a terrible mess of things.'

'And of course Randell always does everything you suggest.'

'He has confidence in my judgement,' Damon agreed, modestly.

I blew a raspberry, but I was still mystified, and when we were in bed together, and out of Roddy's earshot, I had to ask, 'I wish you'd tell me how Roddy's becoming a partner in the firm, with a very minority shareholding, is of any use to us. Or am I going to be promoted too?'

'Not yet. In a business like this, one must hurry very slowly. Events should be seen to take place in an orderly manner.'

'So what event do you expect to happen next?'

'I have no idea. We'll just have to wait and see.'

It occurred to me that he was either lying or the whole business was to him a great game in which he felt himself to be the strongest player – as he undoubtedly was. So, he was content to wait for his opponent, or opponents, to make a move, confident that he could either counter it or take advantage of it. It was quite exciting to be involved, even from the fringes, but I still couldn't see a worthwhile ending. I could not believe that Randell would agree, even under the influence of hypnosis, to give any real decision-making powers to Roddy.

Obviously I was going to have to be patient as well. But

not for very long. Damon and I went down to Hastings for Christmas lunch and an exchange of presents, Damon's being absurdly expensive, and we stayed over Boxing Day as well, returning to town that evening so that I could go to work in the morning – where I found the office agog with rumour and speculation.

Roddy had gone in first, and straight upstairs to the management floor, and when Louise had arrived and found him studying some confidential files and remonstrated, she discovered that he was now a partner. That had everyone whispering wildly, and the agitation grew when Randell arrived, looking rather grim. We could hardly wait for Louise to come down for coffee and spill the beans. 'They've left him,' she announced. 'Everyone. Lock, stock and barrel. His wife, his daughter, and the sons. They all packed their bags and moved out on Christmas Day.'

'Where'd they go?' Jeremy asked.

'They have a house in the country. They've gone there. There's talk of a divorce.'

'All over Webster getting a partnership?'

'It seems like it.'

'Will the boss have a change of mind?'

'I don't think so. They're still as thick as thieves. Anyway, he can't now. Apparently it was all done a couple of weeks ago. The share transfer is perfectly legal and has been registered. The only way he can get them back is to buy them, supposing Mr Webster wishes to sell.'

Everyone looked at me. 'How'd it happen?' Daphne inquired.

'How should I know?'

'For Pete's sake, you live with the guy. You must have had some idea of what was going on.'

'Well, I didn't. If you ask me, it's all a storm in a teacup. What relations Randell has, or does not have, with his family, or with Roddy, is no business of mine.'

'Lucky for some,' Daphne sneered. 'I suppose you'll be promoted next.'

'We'll just have to wait and see,' I riposted.

I was perfectly right about it being a storm in a teacup, at least as far as the rest of the world was concerned, and that included us in the office.

Roddy was given an office of his own, next door to Randell's, and they shared Louise as a secretary. For the rest of us it was business as usual. Possibly the only one of the staff, apart from Roddy himself, who was most affected was me. He actually became less of a friend than before. At home in the flat, he was unchanged, but he explained to me that he could not afford to show me any favouritism in the office.

That was all right by me; it was certainly not a problem I intended to take to Damon. I was frying my own fish. As soon as I could after the initial furore had died down, I got out of the office and went home to my flat. I did this fairly regularly to make sure everything was all right, and although most of my neighbours had got the message that I was no longer actually living there, they had no cause for complaint, and neither did Mrs Thurgold, as my rent was paid quarterly by direct debit. There was only one message on the ansaphone. 'If you really are real, and not some dream from that very odd night, call me.' Then he gave the number.

I gazed at the phone for several minutes before picking it up. Because if it was going to happen, it had to happen now, before my wedding; Damon was beginning to talk about dates. Right now, even if he was my partner, I was still free – well, relatively speaking. Once I was married, it would be adultery. So what the hell? We were coming up to the Millennium. Did ethics really matter any more? Besides, I told myself, at eleven in the morning he would hardly be in. But he was. When he said, after the phone had buzzed for several seconds, 'Hello,' my heart nearly jumped out of my shirt front.

'You wanted me to call,' I said.

'Frances? Frances! My God! I never thought you would. Where are you?'

'At my flat. Would you like the address?'

'I already have that. I got it through your phone number. But you don't live there anymore; so the neighbours told me.'

'I live with my partner, at his place. But I still have mine.'

'Wow! And you'd like me to come round?'

'If you'd like to continue our discussion.'

'I like the sound of that. But . . .' I got the impression that he was making some sort of violent movement at the end of the line. 'I can't come right this minute.'

'I can't stay, either. But we could make a date.'

'When?'

'It'll have to be during the day. I can get out for an hour.'

'Fine. I don't suppose I can call you back?'

'Not here. Call me at work.'

'You mean Randell's?'

'I'm going back there now.' I had set the ball rolling, for my own good, just as Damon was setting balls rolling for his. My trouble was that I had no idea what sort of ball I had, or where it was rolling to. An even greater trouble, and one which I did not have the slightest idea existed at that time, was that I did not really know what I was getting myself into – my sole idea was to get myself *out* of the mess I was in.

Anthony – I still didn't know his last name – didn't call back for a couple of days, so that I began to suppose that he had had both second thoughts and cold feet; we had both been tight when he had made his first advance . . . although he had called the first time, presumably when sober. I spent the time in a state of uncertain excitement, terrified that Damon would notice something different in my demeanour. But he didn't appear to, self-centred and confident as he was. And three days after we had spoken on the phone, Anthony called. 'Name it,' he said.

I checked my diary. 'Tomorrow at twelve. At my flat.'

'Done.'

As I normally took my lunch hour at half past twelve, getting an additional half an hour off was no problem; I told Watson, the new office manager since Roddy's elevation, that I had to go to the dentist. Then I caught a cab home, arriving at five to twelve. The flat, even in my absence, remained perfectly habitable, stocked with such things as towels and tissues, and even a limited booze cabinet, in case he wanted, or needed, a drink. I certainly felt like one, but I decided against it; I was determined to let nothing interfere with my mental processes, and preferred not to remember that I had been perfectly sober during the fiasco with Jeremy. At twelve sharp the street bell rang. 'Come up,' I said into the phone, and dried my hands for the umpteenth time – I was seething with perspiration.

I hadn't changed, or even taken anything off. I wasn't sure how things were going to turn out; I wasn't even sure how I *wanted* them to turn out. I was breathless, and not only because of the possibilities. I couldn't believe this was me; I had never even dreamed that one day I would do a Mae West and invite a man to come up and see me some time.

His fingers tapped on the door, and I let him in. He closed the door behind himself and leaned against it. He was wearing an overcoat, as it was a chilly January day, and a jacket and pullover but no tie. He looked just as attractive as he had at the party.

He felt the same. 'I had forgotten just how much of a looker you are,' he said, and took me in his arms.

I didn't object to that, or the deep kiss that followed; after all, I had set this up. And I was turned on. It's going to happen, I told myself. 'Would you like something to drink?'

'Afterwards, maybe.'

'Makes sense. Well . . .' I gazed at him. 'At least take off your coat.'

'Oh. Yes.' He hung it on the hook behind the door.

'What would you like to do first?' I asked.

'How much time do I have?'

'Until a quarter past one.' I was prepared to forgo lunch.
'That sounds fine. Just let's sit for five minutes.'
'Surely.' We sat together on the settee, and did some more deep kissing, while his hand got inside my jacket and then my shirt. I did wear a bra to work, and he managed to get inside that as well, all very gentle and stimulating. I was doing the same to him, which was more difficult, as I had to work my way through his jumper, which was under his jacket. 'I think we should take these off,' I suggested.

'Good idea.'

I took off my jacket, and he took off his. I didn't see much point in taking off my shirt until we actually went to bed; it was totally unbuttoned anyway. But it was necessary to remove his jumper, which we both did, lifting it over his head, to reveal that underneath he wore a short-sleeved shirt. I noted that on his left wrist he wore a Rolex, not gold but still pricey, and on his right forearm a bracelet, one of those silver things with a name plate. 'That's pretty,' I said.

'I'd forgotten I was wearing it. I'll just take it off.' He made to do so, but I caught his hand and turned the arm over to expose the plate. *To my ever-loving Anthony. Your ever-loving Jane.* Then he got his hand free and pulled the bracelet off, shoving it into his trouser pocket. 'You weren't supposed to see that.'

'Sounds very loving,' I said. 'Is she your current partner, on whom you're having a little cheat?'

'Of course not. This was given to me years ago by an old flame.'

Over the years in my profession I had become adept at knowing when people are lying, such as the female client who, on being shown a property, says, but this is absolutely fabulous, don't you think so, darling, meaning, I wouldn't touch this place with a ten-foot pole and don't you say anything stupid. Besides, I was remembering that conversation with Jane at the Christmas Eve party, just before her father's conversation-stopping announcement. 'I like men who tell me the truth,' I said. 'This was given to you by Jane Randell.'

'Well . . .' He flushed. 'A long time ago.'

'Like hell,' I remarked as the penny dropped. 'She was with you when I telephoned you. I had an idea there was somebody there. So I suppose she knows you're here now.'

'No, she doesn't. She doesn't know who I was speaking to. When she came out of the bedroom to see who it was I waved her away.'

'She told me you were a womanizer. But it's a bit much to set up a date with one woman while virtually in bed with another.'

'I'm sorry. But compared with you she's a carthorse.'

'That,' I pointed out, 'is also unacceptable behaviour. What are you going to tell her about me?' I put my bra back where it belonged and buttoned my shirt. Needless to say, I had gone right off the boil. But this was entirely reasonable. I was angry, and justifiably so. On the other hand, I wasn't sure I would have gone through with it anyway.

'Do I gather you no longer wish to have sex with me?'

'I would like you to leave,' I said.

He gazed at me, and I braced myself to resist an assault, not at all sure I would be able to do it; he was obviously much stronger than I, and I had irrefutable evidence that he was not a gentleman. But he seemed to have second thoughts. 'I will wish you joy of your swarthy friend,' he said. And left.

I found myself crying. This was sheer frustration. I had behaved as perhaps any woman should have done, and yet I knew I had thrown away a golden opportunity to break free. I could easily have accepted him for what he was, had sex, and proved a point one way or the other. I kept telling myself that my reactions had been entirely natural, and had no bearing on my problem.

But I couldn't be sure if that reaction hadn't been at the behest of Damon's curse, as I was now coming to recognize it. I was so miserable, I did a very stupid thing: when I got home from work that evening, Roddy not yet having come in, I told Damon what had happened. He could tell at once that something was on my mind, and was perfectly willing to listen. Naturally I dressed it up a bit. 'He came on to me at that party,' I said. 'Tall, rugged-looking bloke. You must have seen him.'

'I saw you talking with him,' Damon said. 'I could tell he was chatting you up.'

'Well, I thought nothing of it. Then today we happened to bump into each other, and one thing led to another.'

'Led to what?'

'Well, actually, nothing. Just a lot of heavy breathing and tit-tugging. Anyway, you know I couldn't have done anything with him.'

'But did you want to?'

'Well . . . he's an attractive man.'

'You are a wanton little bitch,' he remarked. 'Or are you still trying to prove something?'

'Don't you think I need to?' I snapped.

'I ought to beat the hell out of you.' I held my breath, wondering if he would. If he would dare. His eyes were so angry I thought he was going to. Then he gave one of his liquid grins. 'What the hell? He didn't make it. What did you say his name was?'

'I didn't. But it was Anthony.'

'Anthony who?'

'I have no idea.'

'You nearly got shagged by a guy whose name you didn't know?' He seemed to be genuinely surprised.

'Well . . . I thought it was better that way. We weren't planning on having an affair.'

'Yeah,' he agreed. 'But you met him at the Randell party, you say.'

'That's right.' Of course he would be able to find out Anthony's name and address by having Roddy ask Randell; the boss would certainly know the names of the guests at his party. 'Damon,' I said, 'you're not going to do anything stupid?'

'Me? I don't reckon I've ever done anything stupid in my life.'

'I meant, you're not going to go and have a punch-up or something with Anthony.'

'No way.'

'Promise?'

'I promise you I'm not going to lay a finger on the guy.'

I supposed that was as good as I was going to get.

The business of Anthony got buried in the business of my wedding. It was a strangely unreal period, as if everything about my life wasn't already unreal.

On the surface, it couldn't have been more perfect. Work went well, especially for me, because of my friendship with Roddy, even if he kept to his principle of being stand-offish in the office.

And Roddy also did well; Randell gradually gave him more and more responsibility, and he proved surprisingly good at his job, which of course on the first floor had very little to do with the mundane business of selling real estate but a great deal to do with the firm's finances.

These were also doing well, even if Randell's personal affairs weren't. His wife began a suit for divorce, claiming half his assets. This didn't seem to bother him a lot, although it would have to involve the handing over of some more of his shares, which meant that he would almost certainly lose control of the company. I asked both Damon and Roddy how this would affect our position, if, as seemed quite likely, Randell was ousted as chairman and replaced by one of his sons, or worse, his wife. But they didn't seem worried, and I had the wedding on my mind.

As summer approached it was a time of dress fittings and rehearsals . . . and house-hunting: Damon decided that as a married couple we should have a house instead of a flat. This was fine by me, although as far as I could see it would entail moving some distance out of Westminster. However, having surveyed the specifications of the various properties we had on our books, he chose one in Chelsea. I was appalled. 'Have you looked at the price?'

'No problem. We'll get a mortgage.'

'May I ask your income?'

'I don't have an income.'

'But we've been living high, wide and handsome all this time . . .'

'Capital,' he explained. 'Old Clermont had a lot of it. Mind you, I'm beginning to see the bottom of the barrel.'

'So what do we live on?'

'Your salary and Roddy's contribution.'

'You're sure he'll go along with this?'

'Of course.'

Well, I couldn't argue with that. 'The point is,' I said, 'that if you are going to go looking for a mortgage, the would-be lenders are going to require a statement of assets, and more importantly, a projection of income. To cover this property, both of those are going to have to be pretty formidable.'

'We'll get Roddy to back us.'

'I'm not even sure that ten per cent of the shares in Randell & Company would do.'

'Listen,' he said. 'Let me do the worrying about our finances.'

Sure enough, we got the mortgage and the house. I hadn't really thought about it before, because I never supposed it would come off, but when I had a good look at the place, I was again appalled. Oh, it was quite magnificent, fitted with every possible mod con – it even had its own incinerator in the basement, so we wouldn't have to worry about refuse collection – and in a splendid state of repair, but with its five storeys and narrow staircases it required a high level of physical fitness just to exist. As for anything else . . .

'I'm going to need a servant,' I said. 'In fact, about four.'

'You shall have them,' Damon assured me.

It still seemed entirely backwards that I, who sold real

estate, should wind up living in some kind of mini-palace.
'You want me to keep on with my job?' I asked.
'For the time being. We'll think about it after the wedding.'

This was a less grand affair than he had hoped and I had feared, as we didn't know very many people, and although Harriet and husband and kids flew across for the ceremony, the rest of the guests were mainly from the office. At least I had the satisfaction of watching my big sister turning green. 'Well,' she commented, 'who's a clever girl, then? You do seem to have fallen on your feet.'

'I think you mean on my back,' I riposted.

'You do know that he's . . . well . . .'

'He has what used to be called in the old-fashioned novels I enjoy reading "a touch of the tar". I hope your prejudices aren't seeping through.'

'Good heavens, no,' she lied. 'I think he's tremendous. Is he that good in bed?'

'He's better in bed,' I told her.

We intended to spend the first night of our married life at the Heathrow Sheraton, as we were catching a flight out to Miami next morning, on-going to the Bahamas for our honeymoon. I wasn't too sure about this, but Damon assured me that we wouldn't go near Eleuthera; we were to spend the fortnight in Nassau, where he apparently had a lot of friends he wanted me to meet. I wasn't too sure about that either. But as usual I was happy to go along with what he wanted. The wedding lunch didn't break up until about six, when Roddy drove us out to the airport. 'Gosh, it's going to be strange, not having you two around,' he remarked.

'Just don't do anything stupid till we get back,' Damon warned him.

Roddy kissed me, as usual utterly uninvolved, and drove off. Damon had already gone inside, followed by a porter with our bags. I followed more slowly. I was full of champagne and not at all sure exactly where my feet were, so I sank into a leather upholstered airline-type chair just inside the doors while Damon dealt with reception. I was sitting there in a quiet daze, when I realized that someone was standing above me. I opened my eyes and blinked at Jane Randell. 'Good heavens,' I said. 'What are you doing here?'

None of the Randells save for the old man had been invited to the wedding, and in fact I hadn't laid eyes on Jane since last Christmas Eve. Now she pointed at me. 'Bitch!' she said. I tried to get up, and sat down again, rather heavily. 'You killed him!' Jane shouted.

Heads were beginning to turn. 'Killed who?' I asked, inanely.

'You killed Anthony. My Anthony. You killed him!' She burst into tears.

Eight

The Senior Partner

The word 'appalled' does not even approach my feelings at that moment. I was utterly horrified. Fortunately Damon, having finished at the desk, had heard the rumpus and returned to me, having to push his way through the considerable crowd that had gathered round us.

'What the hell is going on?' he inquired. 'Jane? What are you doing here?'

Jane had collapsed on to the chair beside me, still weeping noisily. 'She killed him,' she moaned.

Now we were joined by an under-manager. 'May I be of assistance?'

'Yes,' Damon said. 'You can get rid of these people. This is a private matter.'

'Ah,' said the under-manager. 'If it is a private matter, perhaps you would be good enough to come into my office.'

'What about our room and luggage?'

'That will be taken care of, sir.' He signalled the waiting porter. We followed him into the office, leaving a discontented crowd behind us.

'This will be fine,' Damon said. 'Now will you push off.'

'Ah . . . there was some talk about a death . . .'

'She's hysterical.'

Jane had again collapsed into a chair before the desk, still weeping. 'The police?' Which was clearly what he really wanted to do.

'You don't want to make a fool of yourself.' Damon grabbed the other chair and pulled it beside Jane, then sat down. I looked at the under-manager; it was only a matter of seconds before my knees gave way. He got the message and held my arm to guide me round the desk to his own chair. This left him standing, but I reckoned he preferred that: it left him in control. 'Now look here,' Damon said to Jane. 'What's all this rubbish? Who's Frances supposed to have killed?'

'Anthony,' Jane sobbed. 'It's all her fault.'

'I'm afraid you've lost me. Who's Anthony?' Of course he knew who Anthony was, but I wasn't going to interfere.

'My boyfriend. Anthony Taggart. She was having an affair with him.'

'You are accusing my wife of having an affair with some guy named Taggart?'

'She was!'

'You care to comment, sweetie?' Damon asked.

'I don't know what she's talking about,' I said.

'She would say that,' Jane snapped. 'They were having an affair. I know it. He virtually told me so. And then . . .'

'He went off and died. And you think Frances had something to do with it? When did he die, anyway?'

'This afternoon.'

'Good Lord! While we were getting married.'

'That's exactly it. While you were getting married, Anthony got into his Ferrari and drove up the M3 at something like a hundred and fifty miles an hour, chased by the police. They must have radioed ahead, because at some junction there was a police car waiting for him. When he saw it, he swerved, lost control, went off the road and hit something, and was killed instantly.'

I clasped both hands to my neck. 'The chap must have been nuts,' Damon commented. 'Had he been drinking?'

'No, he hadn't,' Jane wailed. 'Don't you see, he committed suicide.'

'Well, it was a crazy way to do it. But what's this got to do with us?'

'Don't you see, he did it because that bitch had stood him up and married you.'

Damon raised his head to look at the under-manager; the under-manager rolled his eyes. 'I think maybe you *had* better call the police,' Damon said. 'And tell them to bring a shrink with them.'

'Just what do you mean by that?' Jane demanded.

'That you need calming down. Before you do or say something that might get you into serious trouble. The idea that some guy is going to go out and kill himself because he couldn't have a woman went out with Sarah Bernhardt. He had to be nuts. And the idea that he had been having an affair with my wife is crazy. So they met at your party, and I believe they exchanged a couple of telephone calls after and maybe met once. Is that right, sweetie?'

'Yes,' I said faintly. I was trying to think, to link up – because the link was there.

'Then why did he do it?' Jane demanded. 'We were going to be married . . .' Once again she dissolved into tears.

'Excuse me, madam,' the under-manager said, as he leaned past me to pick up the phone.

What a way to start a honeymoon. Jane was removed, but then the police wanted to have a chat with us. I was terrified that Detective-Sergeant Borrow might appear, but he didn't, and they were very sympathetic, and agreed entirely that any suggestion that our marriage could have had anything to do with Anthony Taggart's car accident was absurd. There was certainly no question of us having to postpone our honeymoon.

In all the circumstances, we had a room service dinner, but I really didn't feel like eating a thing. 'Damon,' I said. 'Please tell me the truth.'

'I shall tell you the truth,' he agreed. 'The truth about what?'

'About Anthony.'

He raised his eyebrows while eating shrimps on toast. 'I would say you know more of the truth about that guy than I do.'

'I was telling the truth when I said we only met once. After the party, I mean.'

'And I believe you.'

'You said you'd forget the whole thing.'

'I did. I didn't even know who Jane was speaking about, first time round.'

I gazed at him. He was lying, of course. But did I dare accuse him of that? 'It's just that . . . you didn't like Jetta Smith-Lucas, and she went off and committed suicide. And you didn't like Anthony Taggart, and now *he*'s gone off and committed suicide.'

'Nobody knows that.'

'Jane says he did.'

'She was distraught. Everyone could see that. To try to kill yourself by smashing up in a car is bizarre, and very uncertain. You're far more likely to wind up in hospital, crippled, or at least with serious injuries. He was just going too fast. He'd probably had a few drinks, and bingo.'

I reached across the table to hold his hand. 'Damon, will you swear to me that you have not seen or made any attempt to influence Anthony's thinking or state of mind since Christmas?'

'Certainly.'

Once again I was sure he was lying, but he was now my husband as well as my master, and I wasn't going to challenge him.

I so desperately wanted to be happy, and Damon certainly knew how to honeymoon. We lay in the sun all day, danced or gambled or just drank all evening, and shagged like mad most of every night – this despite the fact that we had already been doing at least the latter for the past nine months.

Nassau is almost as violent as Central London, given the much smaller population, but with Damon and his friends looking after me I was every bit as safe as if I had had a police escort, and the whole trip was therefore a great success, at least superficially. But I was still having nightmares, and

Demon

suspicions. Actually being in Nassau increased these. 'Where is Mr Clermont buried?' I asked.

'Somewhere.'

'Didn't you go to the funeral?'

'Funerals aren't my scene.'

'But you went to your mother's funeral, surely.'

'Well, I had to, right?'

'Can we go and see her grave?'

'She was cremated. I scattered her ashes myself.'

So I was getting nowhere there. I actually went to the library and looked up the newspapers for three years before. The Clermont case was well covered, but I discovered nothing Roger Gaillard hadn't told me. I tried to convince myself that it was all paranoia on my part. Everyone else seemed perfectly happy, except those closely connected to the deaths, but the point was that these were not closely connected to each other, and in each case the police also seemed perfectly happy. Clermont's family might still feel Damon had been responsible for his death, or in some way had manipulated the inheritance, but they had no proof and they had never heard of either Jetta Smith-Lucas or Anthony Taggart.

Presumably Jetta had some relatives, and she certainly had had that rather nice secretary, who might be quite unable to understand why her employer had put her head into a gas oven when she had had no reason to do so, but none of them could argue with the fact that she *had* put her head in the gas oven, unassisted. And none of them had ever heard of either Anthony Taggart or Clermont.

While even Jane Randell, although she was convinced that Anthony had committed suicide because of me, could not argue the fact that he had died in a car accident while I was standing at an altar tying the knot. And she had never heard of either Jetta Smith-Lucas or Clermont.

Only three people in the world knew that the three deaths were linked in that they were all connected, however tenuously, to Damon Smith. My husband! Who denied that the link was anything more than coincidental. I simply had to believe that it was.

We returned to sensation, at least within Randell's office. And if I had determined to quell my apprehensions, and had at least partly succeeded, what I was told brought them all flooding back, especially as Roddy, who met us at the airport, had nothing more than usual to say. But when I got to the office the next morning both Daphne and Louise were waiting for me, virtually panting. 'Have you heard the news?'

'Clinton has been impeached.'

'Oh, that.' Daphne waved her hand contemptuously. 'Tell her, Lou.'

'Well,' Louise said, 'you know that Mrs Randell and the children walked out on the old man in January, because of you-know-who?'

'Everyone knows that.'

'Well, then Mrs Randell inaugurated proceedings for a divorce.'

'I knew she was meaning to. What are her grounds?'

'Oh, irretrievable breakdown of marriage and that sort of thing.'

'Isn't that a two-year business?'

'I don't think it has to be. The point is, Mrs Randell's solicitor got together with Mr Randell's solicitor last week to discuss the financial settlement. She wanted half, as you can imagine.'

'I can.'

'Well, Randell's man didn't argue. You're welcome, he said.'

I frowned. 'You mean he's giving up the firm?'

'I don't think so. You see, when Mrs Randell's man asked for a statement of the boss's assets, this was again handed over without protest, and the opposition discovered that the boss only holds ten per cent of the shares.'

'Say again?'

'Ten per cent. So all Mrs Randell could claim would be

five, and a divvy up of the two houses and the cash in the bank. But she'd still only have fifteen per cent of the company. And even with her children, only thirty per cent.'

'I'm afraid you've completely lost me,' I confessed. 'I always understood that Randell owned seventy-five per cent, or sixty-five after he'd given ten to Roddy. Who has the other fifty-five per cent?'

Louise drew a deep breath. She had always been a trifle stout; now it seemed possible that she might explode. 'Roddy.'

'You are saying that Randell has given his company to Roddy?'

'That's about it.'

'You mean as a ploy to avoid having to give anything of it to his wife? He'll never get away with it.'

'Well,' Louise said, 'informed opinion is that he may very well. You see, he made the second transfer, the big one, at the beginning of January, properly registered and all that. That was long before Mrs Randell began divorce proceedings.'

'But he knew she was going to.'

'He says he didn't.'

'She'd left him.'

'Ah, but she's done that before when they had a quarrel, and always come back.'

'So what's the situation?'

'Oh, she's taking him to court. She's claiming he had no right to transfer his shares without informing her, but this is a private company and it is not thought she can make that one stick. She's also claiming that his affections had been suborned, and his judgement corrupted, by Roddy.'

I realized I was sweating.

'Can she make *that* stick?' Daphne asked.

'It's extremely unlikely. And if she does take that to court, it could be very nasty. I mean, to suggest your husband is gaga is one thing. Additionally to suggest he's gone gaga because he's suddenly gone gay really is to open a can of worms and scatter them about.'

'Meanwhile, who's running the business?' I asked, having got my breath back.

'Oh, the boss is still doing that. Even if he is actually being employed by Roddy.'

'Isn't that a dead giveaway that there's been collusion?'

'Not necessarily. Lots of takeovers include an agreement that the current boss stays on, at least for a while.'

'Some do,' Daphne remarked. 'Is Roddy still your boarder, Frankie?'

'When last I heard.'

'You'll be a partner yourself, next,' she commented.

My heart was screaming for me to rush upstairs and confront Roddy. My head warned me that I should wait until I got home that evening. There were so many things to consider.

As usual, I was home before Roddy, and as usual, Damon was in the bath.

'Dogs,' he said when I stormed in, panting after having climbed all those effing stairs. 'What this house needs is a couple of really big dogs. St Bernards.'

'They'd have to be in good nick,' I gasped.

'They're used to going up and down mountains,' he pointed out. 'With barrels of brandy strapped round their necks.'

'Listen,' I said, having got my breath back. 'What's going on?'

'Where?'

'You know what I'm talking about. Randell giving Roddy all those shares. In effect giving him the company.'

'I reckon he thought it'd be a good idea. This way the old buzzard can't get her hands on them.'

'She's certainly going to try. And stir a lot of shit.'

'That's up to her. It's mostly going to settle on her.'

'Anyway,' I said, seeking relief, 'Roddy's going to give them back to Randell when it's over, right?'

'Well, that has to be considered.'

'You mean you're planning to swindle the old goat?'

'Never crossed my mind. It's up to Roddy.'

I glared at him. 'You made him do it, didn't you.'
'Who?'
'And you knew he was going to do it. In fact, you knew he'd already done it. That's how we got this mortgage, isn't it? Because Roddy effectively owns Randell's.'
'Well, of course I knew he had the clout. The transfer was made last January.'
'And it was your idea.'
'I was consulted, by both Randell and Roddy. I gave them the best advice I could. And it's all for the best.'
'It's for the best that Randell should lose . . . Just what is the firm valued at, anyway?'
'Twelve million.'
'Twelve . . . You mean you advised him to give away more than six million pounds? To Roddy? You hypnotized him again, didn't you?'
'I didn't have to, after the first time. He's happy to take my advice.'
'Is that what you did with Clermont?'
Damon got out of the bath and picked up his towel. 'You ask too many questions. Sure I hypnotized the old goat. I wanted money, and he had it.'
'You couldn't have known he was going to die. No one thought he was going to die.'
He grinned. 'So I'm lucky.'

Incredibly, the penny still hadn't dropped. This was firstly because I didn't want it to drop; I just couldn't face the possibility that my husband could be a murderer. But it was also because I couldn't bring myself to believe that it was possible to hypnotize someone to die. According to everything I had ever read, it wasn't possible to make someone commit a crime or harm themselves while under hypnosis. Therefore it had to be coincidence.
In any event, all consideration of my position became impossible only a few weeks later when I discovered that I was pregnant! How this happened I have no idea, and I

am not talking about the birds and the bees. I had always used the pill, so the question of pregnancy had never arisen. I had not stopped the pill when we married, because he had appeared to want me to go on working. And now . . .

I was scared stiff, but more of his reaction than what might be happening in my tum. 'I don't know how to tell you this,' I said at breakfast, the day after I had returned from my second visit to the doctor. 'I seem to be pregnant.'

He was involved in poached eggs and *The Times*, and only slowly raised his head.

'I don't know how it happened,' I said. 'I missed my period just after we came home, and thought nothing of it. But then I missed again this month, so I went along to the clinic. They took tests and told me to come back in a week. So I went back yesterday, and was told the news.'

Damon continued to look at me.

'Do you think I should sue the pharmaceutical company?' I asked.

Still no comment.

'At least I could have the pills analysed,' I suggested.

At last he looked away, but merely to fold up the newspaper.

'Would you like me to abort?' I asked. I don't believe in abortions, but by now I was terrified.

'Why should you want to do that?' he asked. 'We're going to have a child. I think that's great. Come round here and I'll give it a kiss.'

Talk about relief! 'What about my job?' I asked.

'Give it another couple of months, then you'd better quit.'

I handed in my notice. Roddy was as usual non-committal. I thought Randell was going to burst into tears. 'You are going to come back to us afterwards?' he begged.

'I don't know, Mr Randell,' I said. 'I'll have to talk to Damon about that.'

*   *   *

'He won't be born hypnotized, will he?' I asked. 'Or she?'

'I don't know. I've never hypnotized a pregnant woman before.'

I held his hands. 'Damon, can't you release me now? For God's sake, I'm your wife. I'm to be the mother of your child. I'm not going to run off and leave you now. And besides . . .' I had had an idea. 'If at any time I suggested moving out, you could hypnotize me again.'

'We'll talk about it,' he said. 'After the birth.'

Breaking the news to Ma and Pa was a different matter.

'Oh, my dear,' Ma said, taking me into her arms for a hug.

This was definitely commiseration rather than congratulation. I pulled my head back. 'Don't you want to be a granny – again?'

'Well, of course I do. But suppose . . .'

'Oh, really, Mummy. Does it matter? It'll be my child. Anyway, you have to look twice at Damon to realize he has mixed blood.'

'That doesn't mean anything. I've read that colour can skip whole generations, and suddenly there is a black child.'

'That is an old wives' tale,' I pointed out. 'And as I said, it doesn't *matter*. Not to me. It's going to be my baby. It can have blue skin with red spots so far as I am concerned. It will still be my boy.'

'It could be a girl,' Ma said. But she realized she'd stepped out of line. 'As you say, we are going to love him. Is Damon happy about it?'

'Of course he is. But you know Damon. He's so laid back it's difficult to tell what he's really thinking. Or feeling.'

Actually, he became more thoughtful and helpful than ever, and wanted to begin interviewing nannies right away, even if the birth was still at least six months away.

But I was happy. Ma and Pa had accepted the situation, after another couple of months I no longer had to go to work, and as Roddy had upped his salary we had all the money we needed.

The drawback with not having to spend all day at work was that I was now spending all day at home, except for such things as visits to the supermarket or the hairdresser, and that gave me too much time to think, about so many things. One of these was my flat. Now that I was married, and to be a mother, I decided to let it go. Mrs Thurgold was very understanding – and she wasn't going to lose as now she could up the rent.

I also found myself doing a lot of thinking about Roddy. I had never really had any doubt that he had also been hypnotized by Damon, and still was. He was now a highly successful if slightly ambiguous figure in the business world. Real estate was recovering, slowly, from the slump that had followed the great boom, and Randell's was thriving. Roddy – 'advised' by Damon – opened two new branches. But the moment he entered the door of our house – in which he had a self-contained flat, although he took most of his meals with us – he reverted happily to being a doormat, almost creating a zombie-like impression. In fact, I even wondered sometimes if he *was* a zombie, as they were also offshoots of voodoo. But Damon had convinced me that that was nonsense, something I was happy to believe. On the other hand, Roddy was definitely not all there. As this could not be reconciled with his business success, I had to assume that whatever he did in the office he had been told to do by Damon. Exactly why Damon needed a perpetual front man I wasn't yet sure, except that it could be some quirk of his personality that made him prefer to pull the strings rather than go up front himself.

But another aspect of the situation that intrigued me, and slightly piqued me, was that Roddy, who at our first meeting had described me as the most beautiful woman he had ever met, had never in the now couple of years we had lived in considerable intimacy made the slightest attempt to touch me, much less flirt with me. He treated me in fact rather like a sister of whom he was not terribly fond. As with everything to do with Roddy, there were perfectly adequate explanations for this.

The most obvious was that he was gay, unlike Damon, who was only gay when it could be used to his advantage. But if he was, it was difficult to decide whom he turned to for emotional or sexual outlet. I was absolutely sure Damon and he didn't have anything going, and as he spent most evenings at home watching TV I didn't see how he could have anything going with anyone else. There remained of course Randell, but they only ever saw each other in the office, and Louise assured me that there was nothing doing there either. Besides, I had my own experience to convince me that Randell liked girls more than boys.

The second explanation was that Roddy was afraid of Damon, or had been hypnotized by him into finding me a turn-off, which was two sides of the same coin. Roddy was the only guy I knew at all well who I had not felt had been mentally totting me up and wondering to himself what that gorgeous chick would be like between the sheets.

Some thoughts for a heavily pregnant woman, and the word 'heavily' quickly took precedence. Soon I was in no condition to care a damn about either office politics or the divorce case.

In fact, the latter seemed to fizzle out before anything really happened with it. Apparently, the Randells were warned by their solicitor that they were pounding their heads against a brick wall. The share transfer had been legitimate, and there was nothing the family could do about it, save buy Roddy out. As that wasn't on, both because he had no intention of selling and they didn't have the financial clout, the only other option was to sell out, and this Roddy was happy to go along with. Just where *he* got the ready to buy their shares was a mystery, at least to me, unless he dipped into company funds, which might just have been illegal, but Damon's and Roddy's finances were a closed book to me.

I did suspect that the entire deal was tied in with the Randell divorce, which duly went through, Alice making off with both houses and the family Rolls. James bought a small flat. His part in all this was totally submerged, although it seemed odd to me that a successful businessman could be seen to give away a multimillion-pound fortune and the company which had created it and not be certified. But Randell's was a private company, not listed on the stock exchange, and had never applied for any government grants, so it remained outside the scope of any investigation, especially now that it was wholly owned by one man, save for Randell's five per cent. I was only happy that the whole business had been sorted out without my having to appear in court to give evidence as to what I had observed of Randell's and Roddy's relationship.

Thus I could concentrate on Baby, who emerged in the summer. To my delight, and relief, everyone seemed over the moon. He was a boy, and looked like me. 'I'll bet he's even going to have yellow hair,' Ma declared. This was obviously very important to her.

But Damon was equally pleased, and even Roddy showed some pleasure; he was going to be godfather. Letters of congratulation arrived from all over the place, but there was also a hate letter, from Jane Randell. It was very brief: *May you and your baby both rot in hell. The woman you swindled out of her inheritance.*

I considered showing it to Damon, but decided against it; he would almost certainly want to do something about it. So I binned it, and concentrated on being a mum. This was a delight. I fed Baby Damon for three months, then weaned him at Damon's request, and, somewhat to my disappointment, was required to hand him over almost entirely to his nurse. She was a nice girl named Clara, who had been picked by Damon from a host of applicants.

'Now you can get on with your life,' he said.

'Doing what?'

'I think you should rejoin the firm,' he said. 'I know Roddy would like you to.'

'You mean as an agent?'

'No, no. He'd like you as his assistant.'

'I wouldn't want to upset Louise. And I've never been a secretary. I can't do shorthand.'

'He doesn't want you as a secretary, stupid. He wants you as an assistant. I think he may even be intending to give you a few shares and make you a partner.'

As if he hadn't organized the whole thing. But the idea was actually rather attractive. It was a joy to return to the office, and as an executive rather than an agent; Daphne and Jeremy had to address me as Mrs Smith rather than Frances or Frankie. It was actually fun working with Roddy, as well; he had a far greater grasp of the business than I had supposed. The work was interesting too. We had very little to do with the selling of properties, or the clients, unless they happened to be very up-market indeed, but long hours were spent with the accountants analysing where everything was coming from and where we should go next. This was fascinating, and with the property market continuing to boom it was all on the up – while as a partner, which quickly happened, my salary had really taken a bump.

Naturally I saw a lot of Randell, but he was rather a sad figure. He seemed to have shrunk, physically, and took less and less part in the running of the business, only supplying, as senior partner, his signature when necessary. After the divorce had gone through, the rest of his family just disappeared from our sight, never to be heard of again. Or so we thought.

Damon kept the old boy happy, and presumably under control, by playing golf with him every Saturday morning. I would say that year was the happiest of my life. Ma and Pa appeared to have become entirely reconciled to Damon, and he and I and Baby Damon spent almost every weekend in Hastings, going down as soon as Damon had finished his golf game. The five of us even went on holiday together, to Spain. I was quite nervous about this, but it went like a dream.

I took up all my old activities, my keep-fit classes to get

my figure back, which was easy, and I even began taking karate lessons. I didn't suppose I would ever need to defend myself, but it gave me an enormous feeling of confidence to know that I could. We also bought a dog. A St Bernard was obviously not quite right for central London, so we settled on a fashionable golden retriever, who barked a lot but was actually as soft as butter. In fact, we called him Butterpaws.

The Millennium was rushing at us, and Damon informed me that he, Roddy and I had tickets for some all-night bash just outside London – at a thousand pounds per head. I considered this wildly extravagant, but it was a huge lot of fun. And then Randell died.

Nine

The Calamity

It happened in the summer of 2000, and was so sudden. As usual, Randell arrived soon after Roddy and myself, said good morning to us both, and to Louise, and went into his office. Again as usual, a few minutes later Louise took in the mail. She normally opened this in her office, and sorted it into Randell's, Roddy's, and mine. There were only a couple for me, both business, and I flicked through them very quickly. I had just tossed them into my in-tray when I heard a strange sound from Randell's office next door. I got up, went to my own door, and found Louise standing in Randell's doorway, staring into the office. 'What's happened?' I asked.

'It's . . . He . . .' She looked absolutely shattered.

Roddy now appeared from his office. 'What was that noise?'

I pushed Louise aside and went into the office. Randell was lying on the floor, on his side. I estimated that he had slumped forward, hit his head on the desk, and then fallen sideways out of his chair.

Roddy had followed me into the room. 'Good God!' he commented. 'What's happened to him?'

'I think he's fainted.' I knelt beside him. And then realized that he wasn't breathing. 'Oh, my God! He's dead.'

Roddy leaned over me. 'Shit!' he commented. 'Just like that?'

'He must have had a heart attack,' I suggested. 'Louise . . .'

'I'll call the doctor.' She ran out of the office to her desk, and picked up the phone. If we were all pretty shattered, none of us felt any extreme grief; as I mentioned before, Randell had rather passed his sell-by date, for any of us.

He had apparently been reading his mail, and in fact a sheet of paper must have fallen from his hand when he collapsed; it lay on the carpet beside him. I picked it up and turned it over, wondering if it contained anything that could have triggered the attack.

Roddy had the same idea. 'What does it say?'

'Nothing. It's absolutely blank, save for this large black spot in the middle.'

Roddy snatched it from my hand. 'Black spot?!'

'You're thinking of *Treasure Island*.'

'Shit,' he said again. 'I'm going to call Damon.'

I supposed that was a good idea; we certainly needed someone to take charge. Louise had rejoined us. 'Dr Brumby is on his way. He's sending an ambulance as well. What about the staff? They'll have to be told.'

Roddy and I looked at each other. 'We'll close down for the day,' he decided. 'You tell them, Frankie.'

'But . . . what about clients' appointments?'

'Whoever has an appointment will telephone their client and postpone the meeting for twenty-four hours. They'll understand when they hear what has happened.'

'You're going to tell all our clients that Randell is dead?'

'Of course. What have we got to hide? Go do it.'

'What about the other branches?' Louise asked.

'Good thinking. Get on to them right away and tell them that Mr Randell has had a heart attack and that we are closing up shop for the day, but will re-open tomorrow.'

'Excuse me, Mr Webster, but we don't know it was a heart attack.'

'What do you think it is?'

'Well, I don't know. We'll have to wait for the doctor.'

'Until he says otherwise, we'll call it a heart attack. Get to it. And you, Frankie. I'll call Damon.'

I took a deep breath as I went down the stairs. Would you

believe that before Jetta Smith-Lucas's suicide, I had never come into contact with death? Three of my grandparents had died either before I was born or certainly before I was old enough to take notice. I had never seen a dead body before five minutes ago, and the shock was just settling in.

But behind the image of poor Randell there was a much deeper shock. I was coming into contact with far too many shocks. Fortunately, this early in the morning, no clients had yet appeared. I almost missed my footing as I went down the steps, and landed in a rush. Jeremy hurried forward to stop me from falling. 'Are you all right, Mrs Smith?'

I nodded, and got my saliva under control. 'Assemble the staff, please, Jeremy.' He raised his eyebrows. 'All of them,' I said. 'I need to address them.'

He hurried round the office, clapping his hands. And the staff slowly assembled, at once curious and apprehensive. Before they were all ready to hear what I had to say, we heard the wailing of an ambulance siren, and a moment later both Dr Brumby and four ambulance men hurried into the office; two carried a stretcher.

Roddy was standing at the head of the stairs. 'Up here.' They went up.

The staff gazed at me. 'As you have gathered,' I said, having got myself back under control, 'there has been a tragedy. Mr Randell has collapsed, and we think he is dead.' There was a rustle of movement. 'In the circumstances,' I went on, 'Mr Webster has decided to close the office for today. Those of you who have appointments will ring your clients immediately and postpone them to tomorrow.'

'Are we allowed to say why?' Jeremy asked.

'Certainly. You will tell them that Mr Randell has died of a suspected heart attack.'

'Does this . . . I mean, will this . . .' Daphne began.

'After tomorrow, it will be business as usual,' I assured her. 'We may close again for the funeral. Mr Webster will determine that. However, your jobs are all perfectly safe. Thank you.'

I returned upstairs, where the ambulance men and Roddy and Louise were waiting while Brumby thumped Randell's chest and took his pulse. But of course he was far too late for any prospect of revival. I looked at the desk, and at the floor, but the piece of paper had disappeared. 'Was it a heart attack?' Roddy asked.

'It certainly looks like it. But . . .' Brumby shook his head. 'It's odd. I have never found anything wrong with his heart, nor has he ever complained about chest pains. He has always been a remarkably healthy fellow.' As the firm's doctor, Brumby had also been Randell's personal physician. 'I'll know more after the PM. You can take him out now,' he told the ambulance men.

They covered Randell with one of the sheets and strapped him on to their stretcher. 'Is there anything we should do?' Roddy asked.

'I imagine the family should be informed.'

'They're estranged.'

'I know that, Mr Webster, but they're still his family. You should also put a notice in the papers. Get in touch with a good undertaker and he'll sort that out for you. The body will be available for burial tomorrow.'

'Should we call the police?'

Brumby raised his eyebrows. 'Why should you do that?'

'Well, sudden, unexpected death . . . Won't there have to be an inquest?'

'Do you think there is something suspicious about it?'

'Well, no, but . . .'

'Then there is nothing you need to do about it. At present there is no need for an inquest. If I discover anything suspicious in the PM, I shall inform the police. And you, of course. My sympathies.' He followed the ambulance men down the stairs.

'He doesn't like me,' Roddy remarked. 'He never has. Louise, would you get hold of a good undertaker. Then I suppose you should stay here to deal with any calls.'

'Yes, sir. What about the family?'

Demon

'They don't like me either. Do you think you could call Mrs Randell and tell her what has happened.'

Louise gulped. 'Yes, sir.'

'There's a good girl,' Roddy said, and closed the door behind her.

'Did you get a hold of Damon?' I asked.

'Yes. But he didn't think it would be a good idea for him to come down. He wants to hear all about it when we go home.'

I gazed at him, and he flushed. 'What have you done with that letter which wasn't?' I asked.

'It's in my pocket.'

'And the envelope?'

'Shit. I forgot about that.'

We both lunged at the desk. Fortunately, Louise had not yet cleared the letters away, and we found the envelope easily enough. The name and address were printed, and the envelope was marked *Most Private and Confidential*, also printed, which was why Louise had not opened it. 'Postmarked Corralby,' I remarked. 'That's somewhere in the West Country, isn't it?'

'It happens to be where the Randell country home is situated,' Roddy said. 'Where Alice is currently living.'

'And you think she sent it to upset him? That is quite absurd.'

'Why?'

'For two reasons. The first is that Alice more than anyone else has to know that there is nothing the matter with her husband's heart. So sending him a possibly disturbing message was not going to have any effect. The second is that if it *was* her, surely she has more nous than to post it from her own village.'

'Then who do you think sent it?' Again we gazed at each other. 'I don't believe it,' Roddy said at last. 'They were friends.'

'I don't think Damon has any friends,' I said. 'Save for you and me. And we're his friends because he wants us to be. At the moment.' Roddy sat down in Randell's chair. 'You do know that he has kept me under hypnosis for the past three years?' I asked. He nodded. 'What about you?'

'Oh, longer than that.'

'To do what?'

'Be loyal. Do whatever he tells me to.' He was lying, but I didn't want to cause any discord at that moment. 'And you?' he asked.

I shrugged. 'Roughly the same. With the addition that I cannot have sex with any other man.'

'Yeah.' The penny dropped. Roddy had also been forbidden to have sex with any other man, which I thought was a bit much as he certainly wasn't having any with Damon either.

'What are we going to do?' I asked.

'What can we do? Only he can end it.'

'And meanwhile you and I are becoming accessories to murder.'

'I can't believe that.'

'I don't want to believe it, Roddy. But there it is.' I could hardly believe I was saying something like that about my own husband and the father of my child. But I had to talk it out, rationally, with someone who was capable of understanding, or I was going to go mad and start eating the carpet.

'You can't make someone die by sending him a letter with nothing on it,' he objected.

'That letter has a spot on it, in the very middle. If someone could by hypnotized into accepting that if he ever received such a letter he would die . . .'

'I don't believe that,' Roddy snapped, vehemently. But he was flushing. He did believe it, and what was more, I had an idea he had seen it work before.

I took a stab in the dark. 'Did you know Clermont?'

'Who?'

'Damon's Bahamian benefactor. You must have heard of that.'

'Oh, well, yeah. I knew him.'

'You were one of his boys?'

'Only for a little while,' he said sulkily.
'But you already knew Damon.'
'Well . . . yeah. I knew him.'
'And Clermont suddenly dropped dead, when apparently in good health, and just after he had willed all his money to Damon.' Roddy blinked at me. 'Isn't it possible that Damon hypnotized him into believing that if something happened, or he received some kind of message, he would die?'

Roddy licked his lips. 'You can't hypnotize someone into doing something like that. You can't hypnotize someone into committing a crime. Everyone knows that.'

'Do they? That's what people, hypnotists mainly, say. And you believe it can happen. I know you do. I can see it in your face.'

His shoulders hunched. 'Even if Damon did do it, there's no proof. No one would ever believe us.'

'There's coincidental proof. That woman Jetta Smith-Lucas. She was hypnotized by Damon. He said that she should walk home without any clothes on. He said he had given her instructions on what to do to break the spell as soon as she got home. Suppose the instructions were to put her head in the gas oven and switch on the gas?' Roddy's shoulders hunched some more. 'And what about that Anthony character? Damon swore to me he never went near him. But suppose he did, and hypnotized him, telling him that the day I got married he should drive his Ferrari as fast as possible along the busiest road he could find.'

Roddy wiped his brow with his handkerchief. 'You're accusing your own husband of murder.'

'I don't want to, believe me. But Roddy, we can't let him go on doing it. You must see that. God knows who he'll murder next.'

'You and me, if he ever finds out we've gone to the police. Anyway, the police would never believe us, even with your coincidental evidence. Okay, so he had a reason for killing Clermont: money. So he had a possible reason for killing both the psychologist and that muscleman: jealousy.

But what possible reason could he have for killing Randell? The old gink had given us everything we wanted. We control the firm. He'd been squeezed dry like a lemon.'

I chewed my lip. 'There has to be a reason. All we need to do is find it.'

'I'm not going to make an enemy of Damon,' he said. 'I don't even know we could do it, go against him, I mean. We're his people, Frankie. We're under his spell. And even if you're right, we didn't kill any of these people. He did.'

'So you reckon we should do nothing about it.'

'Randell died probably of a heart attack, certainly of natural causes. That's the way it is, until someone tells us something different. Until that happens, we keep the happy home . . . happy.' He opened the desk drawers until he found what he wanted, a box of matches. He struck one, and lit the end of the sheet of paper. We watched it burn. My brain seemed to have gone dead. I could no longer have any doubt that I was married to a serial killer – who was also the father of my child. And there was nothing I could do about it.

But did I want to do anything about it, Christian morality aside? It would mean the end of all the cosy domestic happiness I had come to enjoy. If I made it stick it would mean that Baby Damon would grow up knowing that his father was in prison serving a life sentence for murder. Just as I would be stigmatized for the rest of my life as the wife of a murderer. Anyway, Damon apparently only killed for a reason, so who was left for him to hypnotize to death?

So I did nothing. Then. But various ideas of how to cope both with Damon and with my own position were beginning to creep into my mind. Whenever I got my breath back.

Predictably, Damon was apparently as shocked by what had happened as any of us. 'He always seemed such a healthy fellow,' he commented.

'That's what Brumby said,' I agreed.

I knew Roddy would not be able to keep his mouth shut, for all his apparent determination to do so. 'I think it was to do with that letter,' he said. 'Frankie thinks so too.'

'What letter?' Damon looked at me.

'Randell got a personal letter in his mail this morning,' I said. 'He was holding it in his hand when he had the attack.'

'Did you have a chance to look at it?' Both Roddy and I nodded. 'So what did it say?'

'It was a blank sheet of paper, with a single black spot in the centre.'

'You're joking.'

'I wish we were,' I said miserably.

'What sort of black spot? You mean someone had dropped ink on it?'

'No, it was a circle, drawn deliberately and filled in with a black ballpoint.'

'*Treasure Island*!'

'That's what we thought.'

'That's childish.'

'That's what we thought too. But he was holding it when he died.'

'Have you still got it? I'd like to look at it.'

'I burned it,' Roddy confessed.

'Why?'

'Well . . . I thought it might be incriminating.'

Damon stared at him, then looked at me. 'You thought I sent it?'

'Well . . . you didn't, did you?'

'What do you take me for, some kind of asshole? Jimmy and I were good friends. Anyway, give me a reason.'

'We couldn't think of one.'

'So you had a good old chat about the possibilities of me being a murderer.' Again he looked at me. 'I'm your husband, for God's sake.'

'I know,' I said, even more miserably. When he put on his injured innocence act I simply had to believe him. 'We were trying to anticipate anyone else thinking that.'

'The envelope was postmarked Corralby,' Roddy offered.
'Do you still have *that*?' Damon asked. Rather shame-facedly, Roddy took it from his pocket. 'Isn't that where Alice Randell is living?' Roddy nodded.

'But if it was her, she was rather stupid in mailing it locally,' I pointed out. 'Anyway, what reason could *she* have for killing him? He's been milked dry.'

'Revenge, maybe. Or maybe he had hidden assets. You contacted his solicitor?'

'Louise was going to do that.'

'Well, it'll be interesting to see what's in the will.'

The phone bleeped. I picked it up. 'Mrs Smith? Dr Brumby here.'

'Oh, yes, doctor. Have you found out why Mr Randell died?'

'No, I have not.'

'Oh. Right. When will the post-mortem be held?'

'I have performed the post-mortem, Mrs Smith.'

'I'm sorry. You've lost me.'

'There is no visible reason for Mr Randell to have died.'

'But he *is* dead.'

'Absolutely. Look, I wonder if I could come and see you and Mr Webster tomorrow morning.'

I looked at Roddy. 'It's Brumby. He wants a meeting tomorrow morning.'

Both Roddy and Damon were frowning. 'Problems?' Damon asked.

'Seems there could be.'

'Then you'd better have the meeting.'

'That'll be fine, Dr Brumby,' I said. 'What time would suit you?'

'Eleven? I'd like to bring someone with me. If I may. Another doctor.'

'We'll expect you at eleven.' I replaced the phone. 'They can't find out why he died.'

'Doctors,' Damon remarked. 'They're a waste of time.'

* * *

I didn't sleep that night. I was lying in bed beside a serial killer! It was too certain to be argued against. Roger Gaillard had told me that no one had been able to find anything physically wrong with Clermont: he had simply stopped breathing. Now Randell had done the same thing.

And Damon was the only connecting link, as he was the only link with Jetta Smith-Lucas and Anthony Taggart. My brain was going round in circles. I had thought all this before. And there was still nothing I could do about it. Or wanted to do about it? Roddy had said he would not back me up unless the doctor turned up something. Well, Brumby wanted to see us. But suppose he had turned up something, even if he had given no indication of it over the phone?

Again Damon decided to distance himself from what had happened. 'Give me a call when you've seen Brumby,' he said. 'And bring me up to date.'

Neither Roddy nor I said much to each other as we shared a taxi into work, save to agree that we would not mention the strange sheet of paper. At least, he made me promise that I wouldn't.

To my relief, the office was settling down again, and Louise was waiting. 'The announcement is in all the main papers,' she told us. 'The undertakers are awaiting a call as to the funeral arrangements.'

'Isn't Mrs Randell going to decide that?' Roddy asked.

'I don't think so, sir. I did get in touch with Mrs Randell, and she didn't seem terribly interested. Although she did want to know when the will would be read.'

'And?'

'Mr Jefferies suggested this afternoon.'

'That sounds ideal. Now, we're expecting Dr Brumby and a colleague at eleven. Show them straight in.'

Brumby's colleague turned out to be a Dr Prendergast, who was introduced as one of England's foremost forensic scientists.

'I asked Prendergast to come along because this is really

the most baffling case I have ever dealt with,' Brumby said. 'There is absolutely no identifiable cause of death.' Both Roddy and I looked suitably po-faced.

'So,' Brumby went on, looking somewhat embarrassed, 'we wondered if it might be possible for you to shed any light on what happened.'

'In what way?' Roddy asked before I could speak, just in case I said anything stupid.

'May I ask one or two questions?' Prendergast said.

'Anything you like.'

'I've made a couple of notes. You've known Mr Randell for about four years?'

'That's right.'

Prendergast looked at me. 'I've known him for six,' I said. 'Since I first came to work here.'

He nodded. 'Dr Brumby says he has always been in at least reasonable health.'

'As far as I know,' I said.

'You began here as an agent. But recently you have come into much closer contact with him. Is that right?'

'I recently became a partner, if that is what you mean.'

Prendergast nodded. 'You became a partner in December 1997, Mr Webster?'

'That's right.'

'So you have been in close contact with Mr Randell for three years. Would you say he has been suffering an abnormal amount of stress recently?'

'Not recently. I know he was somewhat stressed at the time of the divorce, but that was two years ago.'

'And the business is doing well?'

'Oh, very well. We have expanded over the past two years.'

'Was *that* stressful for Mr Randell?'

'I wouldn't think it was. I handled most of it. In fact, over the past couple of years, Mr Randell has been playing less and less of a role in the running of the company. He has handed it all to me.'

'I see. Then let us come down to yesterday. Did Mr Randell seem the same as usual when he came into the office?'

'I would have said so.' Roddy looked at me.

'Yes,' I said.

'Do you mind if we ask Miss Mazender?'

'Not at all.'

Louise was called, and confirmed that Randell had seemed perfectly normal when he had come in. 'And what did he do after he said good morning?'

'He went into his office, and I took in the mail.'

'Did he open the mail in your presence?'

'Oh, no, sir. I opened the mail before bringing it in.'

'I see. Did you read any of it?'

'I glanced at it, sir, to see if there was anything to which I should draw his attention. The only envelope I didn't slit was one marked personal.'

'Ah. Mr Randell opened that one himself?'

'I imagine so, sir.'

'Did you find it after his collapse?'

'I didn't look, sir. There was so much going on.'

'Quite.' Prendergast turned to us. 'I don't suppose either of you noticed a letter marked personal?'

'No,' Roddy said, in this case actually telling the truth.

'But it must be somewhere. I think it should be found, as it may have some bearing on what happened.'

'I think Mr Randell burned it,' Louise said.

Prendergast frowned. 'Burned it? Why should he do that?'

'I have no idea, sir.'

'All right. What makes you think he burned it?'

'Just that when I checked out the office before going home – this was several hours later, you understand, what with all the telephoning I had to do – I found some ashes in his wastepaper basket.'

'I see. Can you remember how much time elapsed between you placing the mail on Mr Randell's desk and him collapsing?'

'I don't think it was more than five minutes. Less, probably.'

'What you are saying, therefore, is that Mr Randell opened the envelope marked private, almost certainly before reading any of the other letters, read its contents, immediately burned it, and then collapsed.'

'Well . . .' Louise looked confused.

Prendergast turned to us. 'Did either of you observe the contents of the wastepaper basket?'

'We had a lot on our minds,' Roddy pointed out.

'Absolutely. Well, then, did either of you smell anything? You must have come in here within seconds of the letter being burned. There should have been a smell.'

This time he looked at me, and I'm afraid I let the side down. I could feel myself flushing, and stammered a bit. 'As Roddy – Mr Webster – said, we were really very upset. There were a lot of strange smells . . .'

'I'm sure there were. But you'll forgive me for pressing the point. There does seem little doubt that it was the contents of that letter that triggered Mr Randell's collapse.'

'His heart attack, you mean,' Roddy suggested.

'Mr Randell did not die of a heart attack, at least not in a conventional manner. His heart stopped beating, certainly. But as there is no evidence of tissue disease or malfunction before the moment of death, it must have been a massive shock to the system to have killed him. But lacking that letter, I don't suppose we'll ever know.'

'The envelope was postmarked Corralby,' Louise said.

I could have kissed her. She was transferring the heat without involving us in the least. 'Where is that?' Prendergast asked.

'It's a village in Somerset,' Louise explained. 'Where the Randells have a country home. Mrs Randell is living there now.'

Prendergast frowned. 'You think the letter came from Mrs Randell?'

'I don't know, sir. But the envelope was postmarked in the village.'

'Hm. That may be worth following up,' he said to Brumby.

'May we ask exactly how you are proposing to handle this?' Roddy asked. 'Do you regard it as a police matter?'

'Would that bother you?'

'Of course it would. If you are referring Mr Randell's death to the police, you are implying that there is some criminal aspect to what has happened. The publicity would be very bad for the firm.'

'I suppose it would. No, Mr Webster, I cannot see that there is any reason to refer this to the police. Mr Randell's death is mysterious, to be sure, but I can hardly suppose he was murdered. It is just not possible. No matter how bad the news Mrs Randell may have conveyed in her letter, as she must have known her husband's health as well as anyone, she cannot possibly have supposed it would cause a heart attack.'

'Then you'll sign the death certificate, Dr Brumby?'

'I can see no reason why not.'

'I think we handled that rather well,' Roddy said when the doctors, and Louise, had departed.

'An object lesson in how to get away with murder,' I suggested.

'Oh, don't start that again. Both of them agreed that it couldn't possibly be murder.'

'Neither of them know what we know.'

'So what are you going to do about it?'

I sighed. 'There is nothing I can do.'

It is amazing how the human mind can wriggle around a difficult subject until it arrives at a satisfactory solution. Mine was that although Randell's death gave every indication of having something to do with Damon, there was simply no motive. As Roddy had said, Randell had been like a lemon squeezed dry, save for those last five per cent of the shares, and what he had done with them in his will was totally irrelevant in the face of Roddy's ninety-five per cent holding. So, unless something was turned up at the reading of the will . . .

Nothing was. None of the other Randells were present, although their solicitor, Mr Mitchell, was. Mr Wright, Randell's solicitor, read the contents, which were very brief. Randell had left his remaining five per cent of the shares to Roddy, as well as his few other possessions. 'I'm afraid that's it,' Wright said, and looked over the top of his glasses at Mitchell. 'Have you any comments?'

'I can think of several comments,' Mitchell said. 'But none I am prepared to air at this moment. Good day.' He left the office.

'A rum business,' Wright remarked. 'It's always sad when families fall out to this extent. Still, Mr Webster, I assume you are content?'

'Well, I'm grateful to the old— to Mr Randell, certainly,' Roddy said.

'I imagine you should be. May I ask, do you wish to continue being legally represented by this office?'

'Oh, certainly,' Roddy said.

'That kept the old boy happy,' Roddy said as we left to go home and tell Damon all about it. 'Who'd have thought the old buzzard would leave everything to me?'

'Did you ever have anything going for him?' I asked.

'Never. I have an idea he may have had thoughts in that direction from time to time, but Damon would never have stood for it.'

I'd forgotten that, but by now I was remembering something else. I kept it for when we got home.

Damon listened to everything that had happened. 'Well, then,' he said, 'when we bury him on Monday we can bury the whole sorry affair with him. And you can get on with business, Roddy. Sole executive. With Frances, of course. How does that grab you?'

'I wonder what he did with his collection?' I remarked.
'He had a collection?' Damon asked. 'You mean like stamps?'
'Not stamps. Wood sculptures.'
'Come again?'
'Bits of wood. Mostly West African, I think, but there may have been others. Women, and a few men, and some animals, all carved. They were quite exquisite.'
'How do you know?'
'He showed them to me, the first time we were invited there. He had the idea that I should have myself sculpted, life-size. Then he would buy the sculpture, and put it in his room, and give me a little squeeze whenever he felt the urge. Like every five minutes.'
'Sounds cute. Are you telling me there's a life-size sculpture of you knocking about?'
'No, there isn't. I slapped him down. I told you about it.'
'You told me you slapped him down. I thought it was because he was trying to feel you up.'
'It was. That was after he had shown me the sculptures and got himself excited.'
'And you say they were in the flat? That means that Alice has them. Were they valuable?'
'Randell said they were priceless. Unique.'
'Goddam,' Damon said. 'No wonder she hasn't contested the will. She's sitting on a fortune. Ah, well, you can't win them all.' I reflected that it wasn't like him to be so generous.

Brumby duly signed the certificate, giving the cause of death as heart failure, which was true enough: Randell's heart *had* stopped beating.

The funeral took place the following day. There was quite a large turnout, and a good deal of adverse comment was caused by the non-appearance of any member of the Randell family. 'Shocking bad form,' Damon declared. He was cultivating what he considered a convincing line in

U-speak. 'Did I ever tell you that you are out of this world in black?'

He could hardly wait to get home, and as usual once he got into that syndrome all other considerations were driven from my mind. So I was taken entirely by surprise when at breakfast next morning he announced he was taking a trip. 'Where?' I asked.

'Back to the Bahamas. There is someone I need to see.'

'Oh. Right. I'll get on to the surgery and see what Baby requires in the way of shots.'

'No need.'

'I am not taking Damon to the tropics without adequate protection,' I said.

'I said, no need. He's not coming.'

'You mean, we're leaving him here? With Nanny?'

'*I* am leaving him here, with you. You're not coming either.'

'Oh.' I didn't know whether to be glad or sorry. We had never been separated for more than a few hours at a time since he had come back into my life and taken control of it. On the other hand, with him out of the country, I could carry out the plan that had been knocking around the back of my mind for some time. The only reason I hadn't done it yet was for fear of his reaction if he found out. But if he wasn't going to be here . . . 'When are you leaving?' I asked.

'Tomorrow morning.'

I was quite happy with that.

We went out to dinner that night and he was in excellent form. 'Can you tell me what it's all about?' I asked.

'When I come back.'

I wasn't all that interested, anyway.

Next morning I saw him off before going to the office, where I spent half an hour with the Yellow Pages. I found what I wanted, made a list of two or three, just to be safe, then got down to business.

'First time we'll have been alone at home,' Roddy remarked.

'With Baby and Nanny and Cook and Horace,' I pointed out. 'And Butterpaws.'

Horace was the butler.

'Oh, quite,' he agreed. 'We'll have to give them all an evening off sometime.'

'I don't think that would be at all a good idea.'

He made a face, and went back into his office.

He was working late, as he often did, so I went home alone. It was just about six and still broad daylight when the taxi dropped me at the gate, which gave access to the short concrete path to the steps leading up to our front door. I paid him, and got out. I don't remember if there was anyone about on the street, but I imagine there wasn't.

I pushed the gate open, stepped through and walked towards the steps. As I did so, I heard a sound from the well beside the steps, where the dustbins were kept. I turned towards it, and plunged into blackness.

The Court

'I have given this matter considerable thought,' Lord Justice Mahaig said. 'And I have determined that the death of Mr Randell in 2000 and the death of Sir Roderick Webster this year are sufficiently linked to require further investigation. I will therefore admit evidence as to the death of Mr Randell. Did you wish to recall Miss Mazender, Sir Barton?'

If Sir Barton might have considered he had lost an important point, he gave no sign of it in his demeanour: it was his nature to tackle unexpected problems head-on. 'I do not think that will be necessary, m'lud. My next witness will be far more able to shed some light on the matter.' His tone indicated, if it is possible to do so. 'I call Dr Harold Brumby.'

Lord Mahaig used his gavel to quell the rustle of surprise. Brumby came in from the witness room, climbed the steps to the witness box, took the oath, and gave his name, address and qualifications.

'Dr Brumby,' Sir Barton said, 'you were the appointed medical practitioner for Randell & Company.'

'I still am,' Brumby said, and looked at me. 'So far as I am aware.'

'Quite,' Sir Barton said, his expression indicating, not another smart alec. 'You were also Mr Randell's personal doctor.'

'Well, the one went with the other.'

'Quite. You were also Sir Roderick Webster's doctor. So you had the entire firm at the end of your stethoscope,' Sir Barton suggested, seeking to regain any lost control.

'That is one way of putting it,' Brumby agreed.

'Now, Doctor, before we come to the sad case of Sir Roderick Webster, I would like you to cast your mind back to the death of Mr James Randell.'

Brumby raised his eyebrows, and looked at the judge. 'You may answer any questions on that subject, Dr Brumby,' Lord Mahaig said.

Brumby controlled a shrug, and turned back to Sir Barton. 'You were called when Mr Randell collapsed.'

'I was.'

'And what was his condition when you arrived at Randell's office?'

'He was dead.'

'Did you form an opinion as to the cause of death?'

'A very preliminary opinion, at that moment. That it had been heart failure.'

'And did you subsequently discover any reason for it not having been heart failure?'

'Well . . .'

'Please just answer my question, Dr Brumby. You signed the death certificate to the effect that it had been heart failure. Did you not?'

Brumby sighed. 'Yes, I did.'

'There was nothing about the circumstances of Mr Randell's death, nothing indicated by the post-mortem, to suggest foul play?'

'Only his peculiar . . .'

'Please answer the question, Doctor.'

'One moment, Sir Barton,' Lord Mahaig said. 'To what were you referring when you used the word "peculiar", Dr Brumby?'

'Well, m'lud, Mr Randell appears to have received a letter just before he died. This letter he read, it would appear, and then burned. And then he died.'

'Was anyone present when Mr Randell died?'

'Not actually present, m'lud. Mrs Smith, Sir Roderick and Miss Mazender were all quite close, in their respective offices, but none were in sight of Mr Randell when he collapsed.'

'I see. I think it may well be necessary to recall Miss Mazender, Sir Barton. But please continue with your examination of the witness.'

'Thank you, m'lud,' Sir Barton said, with as much sarcasm as he dared. 'So, Doctor, Mr Randell received a letter, which you feel may have had some influence on his death.'

'It would seem possible.'

'But as you have suggested, Mr Randell's behaviour is hardly consistent with that theory. If one receives a letter, the contents of which are so distressing, or so shocking, as to bring on a heart attack, one hardly takes the time to destroy the letter before collapsing. Would you agree?'

'I have said that I found Mr Randell's behaviour peculiar.'

'But that did not stop you from signing the death certificate, without having referred the matter to the police.'

'There was no reason to refer the matter to the police, Sir Barton. As you have pointed out, there was no evidence to suggest foul play, just as there was no evidence that the mysterious letter had anything to do with Mr Randell's death.'

'Absolutely,' Sir Barton agreed, enthusiastically.

'If I may interject,' Lord Mahaig said. 'You say Mr Randell burned this letter before collapsing. Do you, or any of his business associates, have any idea what the letter might have contained?'

'I'm afraid not, m'lud.'

'Well, then, what about the person who wrote the letter?'

'I'm afraid I do not know who that is, m'lud.'

'Surely the envelope gave some clue as to the identity of the sender? A postmark?'

'The envelope was never found, m'lud. It would appear that it also was burned.'

'And no one has ever come forward to admit sending it?'

'No, m'lud.'

'As you say, most peculiar. Very good, Sir Barton, you may continue.'

'Thank you, m'lud. Now let us move forward to the death

of Sir Roderick Webster, which is why we are here today. Again, you were the doctor in attendance.'

'I was called, yes.'

'And what was your opinion as to the cause of death?'

'In the first instance, I had to presume that it was a heart attack.'

'But this time you were not prepared to sign a death certificate. In fact, this time you took the matter to the police, and as a result of this the post-mortem was carried out by Professor Prendergast. Am I correct? Would this have been before, or after, the discovery of this infamous letter?'

'No, you are not correct.'

Sir Barton's head jerked while another rustle ran round the courtroom, and Lord Mahaig gave an admonitory tap of his gavel. 'Just what do you mean by that?' Sir Barton demanded.

'I have never seen this letter you refer to as infamous. And I did not go to the police,' Brumby explained. 'I went, in the first instance, to Professor Prendergast, and suggested that he carry out the post-mortem with me. I had previously associated him with me in the post-mortem on Mr Randell, and he had shared my mystification as to the cause of death. It was as a result of this second shared post-mortem that we went to the police.'

'But as I understand it, you found nothing untoward in the post-mortem. Just as you had found nothing untoward in the post-mortem you carried out on Mr Randell.'

'Exactly. However, when this carbon copy case occurred, we agreed that it was necessary to take the matter further.'

'And so you convinced the police that a murder had been committed, although, like Professor Prendergast when he appeared earlier for the Prosecution, you can provide no evidence to indicate that anything criminal was done to either Mr Randell or Sir Roderick Webster?'

'They both died in virtually the same manner, in actually the same place, and in association with the same person.'

'Come now, Dr Brumby. Mr Randell died in the middle

of the morning and virtually in the presence of three other people. Sir Roderick, who was one of those other people, died, admittedly in the same office, in the middle of the night, while the entire building was empty save for the security guard, who was situated on a different floor. The only common denominator here is the office.'

'With respect, Sir Barton, there is also the matter of Sir Roderick having stripped himself naked shortly before his death. This was, to say the least, peculiar behaviour.'

Sir Barton checked his notes. 'I must correct you, Doctor. There is no suggestion in your report that Sir Rodney had engaged in any sexual activity immediately prior to his death. In fact, Dr Prendergast rejected this suggestion.'

'Agreed. But the fact that he was naked suggests that he was anticipating some such activity when he died. This would indicate that he was expecting a visitor.'

'That has got to be pure speculation, Doctor,' Sir Barton insisted. 'The fact is that you cannot tell us how Sir Roderick died. Apart from that his heart stopped beating.'

'No, I cannot,' Dr Brumby said.

'And you cannot tell us how Mr Randell died. Apart from that his heart also stopped beating. Therefore you have no evidence that either man was murdered, much less both.'

'I have this . . .'

'Evidence, Dr Brumby.'

Brumby sighed again. 'No.'

'Thank you, Dr Brumby.' Sir Barton sat down.

Mr Buckston stood up. 'In his evidence, given yesterday, Professor Prendergast advanced the theory that it might be possible to induce death by suggestion. Professor Prendergast is both a friend and a colleague of yours, Dr Brumby. Have you ever discussed this suggestion with him?'

'I have.'

'And do you consider it a possibility?'

'Yes, I do.'

'Is there, in your opinion, a possibility that the mysterious *letter that Mr Randell received shortly before his death may have influenced that death?'*

'Yes.'

'And is there, in your opinion, a possibility that Sir Roderick Webster's bizarre behaviour immediately preceding his death can have been influenced, or perhaps even commanded, by some external force, some power, perhaps, of hypnotism?'

'I believe that is a very strong possibility, yes.'

'Thank you.' Mr Buckston sat down.

Sir Barton stood up. 'Before you go, Dr Brumby, will you tell us, have you a degree in psychology?'

'No, I have not.'

'I see. Have you ever studied hypnotism?'

'No, I have not.'

'Have you ever heard of a case where someone was hypnotized into dying?'

'Not before these.'

'At the present time, Doctor, these are unfounded allegations. I wish to know if there is any medical record of deaths like these, anywhere in the world.'

'Not in the civilized world.'

'Would you agree that if you were not connected with this case, but might be having a drink in a pub or in your club, and a friend came up to you and said, old so-and-so has died, hypnotized to death, they say, you would not regard that as the most utter nonsense?'

'I very probably would, without more detailed knowledge. However—'

'Thank you, Dr Brumby,' Sir Barton said.

Ten

The Anger

Pain! Uncertainty! Sheer bloody terror! I was blindfolded, and there was also sticky tape across my mouth. My wrists were bound behind my back, and my ankles were also tied. I was lying, on my side, on something fairly soft. I reckoned it was a car seat, and the car was moving, not very fast. Well, they wouldn't want to be stopped for speeding at this moment. They! It had to have been more than one. I had been assaulted, laid unconscious, virtually at my own front door, and was now being carried . . . where? And for what purpose? Presumably there was rape somewhere in the equation, but they couldn't be in a hurry; I was wearing my dark blue trouser suit, and so far as I could tell my pants hadn't been removed.

    That was the only reassuring aspect of my situation. I had been laid unconscious at my own front door. How? My head was hurting, but not as severely as I would have expected had I been hit on it hard enough to knock me out. But there was also a pain, much more sharp, in my left arm, above the elbow, and my whole body felt odd. I had been injected, with something, through my jacket. But a knockout dose was not something that would wear off very quickly. Therefore I must have been in this vehicle for some time. What I must not do, I told myself, is panic. I have been kidnapped. Very elaborately. Very carefully planned. For ransom? Or rape and murder?

    I panicked, and thrashed to and fro while screaming as loudly as I could. The results were disastrous. I could only make a sort of 'mmm' sound at the back of my throat, and while rolling about I fell off the seat on to the hard floor of the car, on my back. As my hands were behind there this was extremely painful, as were the following two slaps I received on the face from someone apparently leaning over from the front seat. Following this my tormentor squeezed my crotch, very hard. This was as humiliating as it was painful, and left me panting, which under the gag almost had me choking.

I decided to be patient, once I had rolled on my side to take the weight off my hands. Obviously there was nothing I could do until they untied me. Meanwhile my brain was spinning. I had no idea what time it was, but it had to be at least an hour since I had been snatched, probably more. Nanny would be wondering why I hadn't come home, but she was not an inquisitive soul. On the other hand, Roddy would be coming home around now. He knew I had been going straight there from the office. What would he do? The thought that my life might depend on what Roddy might do was terrifying. If only Damon were here. But these people had to have known that Damon wouldn't be here. That was actually a little encouraging. If what they were doing depended on Damon being away, it had to be ransom; if it were meant to be a quick rape and murder they wouldn't have cared whether he was here or not.

The car was slowing. At last. Then it stopped, and one of the doors opened, followed by a creaking sound as a gate was pushed back. The car moved forward again, quite some distance, and I had the sensation of turning a corner. Then it stopped. I was left lying there for several more minutes, then I heard feet crunching on gravel, and a moment later the back door was opened. Someone seized my ankles and pulled me out; I had to press my wrists into my back to avoid having an arm broken. As I came out of the car into the quite chill night air someone else held my shoulders to lift me up; then a shoulder was driven into my stomach and I realized I was being carried, head and legs hanging down, gasping for breath, while the bastard had his hand on my thigh to hold me in place. Doors opened and shut, and even through the blindfold I was aware of light. I was carried upstairs, through another doorway, as I could tell because I bumped my head, and was then thrown on to a bed, or at least a mattress.

Apart from my now feeling so dodgy I wasn't sure that I *could* move, I felt it was safest not to, so I lay as I had fallen, for several more minutes, trying to pull myself together; this was difficult, as I was not only physically uncomfortable but was now aware of a horrendous thirst. I did, however, realize that there was only a glimmer of light in this room, and that there was a good deal of rustling surrounding me. Then at last I felt hands on my head, and the blindfold was taken away. I blinked into gloom, and the tape at my mouth was seized and pulled free, most painfully. 'Oh,' I gasped.

I was rolled on my face, and my wrists untied, while other hands were untying my ankles. Only then did I realize that my shoes had come off. I lay on my back, panting, and saw that there were three people in the room with me. The situation had been reversed, for where I was now free, my captors had donned long black sleeved gowns, worn with black hoods; as they also wore black gloves the only part of their bodies that was visible were their eyes. I did not suppose this inquisitorial garb was intended to frighten me, only to entirely conceal their identities. As I had surmised, there was no light in the room, the gloom adding to their concealment, but through the half-open door I could see light in the hallway. I sat up and rubbed my wrists and ankles to restore circulation, but I was beginning to feel that for the moment at least I was on a reasonably level playing field. 'I need a drink,' I said.

They looked at each other; then one left the room. One of the remainder now held my arm, pulling me off the bed, and directing me to a table in the corner, before which there was a chair. I was made to sit in this, and a piece of paper was laid in front of me. I blinked at it, and the other person shone a flashlight over my shoulder. I read: *I am in the hands of bold and determined people. My life is set at ten million pounds. On receipt of this letter start making arrangements for finding this money. Further instructions will follow. Going to the police will be useless; you will not find me and I will be killed. Please obey all the instructions.*

Another piece of paper was placed on top of the letter. This merely said: *Sign it.* 'You have got to be nuts,' I said.

The third kidnapper now returned with a glass of water, which was handed to me. It tasted like nectar. Another sheet of paper was produced: *If you do not sign the paper, we will hurt you.* 'Bugger off,' I said. 'This is impossible. Who do you want to send it to? Roddy Webster, or my husband? There is no way either of them can raise ten million pounds.'

More paper: *He can sell Randell's.* Which left me in no doubt who my kidnappers were, or at least, who they were working for. But I felt it would be a mistake to let them know that I had identified them; even if the absurd ransom were paid, they wouldn't ever be able to let me go.

Once again the paper calling for my signature was placed in front of me. I tried desperately to think. Signing the paper would at least buy me some time. And it would put Roddy in the picture, and Damon too; Roddy would surely get in touch with him immediately. I had no idea what they would do, what they *could* do, but it would be something. Not to sign it would mean . . . I had no idea. Something unpleasant. But to change my mind and sign now, after having refused, would make them suspicious. I had to chance my arm, at least briefly. The paper was waved at me again. I shook my head. They were standing one to either side, and one behind me. The one behind me seized my arms and pulled them back. I tried to rise, and the two beside me held my shoulders and pushed me down again.

The one behind me now taped my wrists together again. I wondered if screaming would do any good, but as they hadn't taped my mouth this time, I realized they wouldn't care if I did; where we were was obviously remote.

The one behind me was now holding my shoulders, pressing down on them to make sure I remained in the chair, while the other two turned it so that the table was no longer in the way. Then one of them started work on my front. My jacket was already open, so this person, revealing as she took off her gloves not only long and well-manicured nails but also soft hands, unbuttoned my blouse. There could be no doubt who *she* was, which was disturbing, both because to be duffed up by a woman seemed so much more unpleasant than to be duffed up by a man, and because Jane Randell, if she still believed I was responsible for the death of her Anthony, had more cause to wish to hurt me than either of her brothers.

My shirt open, she lifted my locket to peer at it. If she takes that, I thought . . . But she let it flop back and proceeded to unbuckle my belt, release the zip, and pull my trousers down about my knees. I felt this was enough. I didn't want her to get serious. 'All right,' I said. 'All right.' She ignored me in favour of pulling down my thong. I kicked at her, vaguely, but missed. 'I'll sign the letter,' I said, beginning to pant. For reply she pushed up my bra to expose my breasts. 'I'll sign the letter!' I shouted.

She snorted, but the chair was turned round and presented to the table again, and the tape pulled from my wrists. Again I rubbed them together, and made an abortive attempt to pull my bra down, only to be slapped on the side of the head. That made me almost as angry as I was already frightened and humiliated. I resolved to get these buggers, somehow. Or have Damon get them. A pen was placed in my hand, and I leaned forward and signed the letter, which was immediately put in a waiting envelope. That done, I tried to stand up to pull up my thong and pants, only to be pushed down again and have my arms seized and carried back and my wrists again taped. 'What the fuck?' I demanded. 'I've done what you asked.'

Jane had been writing again, and now she held up the piece of paper. *We like you the way you are.* 'You bastards,' I said. 'You—'

Another slap on the face made my head spin, and before I could recover I was pulled up and bundled across the room to the bed and thrown on it. Then Jane pulled my pants and thong right off to leave me naked from the waist down. Her brothers taped my ankles together. Then she rolled me on my face and hit me on the bottom. This was obviously something she had wanted to do for some time, because the blow was delivered with such force I shrieked in pain. But at least they now all left the room, closing the door, which left me in darkness and about as black a mood as I had ever known.

I lay still for some seconds, aware of some discomfort. I was again thirsty, and now I was hungry as well. And angrier than ever. I couldn't even look at my watch to find the time, but I reckoned it had to be about ten o'clock. Way past supper time.

I heard a car engine, slowly fading. At least one of them had left the house. Perhaps they all had. Be rational, I told myself. In all the movies I had seen, the hero, or the heroine, left alone, even if tied up, had managed to get free. I had to be able to do the same.

Kicking and trying to rub my legs together had no effect at all. It had to be my hands. But straining on the tape wasn't successful either; it had been wrapped round several times. I had to use something. Trouble was, although I hadn't had the time to study the bed very carefully, I was pretty sure it didn't have any uprights against which I could attempt to set up any kind of friction.

I checked on this by swinging my legs to and fro, and then rolled about until my head was at the bottom of the bed and I could perform the same manoeuvre the other way round. But there was nothing there.

The table. Cautiously I got my legs off the bed and then slowly lowered myself behind them, face pressed into the mattress. Even so my knees hit the floor with a thump. I remained kneeling against the bed for several seconds, but there was no sound from elsewhere in the house. Maybe I was indeed alone. I had to lie on my side and reach the table by a series of wriggles, like a snake, and when I finally got up against it, and sat up to rub my wrists against the legs, it promptly shifted, sliding noisily across the floor and causing me to overbalance and fall down again. That left me dizzy for a moment, and before I could recover, the door opened. What is more, the overhead light was switched on.

I rolled over, and saw one of the brothers standing in the doorway. He had taken off his ridiculous black robe and hood, and wore shirt and pants. 'Just what are you trying to do?' he asked.

'Getting free, you stupid bastard,' I said.

'I ought to give you one.'

'Fuck off,' I told him.

He came towards me, and I braced myself for a kick, but he merely grasped my shoulders, dragged me up, and sat me on the chair. 'Did anyone ever tell you—'

'Lots and lots,' I said.

'I'm going to shag you,' he said.

'You'll be lucky.' But at the same time, an idea suddenly took shape. Damon had forbidden me ever to want sex with another man, or ever to be able to *have* sex with another man. But that did not include rape, surely? I was not going to enjoy it. Who does? But if I was forced, there would be nothing I could do about it. And then . . . ? It was certainly a chance worth taking, especially if it was going to happen anyway. But I had to be careful. If I suddenly appeared to welcome the idea he might get suspicious. 'What about your siblings?'

'They've gone out to post your letter. They're going a long way, to make sure it can't be traced back to here. They won't be back for a couple of hours.'

'And when I tell them about your libido?'

He grinned. 'They'll probably have a go at you themselves. David will, anyway.'

'So which one are you?'

'I'm Charlie.'

'That figures.' I was trying desperately to think. This Charlie wasn't actually as tall as me, and I doubted he was any stronger. I wondered if he'd ever done karate. If I could just get him to free my hands . . . It was certain I would never have a better opportunity than right now. 'So you want to have sex with me,' I said. 'I might go along with that. After I've had something to eat.'

'You wish to eat?'

'I'm sorry. It's a quaint habit I've accumulated over the years. I'm no good in bed except after dinner.'

'Shit!' he remarked. 'I'll go see what I can do. But first . . .' He picked up the roll of tape. It had been on the table but had fallen off when I had pushed it. This he now passed round my thighs and the chair seat, several times, strapping me into position. Then he did the same to my chest, using the opportunity for some tit-tugging. Then he did the same to my ankles. I really was trussed up, and could only breathe very hard. 'If you mess about,' he said, 'you'll fall over and hurt yourself. I won't be long.'

He left the door open, and I heard his feet on the stairs. I was seething, so much that it never occurred to me to consider what might be the implications of what was going to happen. My only ambition at that moment was to get free and clobber the bastard. But I was going to have to be patient. He actually wasn't very long, returning with a couple of badly cut sandwiches. He placed the plate on the table, sat beside it. 'Open wide.'

'I am quite capable of feeding myself.'

'I'm going to feed you. You want it, or not?'

I opened my mouth, and he pushed one end of the sandwich in. I bit and chewed, and swallowed; it was surprisingly tasty. And at least he couldn't possibly fuck me while I was sitting in a chair. Now I began to worry that if I took too long the others might come back. I swallowed the last of my sandwich, and attempted an ingratiating smile. 'I think I've had enough. I can eat the other one later.'

He looked uncertain. 'You going to fight me?'

'Certainly not,' I assured him. At least not until afterwards.

He licked his lips, and began unbandaging me. 'I want you to take your shirt off,' he said. 'I want to see those tits.' My arms were free, and I obligingly shrugged off my jacket and then my shirt, then unclipped the bra. He went for them immediately, both fondling them and lowering his head to kiss and suck the nipples. I found it revolting, but I think I would have found it so anyway, spell or no spell. Certainly I could have clobbered him then; he was totally helpless. But I was determined to carry out my plan.

He led me to the bed, and began kissing and sucking the rest of me. I was now becoming quite anxious; time was passing. 'Come on, come on,' I said. 'I want you in me.' At last he obliged. As, despite his efforts, I was in no way ready, it was both painful and unpleasant . . . and slow. It took him what seemed an age to ejaculate, but he finally made it and then began panting into my neck. And I heard a car engine in the drive. 'Shit!' I muttered.

He raised his head. 'Whatsa matter?'

'You,' I told him, rolling him off me and getting on top; then I rolled him again on to his face and delivered a karate chop on the base of his neck with all of my strength. He never uttered a sound, just subsided. I wondered if I'd killed him, but there was no time to find out. The car engine had stopped, which meant they were probably already in the house. I dragged on my pants, shirt and jacket, stuffed bra and thong into my pocket, switched off the light, and stepped on to the landing; there was no time to look for my handbag.

Now I could hear feet on the lower stairs, but being barefoot myself I was making no noise. I studied my situation as best I could in the gloom. There was a room opposite, and the door was open. I went into there, just in time, as someone switched on the light for the upper stairs. This was a junk room, with a very dilapidated bed and mattress, and various household items scattered about the floor – including a discarded iron frying pan. I grasped the handle in both hands and felt a lot better. The feet were coming closer. 'Charlie?' Jane called. 'Where the hell are you?'

'I'll bet he's having a go at her,' David said from below her.

'Silly bugger.' Jane reached the landing and switched on the light in the bedroom. 'Holy shit!' She ran into the room. 'Charlie? Charlie! My God! David!!'

'What's the matter?' David's shoes clumped on the stairs.

'It's Charlie! She's laid him out. I think she's killed him. The bitch!'

'Charlie?' David reached the landing, panting.

I did not suppose my position could be improved. Jane was in the bedroom, kneeling on the bed, peering at her brother. David was in the doorway, his back to me. I stepped behind him, the frying pan above my head, and brought it down with all my strength. Like his brother, he did not utter a sound, just struck the floor in a collapsed heap and with a dull thud. Jane turned, staring firstly at him then past him at me – and the frying pan. 'Shit!' she muttered.

'You're in it,' I agreed. 'Who has the car keys?'

She stood up. 'You have committed murder.'

'Once you've done it once, it comes easy,' I said, advancing behind my frying pan. 'The keys.' To my relief I saw Charlie's eyelids starting to flutter. But that meant I didn't have any time to waste. 'I really would enjoy hitting you with this.'

'David was driving,' she said. 'The keys will be in his pocket.'

'Then you just stand still,' I recommended, and backed through the door again. David was just starting to stir as well, but he was a long way from consciousness. I fumbled in his pockets, keeping an eye on Jane all the while. She stared at me, obviously trying to will herself to attack me, but too afraid of both the frying pan and the way in which her brother had been laid out.

I found the keys in a few moments, and stood up. 'Now,' I said, 'you stay right here and look after your siblings. If you come downstairs I am going to hit you with this. I'd really like to do that, so don't chance your arm.'

Five minutes later I was behind the wheel of the car.

Eleven

The Truth

It was only on the drive home that I realized how agitated I was; my hands were shaking. I was relieved that my journey began in the country; had I been in a town I might well have been stopped by a policeman anxious to find out why the car was drifting to and fro across the road.

Partly my emotions were frazzled by the physical battering I had had; I felt as if I had been run over by a meat grinder. But there was also the trauma of what had happened, of actually being kidnapped. Not to mention the trauma of having had sex with a man other than Damon for the first time in four years. There was also the question of how I was going to handle this without admitting a whole lot of people, mostly policemen, into the very heart of my affairs, something I did not wish to have happen.

But gradually my nerves settled down, and then my overriding emotion was elation, that I had dealt with those three upper-class thugs in a way they weren't going to forget. Which brought up the question of what were *they* going to do about it? Save have a good sweat, as they would have to assume that I would be heading straight for the nearest police station. I wondered if the formidable Alice had known what her offspring were planning, or if, indeed, she had planned it herself. If she had, that put a whole different complexion on the situation. Maybe she *had* sent that black spot to her husband, maybe relating to some incident in their past, unknown to us. That was certainly something worth investigating, because if it were true, then maybe my suspicions of Damon were unfounded. Oh, how I wanted them to be unfounded.

As I did not know if the car I had stolen was already a stolen car, and in any event I did not wish it to be traced back to me, I abandoned it a mile away from the house; this was in any event just before it abandoned me by running out of gas.

By now it was well past midnight. It had taken me some time to discover where I was in the country, or which way I needed to go to get back to London: the car did not rise to a GPS system. But once I got my bearings it was fairly straightforward, save that by the time I abandoned the car it had started to rain. And I had no shoes. Shades of poor Jetta Smith-Lucas, I thought as I sloshed through the puddles, each seeming colder than the last, so that I began to lose all feeling in my toes, while my hair was plastered on my head. It was half past one before I finally stood on my own doorstep and rang the bell. The house was in darkness. So who had been worrying over my failure to come home? I wondered. But then Butterpaws began to bark, and lights came on, and a moment later the door was opened by Horace, wearing a dressing gown over pyjamas and looking amazed. 'Mrs Smith?'

'It's not her ghost, yet.' I stepped out of the rain. Butterpaws bounded past the butler to hurl himself into my arms. 'I'm sorry to get you out of bed in the middle of the night, Horace, but I seem to have lost my handbag, and with it, my key.'

'Your handbag is here, madam.'

And there it was, on the table just inside the door. 'Can you explain that?'

'I believe Mr Webster found it, madam. At the foot of the outside steps. But madam, are you all right? Has there been an accident?'

'That is one way of putting it. Now I am going to have a bath and go to bed. Thank you, Horace.'

He looked as if he would have liked to pursue the matter, but decided against it. I freed myself from Butterpaws' attentions, went to the stairs, and Roddy appeared, also wearing a dressing gown over pyjamas; his were mauve. 'Frances?! My God! Where have you been? What has happened to you?'

'Not a lot. And then, maybe, quite a lot.' I climbed the stairs, dripping on to the carpet. 'Come upstairs and I'll tell you.'

He looked down at Horace, who waggled his eyebrows, and then hurried up the stairs behind me. 'I found your handbag outside when I came in. I couldn't imagine what had happened.'

'So what did you do?' I asked over my shoulder, starting on the second flight.

'I didn't know what to do.'

'So you did nothing.'

'Well, I had no idea what you might be doing.'

'Having dropped my handbag and walked away from it.'

'Well . . . I didn't know what to think. Where have you been? What happened to you? Why have you been walking barefoot in the rain?' I opened my bedroom door and went in. He hesitated in the doorway. 'Oh, come in, do,' I said. 'Is Damon all right?'

'Well, yes. Nanny put him to bed at the normal time.'

'Did he ask after me?' I stripped off my soaking garments; well, there were only three of them left, although the bra and thong had also got soaked, even in my jacket pocket.

'I don't think he did.' Roddy was studiously staring at the wall. I went into the bathroom and turned on the hot water. 'Do you realize you have bruises and things?' he asked. He hadn't actually been looking at the wall after all.

'Yes, I do,' I said. 'Come in here and sit down and I will tell you what happened. But I want you to understand that none of this is to go any further unless I say so.'

He sidled into the room and perched on the toilet seat, while I added a liberal portion of herbal bath relaxant and then sank into the foam. 'Would you like something to drink?' he asked, as an afterthought.

'Not right now. Just listen.' I had to be careful how much I told him. Certainly he couldn't know that I had been raped, at least until I had worked out exactly what might have devolved as a result of that. I felt not the slightest bit sexy at bathing with a man sitting and watching me. This might have been because it was Roddy, who was almost a brother to me, or it might have been because in my present mood I wouldn't have felt sexy even if he had been Brad Pitt. Or it could have been that allowing myself to be raped hadn't done me a damned bit of good. But I didn't want to consider that right then.

So I told Roddy everything that had happened, apart from the rape, advancing my attack on Charlie, as it were, to just prior to the event. He listened in silence while I soaped and soaked. When I had finished, he asked, 'You mean they let you see their faces? Let you see who they were?'

'I don't think they meant to. Things just got out of hand.'

'What are you going to do?' He seemed more agitated now than before.

'I haven't made up my mind yet.'

'Do you want me to call the police?'

'Definitely not. Damon would throw a fit.'

'He's going to throw a fit anyway.'

'Only if we tell him what happened.'

He frowned. 'We can't keep any secrets from Damon.'

'Why not?'

'But if he asks us . . .'

'Why should he ask us? We'll concoct a story to tell the servants, about how I was in an accident, but we don't want to bother Damon by telling him.'

Roddy scratched his head. 'He'll know. He always knows.'

'That's not so. He's able to command certain parts of our brains to make us obey him, but he can't possibly know what's going on in the rest.' I got out of the bath, wrapped myself in a towel. 'Don't let me down in this, Roddy.'

'I won't,' he promised. 'But . . . what *are* you going to do about it.'

'I think it might be interesting to discover what *they* intend to do about it,' I said.

This decision was the easier to take, because of course, having handled it the way I had, I had no proof to offer anyone that the Randell family had been involved at all; it would be their word against mine. But all I wanted to do was rest; I was far more shaken by what had happened than I had first realized.

So with Roddy's blessing I took the next three days off work, just lying about the house and playing with Little Damon and Butterpaws. I heard nothing from the Randell camp – apart from the arrival, the next day, of the ransom demand, addressed to Roddy, which we binned. And at last curiosity got the better of me. I got the number of the house in Corralby from Inquiries, and telephoned. 'Mrs Randell's residence,' said a voice I hadn't heard before, and which I reckoned must belong to the maid.

'May I speak with Miss Jane Randell, please?' I asked.

'I'm sorry, but Miss Jane isn't here.'

'Then would you tell me where I can get in touch with her? It's rather urgent.'

'I'm afraid Miss Jane is out of the country. She's gone on holiday.' She'd done a bunk.

'And Mr Charles? Mr David? Are they out of the country too?'

'That is correct, ma'am.'

'But Mrs Randell is there, isn't she? Let me speak with her.'

'Mrs Randell has also gone on holiday, madam.'

'Ah,' I said. I wondered if they'd be coming back.

I knew I couldn't lie around for ever. There was that plan I had been working on before the Randells had acted up. This had to be done before Damon returned, and he was due back any day now. Back to the Yellow Pages.

There was quite a wide choice, and I kept remembering my

experience with Jetta Smith-Lucas . . . and her experience with Damon. So I took the first on the list. His name was Addamms. I assumed he spelt it that way for effect. But I was also determined to play this one from on top, as it were. 'I'd like you to come and see me,' I said.

'To show me the venue. Of course.' He had a smooth and caressing voice. But that went with the profession. 'Can you tell me, Mrs Smith, is it to be a children's or an adults' party?'

I didn't want to frighten him off. 'A children's party,' I said.

'Very good. When would be convenient for me to call?'

'How about this afternoon?' I suggested.

I was quite nervous, less about the actual meeting with the man than about exactly how I was going to approach the matter without giving away more than I wanted to. I actually didn't want to give away anything at all.

Mr Addamms was reassuring. He was not very tall – shorter than me by several inches – was plump and balding, wore a beard and horn-rimmed spectacles, and had that gentle voice. He made me think of an old-fashioned family GP. 'What a lovely home you have here, Mrs Smith,' he commented, having been shown into the lower drawing room by Horace.

'Thank you. Would you like something to drink?'

'Perhaps later.'

'Well, do sit down. I should begin by asking what you charge.'

He had been sizing up the value of the house and the furnishings. 'I charge two hundred pounds for a one-hour show.'

He looked at me somewhat anxiously. 'That seems reasonable,' I said. He gave a little sigh of relief. 'However,' I went on, 'there isn't going to be a show.'

He took off his glasses to polish them. 'I'm afraid I do not understand.'

'I need information and advice,' I said. 'If you will give

me an hour of your time and knowledge, I will pay your fee of two hundred pounds.'

He replaced his glasses, looking brighter. 'What is it you wish to know?'

'You are a professional hypnotist.'

'Yes.' He was again uneasy.

'Is your business just a prolonged party trick, Mr Addamms, or is there something deeper behind what you do?'

'Hypnotism is a serious business,' he protested. 'It is humiliating to have to make a living out of distracting people, whether they be children or adults. Unfortunately, society is not yet ready for the proper application of my science. And that of my colleagues, to be sure. Such an application, I am certain, could make a vast difference to the safety and prosperity of society.'

'Tell me about it. How long has it been used?'

'Oh, for centuries. The ancient priesthoods of Egypt and Babylon used hypnosis extensively. You must remember that they were dealing with essentially simple and uneducated people, who believed everything their priests told them. The sheer maintenance of the power of the priesthood was a form of mass hypnotism, if you like. There is considerable evidence of its use in early Christianity as well.'

'But not now.'

'Well . . .' He rubbed his nose. 'I suppose it is possible to say that all organized religion is an aspect of mass hypnotism in that people do certain things, believe certain things, not because they actually wish to, but because they are told to do so.'

Another anxious look; how religious was I? 'I'm more interested in the modern usage,' I said. 'I want to know about the one on one, as practised by you and your associates.'

'Well, modern hypnotism is generally regarded as beginning with Franz Mesmer, hence the term "mesmerism". He was an Austrian doctor working in Paris during the French Revolution. He didn't really know what he was at, in the beginning. He was experimenting with cures for all manner

of diseases, suspecting, as most doctors would agree today, that so many illnesses begin in the mind. I don't mean that they are imaginary, but that a chronically unhappy mind can give birth to real physical ailments. Anyway, he found that by making his patients sit in a tub of water, and passing iron bars over their bodies while talking to them in a gentle voice, he could cure their disease, or more properly, their dis-ease. Then he discovered, entirely by accident, that his "cure" worked even without the iron bars. He thus devolved the theory that he personally possessed some kind of animal magnetism which enabled him to influence people. We've come a long way from there, but the concept that the ability to mesmerize people had something to do with metal and magnetism lasted a long time. What discredited the whole idea was a fellow named John Elliotson, a doctor in the 1840s, who practised mesmerism, or hypnosis as it was now being called, from the Greek word for "sleep", while carrying out operations, and is even supposed to have done amputations with no other anaesthetic than hypnosis. But like Mesmer, he believed that he possessed a mysterious metal-based "fluid" which he could transmit to his patient, only he thought it was based not on iron but on nickel. However, the then editor of *The Lancet* didn't believe this, and in one of Elliotson's operations secretly substituted lead for the nickel. The patient was still hypnotized, but the theory was, as I say, discredited.'
Another somewhat anxious pause.

'Fascinating, Mr Addamms,' I said. 'So, what exactly do you do?'

'Oh, I am strictly an entertainer, Mrs Smith.'

'Tell me about it. Can you hypnotize anyone you choose?'

'Ah . . . it helps if the person is happy to be hypnotized. Or if, perhaps, they do not have a very forceful personality.'

'I can see that would work very well with most children. What about adults? Isn't that much more difficult?'

'Well, yes, it is,' he acknowledged.

'But you can do it.'

He flushed. 'Perhaps some preparation is necessary.'

'You mean you employ a stooge.'

'Well, it sort of primes the pump.'

'Hypnosis by extension,' I suggested. 'If Joe Bloggs can be hypnotized, your audience is more likely to accept that you really can do it, and thus be more ready to accept hypnosis themselves.'

'Well . . .'

'Now tell me, is it true that you cannot command someone under hypnosis to do anything that is against their nature, or that they know to be wrong?'

'That is generally accepted,' he said, more cautiously yet.

'I wish to know if it is true.'

'Well, there are degrees of perception as to what is right, and what is morally acceptable. These degrees alter all the time in our modern society. A lot also depends on the mental strength of the subject.'

'So that it *is* possible to make someone do something they should know is wrong, or socially unacceptable.'

'It is *possible*, in certain cases. But of course one would never do that.'

'Of course,' I agreed. 'Now tell me this: is it possible to hypnotize someone who is determined to resist you?'

'It would be very difficult.'

'Is it possible, Mr Addamms?'

'I suppose it could be possible, given the right circumstances.'

'Have you ever done it?'

'Well, no. But you see, when I attend a function, if one of the guests makes it perfectly plain that he, or she, does not wish to be a subject, it is not my place to force them.'

'Quite. So, if you wanted to hypnotize me, and I absolutely refused to be hypnotized, you couldn't do it.'

'Absolutely,' he said enthusiastically. 'Anyone can see that you are a very strong character.' Thinking of his two hundred pounds.

'What would you say if I told you that I had once been hypnotized? Against my will.'

'The circumstances must have been very unusual. Or . . .'
'Yes?'
'The person who did it must have had an even stronger character than yours. Much stronger. Unless . . .'
'Yes?'
'The hypnosis could have been related to some physical object, which to you was sufficiently important to act as a back-up, shall we say, to his, or her personality.'

I stared at him, as all manner of understandings suddenly began to tumble through my mind, as yet chaotic, but slowly taking shape. But there were other things I needed to know. 'When you hypnotize somebody, you make them do, or say, whatever you command; then you snap your fingers or whatever and they come out of it. Right?'

'Loosely, yes.'

'And before you do that, you tell them that they will forget everything that they have said or done while under hypnosis.'

'That depends on what I have made them say or do. If it has been anything embarrassing, usually yes.'

'But you can also tell them to remember everything that happened.'

'Oh, indeed.'

'But in fact, you don't have to release them from their hypnotism at all, do you?'

'I'm not sure I understand you. Not to release a subject would be unethical.'

'Oh, quite. But let's suppose you had someone under hypnosis, and you had a heart attack and died before they could be released. Would they then remain hypnotized for the rest of their lives?'

'Bless my soul,' he remarked. 'There's a macabre scenario.'

'Would they?'

'Well . . .' He took off his glasses and polished them. 'I don't really know, Mrs Smith.'

'Should such a thing happen, would it be possible for

friends of the subject, the hosts of the party, perhaps, to send out for another hypnotist to release the subject?'

'Well, they could, of course, but . . .'

'Yes?'

'Well, you see, Mrs Smith, hypnosis is a very personal thing. It is almost a form of thought transference, from master to subject. For example, if I were to hypnotize you— I know I wouldn't be able to do it, but supposing I could, only you and I would know what had passed between our minds. I would know it consciously, you would know subconsciously. You would never be able to identify it, at least while you remained under hypnosis. But it would be *there*. Now, for someone else to get in on the act, as it were, he or she would have to be able to get into your mind. Obviously there wouldn't be much point in attempting to get into mine, if I were dead. But it would be next to impossible to get into yours, if you were under hypnosis.'

The temptation to tell him everything was enormous, but so were the risks. If I did, and he couldn't help me, he'd be in a position to blackmail me for the rest of my life. But he would be in that position even if he could release me; he was very unlikely to leave it there, no matter what he might promise, and what might happen if he started to probe into Damon's mind I didn't like to think. Besides, I now had that other idea. 'Supposing,' I asked, 'the subject had been hypnotized with the aid of some outside force, as you suggested just now, and was then left by the death of the hypnotist. Could her, or his, position be reversed by the discovery of the outside force, or talisman, and perhaps its destruction?'

The glasses came in for some more polishing. 'There's a tricky one. I would have to say, Mrs Smith, I really don't know. What we are doing is leaving the realms of hypnosis, which in my experience has never been anything more than a party trick, and going into the realms of the occult. This is not something I know much about. Nor wish to,' he added hastily. 'I would say though that one needs to tread very carefully when one delves in the occult. Here again, you see, it would be possible to expect that the hypnotist, if using some additional force, will have imparted part of his own persona into that object. To find the object, and destroy it, might have incalculable consequences upon both the hypnotist's and the subject's character. Of course, in your hypothesis, the hypnotist would be dead, but no one could say what effect the destruction of the force might have on the subject.'

'So, rather than take that risk you would condemn the unfortunate subject to a lifetime of hypnosis.'

'Well, she, or he, would be unaware of it.'

'Not if they had been told to remember it.'

'Ah. Yes.' He was now beginning to look extremely hot under the collar. 'May I ask, Mrs Smith, this *is* a hypothetical case we are discussing?'

'Of course. What makes you think it is not?'

'It is merely that you have gone into such detail that it almost sounds as if you were describing something of which you have personal knowledge.'

'It is a subject in which I am interested. And you have been most helpful, Mr Addamms. I'll just write you your cheque.'

The moment Addamms left I ran upstairs to my bedroom, and locked the door behind myself. My emotions were in such a jumble they really precluded rational thought.

I sat on the bed, and slowly, carefully, lifted the necklace over my head and laid the locket on the bed beside me. I had of course taken it off before, but not very often – I even bathed with it round my neck, as a rule. It simply had never occurred to me that there could be anything occult about it. I had even forgotten the very odd manner in which Damon had found it and returned it to me. But had he found it? Or . . .

I picked it up and inspected it very carefully. I never had put a photo into the locket itself. But it certainly seemed the original article. How to prove it? Presumably any competent jeweller should be able to set a date on it. Any date before the day I lost it in Eleuthera would prove that it was the genuine article. But would *that* prove anything? The locket *had* to be genuine. There was no way even Damon could have found an exact replacement in a place like Harbour Island in a couple of hours.

But he had found it, somehow, and he had put a spell on it. I began to feel quite creepy, as this was way beyond any experience I had ever had, or had ever believed possible. One half of my brain utterly rejected the idea. The other kept telling me that perhaps this was the only way I would ever be able to free myself. Then I remembered Charlie. Suppose I was already free? How was I to find out? I had had too many unfortunate experiences in the past even to consider trying another one. Besides, it was no longer about sex. I didn't really care if I never had sex again, with anyone. It was about freeing my mind. And I could prove that I had accomplished that very simply, by packing my bags, and Baby Damon's bags, and moving out. But that had been practical even before Charlie, with Damon away. The crunch would come when Damon returned, and commanded me to move back in. I wasn't sure I would be able to take the scene that would surely follow a refusal. I had to admit, at least to myself, that I was deathly afraid of what he might do.

As for destroying the locket . . . Because, if it was carrying or assisting the spell, I knew it would have to be destroyed. Just ceasing to wear it would not do. As long as it was around me it would continue its influence. But to destroy it without being sure . . .

And then some more of what Addamms had said came back to me. Suppose destroying it did have a bad effect on Damon's personality. Seeing as how he had apparently killed several people just because they had got in his way suggested that his character was pretty unhealthy anyway. But he was the father of my son.

And then what about me? Apart from the fact that I had so far loyally supported Damon in everything, and that was a result of the spell, I was pretty pleased with my personality.

Certainly I didn't want to alter it in any way. What *was* I to do?

I was back to an awareness of how lonely I was. There was absolutely no one to whom I could turn for help or advice.

I picked up the threads of my life again, went to the office, gave directives, smiled at the staff . . . The official word, as spread by Roddy, was that I had had a car accident. We didn't elaborate. Every spare moment away from work I spent with Little Damon, trying to use his unwitting company as a means to a decision. But it was gradually hardening in my mind. I had to make the decision and make the break. And it had to be done before Damon returned. Next morning there was an e-mail: LANDING HEATHROW ZERO EIGHT HUNDRED TOMORROW. TREMENDOUS NEWS.

'What on earth is he at?' Roddy asked.

'Haven't a clue,' I said, my brain racing away at a tangent. I had twenty-four hours. Would it not be better just to confront him, and tell him that I knew his secret? He'd simply laugh at me. But suppose, thanks to Charlie, I was actually free? I know all of these reflections make me seem like a ninny, but the decisions were all so irrevocable. Maybe I've just never been very good at making decisions. So I decided to wait.

Roddy and I both went to Heathrow to meet Damon's plane. He was every bit as ebullient as he had appeared in the e-mail, bustled out of the customs hall behind a porter with his bags, approached me with arms outspread; I was glad I had held fire. 'Darling,' he announced. 'I have been so lonely without you. How's the boy?'

'Looking forward to seeing you.'

He peered at me; although my bruises had faded, there was still a slight stain on my cheek. 'Who hit you?'

'Oh, that. I was in this taxi which hit another car and I bumped my face.'

'Goddammit. We'll sue the bugger.'

'Oh, really, I'd rather forget all about it.'

He released me to shake hands with Roddy. 'All well?'

'Oh, indeed.'

'You know about this accident?'

'I was worried stiff.'

'Yeah. Well, we'll talk about it. But first . . .' He escorted us to the taxi rank, the patient porter following. 'Have I got news for you.'

We fitted ourselves into the back of the taxi, Damon beside me on the seat, Roddy on the jump seat opposite. 'Well?' I asked.

'How does Sir Roderick Webster grab you?'

Roddy goggled at him. 'You're kidding.'

'I never kid, Roddy.'

'But . . . I don't get it.'

Neither did I. 'He's not even English,' I pointed out.

'There's the point,' Damon said. 'If he was English, there wouldn't be a hope in hell. But he's Bahamian. They can have their own knights. I've spent the past fortnight chatting up the more important members of the government over there, pointing out what a great job Roddy is doing, how successful he's been, what an ambassador he is for the Bahamas . . . and how much more successful he is going to be with a handle. It took a little work, but in the end they went for it. You'll be in the next Honours List.'

'Holy shit!' Roddy said. I could have echoed him. The sheer effrontery of it took my breath away, especially as I couldn't have any doubts about how Damon had achieved his objective. And once I had supposed that he lacked the imagination ever to use his unholy powers for anything other than personal gain! 'Sir Roderick Webster,' Roddy said, reverently. 'Oh, if the old lady could only know.'

'She's probably shifting a few daisies already,' Damon said.

I could hardly wait to get home and find out just what he was at, or at least try to do so, but Roddy was desperate to let the office know what had happened. Both men felt, as Damon officially had nothing to do with the firm, that I, as second-in-command, should actually break the news.

So we dropped Damon off at the house, where he could see Little Damon and have a bath and a lie-down after his long flight, and then continued to the office, where I assembled the staff and told them that we had just received news that the boss was to receive a knighthood from the Bahamian government. Although they were obviously as surprised and mystified as I had been, they were also delighted, and clapped their congratulations, their happiness increasing when Roddy announced that in view of the news he was authorizing a bonus across the board. Louise was so excited that she actually kissed him, much to his embarrassment.

Then she left us alone, and I sat across his desk from him. We gazed at each other for several seconds; then he said, 'He certainly is full of surprises.'

'You do realize that he hypnotized at least one member of the government,' I pointed out.

'Well, we don't know that.'

'Oh, come now, Roddy. None of those guys have ever heard of you. And if they have heard of Randell's & Company, which is highly unlikely, they can't possibly know that it's owned by a Bahamian.'

'Why not? Governments keep their eyes on things. Far more than you realize.'

'And don't you realize that if the Bahamian government *had* been keeping their eyes on you, which again is highly unlikely, and decided to reward your efforts, they would have informed you before some friend who has nothing to do with the business?'

'Hm. Probably Damon met some of those guys at a party, and when they discovered he was a friend of mine they told him the news.'

'Oh, for God's sake.' I gave up. 'Anything you say. You're the boss. Would you mind if I took the rest of the day off?'

'You want to be home with lover boy, eh?'

'As a matter of fact, yes. We *have* been separated for two weeks.'

'So, be my guest. I'm going to have to have the name plate changed.' He was still on cloud nine.

I got up. 'I'd wait until it actually happens.'

'You still think he had something to do with Randell's death?'

'Well, you certainly wouldn't be getting a knighthood if you didn't own the company.'

He rubbed his chin. 'What about those others? You going to tell him?'

'I haven't decided yet. And you remember that you promised the decision would be mine.'

'Oh, sure. I remember. Well . . . have fun.'

I went outside. 'Oh, Mrs Smith,' Louise said. 'Isn't it exciting?'

'I'm sure it is.'

'To work for a sir. I've always wanted to work for a sir. I wonder why Sir Roderick has never married. Do you know why, Mrs Smith?'

'Sir Roderick has never married because he doesn't go for women,' I said, somewhat brutally.

'Oh,' she said. 'Oh!'

I took a taxi home, to a quiet house. Little Damon and Butterpaws were being walked by Clara, and I gathered from Horace that Damon was in bed. I took off my shoes and went upstairs as quietly as I could, crept into the bedroom. The drapes were drawn, and I waited for a few moments to allow my eyes to become accustomed to the gloom. I was still waiting when he said, 'Come to bed.'

'I didn't mean to wake you.'

'Well, you did.'

I undressed. 'I'm a noisy girl.'

'You didn't make a sound. Don't you realize I know where you are and what you are doing all of the time?'

Hype? Or a frightening reality. I slid into bed beside him, and there was no conversation for several minutes: the past fortnight was the first time we had ever been separated for any length of time since his return to my life. 'So tell me what I have been doing while you were away,' I challenged when we were both lying on our backs.

'Claiming to have had a car accident.'

'Claiming?'

'Well, you didn't, did you? Tell me what really happened.'

I stared at the ceiling. 'I had a car accident.'

'What was the date?'

'Oh . . . Tuesday before last.'

'Right. And you were in a black cab?'

'Yes.'

'What was the number?'

'How should I know?'

'Okay. You say he ran into another car.'

'No. Another car ran into us, when we stopped at a light. The driver wasn't paying attention.'

'Right. What make was the other car?'

'Oh, for God's sake.' I tried to think of the most common car on English roads. 'A Ford Fiesta.'

'Right. That should be enough to go on. I'll get on to the cab company tomorrow and check it out.'

'Why do you want to do that? I'd rather forget the whole thing. Let the taxi company take action against the driver, if they wish to.'

'I am going to check it out, darling, to prove to myself, and to you, that you are lying.'

I raised myself on my elbow. 'You think I am lying?'

'I know you are lying.'

'Well, then . . .' I lay down again, and drew a deep breath. 'I would like a separation.' First things first.

'You wish to leave me?'

'I think we should try living apart for a while. We need a chance to think about things.'

'You mean you want to have a whirl with this lover of yours. The one who knocks you about.'

'I do not have a lover,' I snapped. 'I said, we need to think about things.'

'What makes you think you can leave me?'

'What makes you think you can stop me?'

He rolled on his side to look at me. 'I can stop you, because you are mine, now and always. You know that. Why fight it? You know that, just as you know that you are eventually going to tell me the truth about this guy who hit you.'

I gazed at him. 'So that you can kill him, as you killed Anthony, and Jetta, and Clermont . . . and Randell?' I found I was holding my breath.

'Why, yes,' he said. 'That is what I will do.'

Twelve

Nemesis

I was too surprised to react for a moment; I had never expected him to admit it.

He grinned at me. 'You've always known that, haven't you?'

'I've always suspected it. And refused to believe it. For God's sake, why?'

'Well, let's see. Clermont had something I wanted, badly. Money.'

'And you told him he was going to die.'

'Something like that. It wasn't difficult. He was obsessed with guilt about being gay, kept going on about how he, or his partners, could never catch AIDS because he made them wash very carefully both before and after sex. So I told him that if any of his boyfriends did get AIDS, he'd die. He laughed at that, but then one of them did turn up to tell him he was dying of AIDS, and bingo.'

'But . . . you must have had an accomplice.'

'Doesn't everyone?'

I gasped. 'Roddy!'

'Spot on.'

'And then . . .'

'He just disappeared again. No one had any idea he'd been near the house.'

'And you promised him . . .'

'I promised him he'd be rich, famous and titled. I always deliver on my promises.'

That explained a great deal, even if it left me in an even

more dangerous position than before. It meant that Roddy was not, and never had been, trustworthy. And I had bared my soul to him more than once. 'And then, Jetta Smith-Lucas? She had nothing you could possibly want.'

'She was getting a handle on you. Besides, I have never met a woman I so instantly disliked.'

'But to kill her . . . What did you tell her?'

'You were there.'

'Yes, but how did you make her kill herself?'

'I told her she wouldn't remember anything of what we had said and done until she got into her own house. Then she would remember, and she would be so ashamed she'd put her head in the gas oven.'

I was sweating. 'And Anthony Taggart?'

'That bastard was after you.'

'No, he wasn't,' I protested. 'We tried, but it didn't work. Your spell, I suppose.'

'He'd have tried again. Anyway, I got his address and went to see him. He wasn't difficult to hypnotize, so I told him that the day you got married he'd get into his car and drive as far and as fast as he could until he ran out of gas. I didn't care whether he was killed or not. I was pretty sure he was going to have a smash-up, which would teach him a lesson.'

'And then Randell?'

'How was I to have Roddy knighted until he was the boss of the firm? He was one of the easiest. I found out he was a great fan of Robert Louis Stevenson, and that his favourite book was *Treasure Island*. Some guys just never grow up, do they? So I told him that one day he would receive the black spot himself. He laughed at me. But he believed, in his heart.'

I drew a deep breath. 'So what are you going to do to me, now that you have confessed all this?'

'Confessed what?' he asked. 'Do you suppose any policeman in the world would believe a word you were saying if you went to them with that story? Anyway, it's marriage bed talk. That's not admissible evidence.'

'Well, then,' I said. 'You have nothing to fear if we separate.'

'I have nothing to fear either way. But I don't want us to separate. You're my wife. And you're the mother of my son.'

'And you reckon I couldn't leave you anyway, because I'm still hypnotized.'

He grinned. 'Aren't you?'

'I think we should put that to the test.' I swung my legs out of bed and got up. To my surprise he just lay back and watched me. I showered, then dressed, put on a face, then took a small suitcase from the wardrobe and packed various essentials. It was of course a trial run, both to see if I could do it, and to see what he would do if I could. The business of moving all of my gear out would have to wait. As for financing the split, I didn't see that as a problem in the short term; he had never asked me for any contribution to the housekeeping, and as I was earning a very good salary, I had a considerable balance in my savings account. I closed the suitcase. 'I will let you have an address. I will return at some stage for the rest of my clothes, and to pick up Damon and Butterpaws.'

'You've had your fun,' he said. 'Now come back to bed.'

He still hadn't moved. 'Those days are done,' I said.

'Come back to bed,' he repeated, his voice taking on a quality I had only heard once or twice before. There was nothing caressing about this tone.

'No,' I said. 'No, no, no.' But I was putting down the suitcase.

It hadn't worked! I hated myself, I hated Damon, I hated the whole world. Because I was as much of a slave as I had ever been. Perhaps more so.

Naturally, I rationalized. I reminded myself that it had only been a trial run, that I had gone at it bald-headed, virtually on impulse, that I had not given adequate thought to Little Damon, and how I was going to get him out of the house, that I had not prepared anywhere to go, and above all that I had made the mistakes of telling Damon what I was doing and then attempting to eyeball him. I had also learned that my rape had been nothing more than an unpleasant experience.

But there remained the locket. I understood that getting rid of this had to be planned as carefully as everything else; I was just about prepared to believe that he did know where I was and what I was doing all of the time. At least in the abstract. And he would certainly spot right away if I wasn't wearing it. Having actively determined to work towards getting him out of my life – any idea of bringing him to justice had to wait on that first step – my first task was to restore our relationship.

This wasn't difficult, for Damon, as usual, was perfectly happy to forget our little spat or my attempt at rebellion. I cemented the situation by telling him about my kidnap. It really is impossible for me to put my hand on my heart and say that I did this voluntarily and as part of my master plan, and not because of his control of my mind. That was the problem with his control: so many of the things he wanted from me were things I wanted to do or give him anyway.

As for the Randell clan, I reflected that they deserved what might be coming to them. Damon listened in silence, again as usual. When I was finished, he said, 'That bastard actually raped you? And you didn't go to the police?'

'I wanted to talk to you about it first. I didn't know if you'd want the police interfering with our lives. What with . . . well, everything.'

'That was good thinking. Then why did you tell me that cock and bull story about a car accident?'

'I . . . I was afraid of what you might do.'

'What would you like me to do?'

'Forget the whole thing.'

'Some bastard rapes my wife and you expect me to forget it?'

'Please. Don't you think you've taken enough lives?'

'There are too many people in the world as it is,' he riposted.

'Damon, I'm begging you. I don't want you to kill anyone else on my behalf. Anyway, he's left the country. They all have.'

He grinned, and rumpled my hair. 'They'll come back.'

I'm sure I can be forgiven for being somewhat cold to Roddy over the next few weeks. Especially when he had the effrontery to say to me, 'So much for keeping secrets, eh?'

'I'm sure you know all about that,' I remarked.

'What did he say when you told him?'

'You know Damon. He doesn't ever say a lot.'

He took me outside to show me his new name plate, even if he hadn't yet received the accolade.

Ma and Pa were, as usual, noticing things.

Ma seized her opportunity when Little Damon and I went down alone to Hastings. Damon was playing golf with some bigwig. Although he claimed that his obtaining a knighthood for Roddy was simply a reward, I didn't have any doubt that was also a part of his plan to achieve . . . whatever he next intended to achieve.

'Is there anything you'd like to tell me, dear?' Ma asked as we drank tea, Pa being ensconced in the telly, where Little Damon joined him.

I brooded for few moments before replying. Dare I implicate them? But then, I reckoned they were implicated anyway, simply by being my parents. I couldn't risk telling Ma the whole truth, but she could help me enormously. 'I suppose you could say there are problems,' I confessed.

'Oh, my dear!' She held my hand. 'Another woman?'

'Ah . . .' It was tempting to take the easy way. But I decided against it. 'I don't think so. It's I suppose what they call an irretrievable breakdown.'

She frowned at me, perhaps for the first time noticing the

last trace of the bruise on my face. 'He hasn't been knocking you about?'

'No, no, nothing like that. I really don't want to go into details, Mum, but I do want to leave him.'

'You mean, get a divorce. Well, I always—'

'Please don't say it. I'm not even sure I want a divorce. I do want us to separate for a while. Trouble is, he won't hear of it.'

'He can't stop you. It's not as if you were his prisoner or something.'

'Ah . . . no, of course not. But I'm sure he'd make life very unpleasant. Certainly he'd be after Little Damon. Unless I can sort of disappear for a while.'

'You mean, come here?' She was doubtful.

I obliged her by shaking my head. 'That wouldn't do any good. Here is the first place he'd look. No, what I thought was, if you could take a place for me, a flat or something like that, so that I could just move down there. I'd finance it, of course.' I paused, hopefully.

She was still doubtful. 'You mean, take it in my name?'

'No. He'd trace that quickly enough. What we need to do is for you to find me a flat, somewhere reasonably remote from Central London, and lease it so that I can move in whenever I decide to pull the plug. You'd take it under a false name.'

Mummy looked more doubtful yet. Things like false names were not her cup of tea. 'Wouldn't it be simpler for you to find the place? I mean, you're in the business.'

'That's why I can't do it myself. Damon's friend Roddy now owns the firm, and he'd know if I rented anywhere. It has to be done entirely outside the office, through some other realtor.'

'You mean, when you leave Damon, you're going to give up your job?'

She did have this ability, disturbingly, to go straight to the nitty-gritty. I hadn't really considered all the aspects of what I was planning. 'Those are things I'll have to work out,' I said. 'Just find the flat and rent it.'

I could put off any other decisions until that was done.

But before anything could be done, I was again, and as usual, thrown right off balance by Damon's announcement that we would celebrate Christmas and New Year's in the Bahamas. 'I thought you said you had tickets for some bash here,' I protested.

'I do. But things have changed. Roddy has to collect his knighthood. The investiture is to take place on the second of January. So we have to be in Nassau for that.'

'What about Little Damon?'

'Oh, he'll come with us this time. There's time for him to have his shots, and for you too.'

'And Butterpaws?'

'He'll stay here. Horace can look after him. It'll only be for a week.'

It did sound rather exciting, even if Ma had to be convinced that I was serious, about anything. 'You're going off to the Bahamas with him? What about this separation?'

'That'll happen when I come back. Just find me that bolthole.'

She looked more dubious than ever.

In the event, the Bahamas trip was just as successful as our honeymoon. Everyone seemed to know Damon, and a lot remembered, or claimed to remember, Roddy, who, naturally, was like a dog with two tails.

There was a reception for us when we arrived, and we were with the governmental party to watch the fireworks on the thirty-first, while two days later there was the investiture. I'm bound to say that Roddy looked every inch a knight. Events like this made me wonder if I had not dreamed the whole thing, whether I really wanted to split, with all the immense hassle that would involve. By the time we got home, after a very convivial flight, I had almost decided to see if it wouldn't work, whether or not he was a serial killer.

We landed at eight, and took a taxi home. 'I think the office can do without us today,' Roddy said. 'I'm for a bath and bed.'

'Me too,' I agreed. Little Damon had fallen asleep in the taxi, so I carried him into the house, to be greeted by Horace, gravely, as usual, and Butterpaws, boisterously, as usual. Clara was also waiting, and I handed Little Damon to her. 'Don't wake him up, if you can avoid it,' I said. 'He can have a bath later.'

'Yes, ma'am.' She carried him up to his room.

Damon followed me into our suite, and I turned on the taps. 'You bathing?'

'You go ahead,' he said. 'There's some mail here.'

'Anything for me?' I asked as I undressed. This was a rhetorical question, as I very seldom received mail.

'Just looking.' He slit an envelope.

'So?' I stepped out of my thong and turned to face him as he turned to face me, a sheet of paper in his hand.

'This is from your mother.'

'To you?'

'No. To you.'

'You opened my letter?'

'Well, it's marked private and confidential. I can't have my wife receiving private and confidential mail without finding out what it is.'

'You bastard!' I stretched out my hand. 'Give it to me.'

'I'll read it to you,' he suggested. I attempted to snatch it, and received a push in the chest that sent me staggering across the room to sprawl on the bed. *Dear Frankie*, Damon read. *I hope you had an enjoyable time in the Bahamas, even if you had you-know-who to cope with. I am writing to say that I think I have found just what you want. It's a neat little two-bedroom flat in Bournemouth, nicely furnished and not too expensive. If you could come down sometime soon, alone, we could drive over together and you could look at it. Call me with your plans. Mum.*

I was panting, as much with apprehension as with the

effects of the push. Ma was so innocent. If only she'd waited until she knew I was back. She must have known I would call her as soon as I had got over my jetlag.

Damon had crossed the room and was standing above me. 'Still up to your little tricks,' he remarked. 'Your attempted little tricks.'

I sat up, pushed hair from my eyes. 'If I want to have a *pied-à-terre* I am going to have a *pied-à-terre*.'

'No you are not. Not unless you are going to share it with me. Who *were* you meaning to share it with? Charlie Randell?'

'You really are a bastard.'

'Okay. So get on the phone to your mother and tell her to forget the idea.'

'I will not.'

'Darling,' he said, speaking very reasonably, 'you can't fight me. You know that. Why keep trying?'

'I am going to fight you for as long as I have to,' I said.

'You are a silly little bitch. Okay. If you won't telephone your mother, I'd better go down and have a chat with her.'

'You are not to go near her.'

'Who's going to stop me?'

'I am.' He grinned, and turned his back on me to go into the bathroom. 'Bastard!' I shouted, and jerked the locket from my neck, breaking the chain, and then hurling it at him. This wasn't how I had intended it to happen, but I had lost my temper.

It struck him in the middle of the back. The locket was of course neither large enough nor heavy enough to hurt him, but he felt the impact, and turned to look at me, then at the locket lying on the floor. When I looked into his eyes, I was afraid. But I was not about to stop fighting. 'You see,' I said. 'I know all of your tricks as well.' Praying that I was right.

He stooped and picked up the locket, looked at the chain. 'We'll have to have this repaired.'

'I am not going to wear it again,' I said. 'Ever.'

Slowly he came towards me, and I propelled myself

backwards across the bed. But he was quicker than I was. When I saw he was going to reach me I turned on my knees to get off the bed and make a dash for the door, but he caught my hair and jerked me backwards. The pain was considerable, and I cried out, but before I could catch my breath he had slapped my face, once, twice, three times, hard. I tasted blood and collapsed across the bed, tears streaming from my eyes. But they were tears of anger at least as much as pain or fear, and despite all three emotions I felt a wild sense of exhilaration. No matter what happened now, I had defied him – for the first time in five years. Then I realized that I had actually defied him, by refusing to call Ma, *before* I had taken off the locket. Perhaps the rape had worked after all. I was free!

Mentally. But not physically. Damon had released my hair and now he left the bed. That was another relief, as I was anticipating another rape, or at least a beating. But instead he picked up the house phone. Roddy was clearly fast asleep already, because it rang several times before being answered. In that period I sat up, wiped blood from my chin, and tried to get my thoughts together. At the moment they were centring on making a dash for the door, even if I knew I wouldn't reach it.

'Oh, for God's sake, wake up,' Damon said into the phone. 'I want you down here. Yes, in my bedroom. Now.' He replaced the phone, returned to the bed, and stood above me.

I licked my lips and tasted more blood. 'If you touch me again, I'll kill you,' I said, trying to get as much venom into my tone as he could get into his.

'You're begging for it,' he said. 'Just what have you told your mother about you and me?'

'Find out.'

'I shall do that. Come in, Roddy. And lock the door.'

Roddy sidled into the room. He looked at me, and then at Damon. 'What's happening? The servants seem to be agitated.'

'As far as they are concerned, Frances has had a nervous breakdown. Now, I have to go out. I'll be gone for several hours. I should be back this afternoon. For that time I wish you to stay in here with Frances. Make sure she stays here too, does not use the telephone, and in general behaves herself.'

Roddy looked at me again, and licked his lips. 'For several hours? But how do I sleep?'

'I imagine Frances needs her sleep as well.' Damon opened the top drawer of his bureau and took out a small box, long and thin. 'I am going to put her out for a while.'

'You dare!' I said.

From the box he took a hypodermic, which he now proceeded to fill from a vial that was also contained in the box; I hadn't even known he had such a thing, much less anything to put in it. 'This is powerful stuff, so I can't give her too much. It'll put her out for about three hours. When she wakes up, if she's fractious, give her another shot. That should take care of things until I get home.' I scrambled off the bed and ran for the door. 'Get her,' Damon said.

Roddy reached me and threw both arms round my waist. 'Bastard!' I shouted. 'Help me!' I screamed. 'Horace!'

'The servants!' Roddy panted, dragging me backwards across the room while I tried to turn and strike at him with my nails.

'I'll deal with the servants,' Damon said. 'I'll tell them to send up some lunch in due course; let's say one o'clock. By then this shot will have worn off, so you give her another one at twelve; I'll refill it for you. When Horace brings up the lunch, allow him into the room so that he can see Frances sleeping peacefully. For God's sake, keep her still.'

I was making more abortive efforts to get free, but Roddy was stronger than he looked, and holding me as he was from behind I couldn't get at him, save by hacking backwards with my heels, which didn't seem to be working. Now Damon came round in front, and grinned at me. 'When I come back,' he said, 'and you have calmed down a bit, we'll have a nice long chat.'

He held my arm and pulled it straight. I kicked at him, but he caught my leg without difficulty, and tucked it under his arm while he tested the syringe with his free hand. I tried kicking with the other foot, but before I could get it up the needle had pricked my flesh and he had stepped away, leaving me panting. 'You can have the pleasure of putting her to bed,' Damon said. 'You can even get in with her, if you like. Just remember—'

'I'll remember,' Roddy said. 'I'm not likely to forget.'

'Bastard!' I panted. 'Both of you. When I . . .'

It took me several minutes of half-consciousness to understand where I was and what had happened to me. Understanding was assisted by the gentle snoring from beside me; Roddy lay on his back, beneath the sheets, breathing rhythmically and heavily.

I investigated myself. I was naked, and somewhat bruised. My arm hurt, as it had done when the Randells had injected me. I felt definitely woozy. And I was hopping mad. I could remember everything.

Damon had gone down to Hastings. To find out how much Ma knew about us? Ma knew nothing about us, really, so he would draw a blank there. But would he accept a blank? Or would he . . .

I eased my legs out of bed and then stood up. Roddy never moved, except to utter a few more snores. As a gaoler he was a write-off. Or Damon had miscalculated both the size of the dose and the strength of my constitution.

I looked at my watch; it was just after eleven. As I had been injected about nine, I had actually been out for two hours instead of three. Damon would only just have got to Hastings. There could still be time. But first, Roddy had to be dealt with. I didn't bear him any ill will; I knew he was Damon's slave, as I had been. But I was still prepared to bat him over the head if I had to, if I could find something to bat him with. I looked around the room. Damon's golf clubs were in his wardrobe, but I really didn't like the idea of hitting Roddy with a number seven iron: that could be fatal.

Then I realized I didn't have to hit him with anything. Lying on the dressing table was the hypodermic syringe, fully charged as Damon had promised. I didn't know for how long it would lay Roddy out, but half an hour was all I wanted. I picked it up, moved back to the bed, and listened to another series of trumpets. I remembered that it had taken a minute or two for the drug to work on me. But once it was in him, it *would* work.

I knelt beside the bed, gently eased back the sheet. He was naked, save for a gold St Christopher medallion on a matching chain round his neck. That was fine by me. I didn't really know anything about injecting people, so I merely took a deep breath, and virtually stabbed him with the needle. He gasped and opened his eyes, but before he could move I had emptied the syringe, and was leaping away from the bedside. Roddy sat up, with his right hand slapping his left arm where he had been punctured. 'You bitch!' he said.

'Sauce for the goose,' I pointed out.

He stood up, uncertainly. 'I am going to bust your ass,' he said.

Clearly he was very angry; he had never spoken to me like that before. But I had backed right across the room to the wardrobe, and now I did take out one of Damon's clubs. 'Come and try it,' I suggested.

He glared at me, took a step towards me, then gave a little sigh and collapsed like a house of cards, going straight down to hit the carpet with a terrible thump. I dropped the club and went to him. He was out cold. I felt I should get him on to the bed, but I just couldn't lift him sufficiently. So I took the pillows and put them under his head, straightened him out, then pulled the covers from the bed as well and draped them over him. I reckoned he should be quite comfortable until he woke up.

I dressed myself, checked my handbag to make sure I had money and cards, renewed my face and brushed my hair, put on my coat and stared at myself in the mirror. I looked perfectly normal.

I opened the bedroom door and stepped outside, nearly tripping over Butterpaws, who was loyally sleeping across the threshold. I went down the stairs, and encountered Horace coming up. 'Call me a taxi, will you, Horace,' I said. 'For Victoria.'

'Yes, madam.' He hesitated. 'Are you all right, madam? The master said you weren't very well.'

'I felt ill earlier. But I'm fine now.'

'Yes, madam.'

He hurried off to call the cab, while I considered telling him not to disturb Sir Roderick. But I decided against it. As far as he knew, Roddy was sleeping off the overnight plane journey in his own bed. It would not occur to him to disturb him, unless he felt something was wrong.

I went upstairs to the nursery. 'He's fast asleep,' Clara said. 'Are you all right, madam?'

'Yes, I'm all right. I'm going out for a couple of hours. I'll be back this afternoon.'

I went downstairs again. 'The taxi is here, madam,' Horace said. 'About your lunch, Mr Smith said we were to take a tray up to you at one o'clock, but—'

'It's only half past eleven,' I agreed. 'Actually, I've decided to lunch out.'

'Yes, madam. May I ask if you'll be in for dinner?'

'I expect so.'

'And Mr Smith?'

'I imagine he will be home as well, Horace.' I really had no idea. I had no idea what I was going to do, what was going to happen. I was again gripped by a wild exhilaration. I was free! Or I thought I was. The next few hours would prove it.

I caught the next train to Hastings, sat alone in a first-class compartment, fingers tight on my handbag. I was doing something positive with my life, for the first time in so very long. I was utterly confident, save for that two-hour start he had. But Pa would be there, and he could hardly hypnotize them both together.

It was two o'clock when I reached the south coast. By then I was really hungry, but there was no time to eat.

Hastings has the reputation of being about the warmest place in England in the summer. It can also be one of the coldest in winter. There was little wind, and the Channel was sullenly grey, as were the clouds. Ice crackled beneath my boots as I hurried to the apartment building.

I took the lift and rang the bell, and after a moment the door was opened . . . by Ma. 'Frankie!' she cried. 'How lovely to see you. Damon said you were all tied up. But you only just caught me. I was just going out.'

I stepped inside and closed the door. 'You've seen Damon?'

'He's here now.'

'Well, hello, darling,' he said from the lounge doorway.

I looked from one to the other. He was as ebullient as ever, and Ma looked even more cheerful than usual. But that was in itself sinister.

'Where's Pa?' I demanded.

'At the pub.'

'The . . . Pa never goes to the pub.'

'He suddenly felt like it.'

I turned to Damon. 'You bastard!'

'Now, Frankie, dear, you mustn't be rude to your husband,' Ma said. 'I'm just going out for a few moments, and then I'll make us all a cup of tea.'

'Where are you going?'

'Just across the street, darling.'

I felt quite sick; he had got at them both. 'Oh no you don't,' I said.

'You can't tell your mother what she can or cannot do,' Damon protested.

'He is right, Frankie,' Ma said.

'You are going nowhere until we have sorted this out,' I

said. I tried to step past her to block the doorway, and Damon grasped my arm and jerked me to one side.

'You really are too old to be fighting like children,' Ma remonstrated. She stepped outside.

'Let me go!' I tugged at Damon.

'I ought to belt you a good one,' he said.

'And I ought . . .' Suddenly I wanted to do it. I grasped his arm, twisted and transferred all my weight as I had been taught to do at karate class. He gasped and sailed over my thigh to hit the floor with a thump.

I turned to the door to follow Ma, and he gave a shout and charged at me. I turned, hands poised, and legs as well, and as he came up to me swivelled on my left leg and kicked with my right. My boot caught him on the side of the jaw. He staggered backwards, then came back again.

This gave me the time to reach the door and pull it open. 'Mum!' I shouted. 'Where are you, Mum?' There was no reply. I ran outside, and listened to the lift. It was going down. Desperately I pushed the buttons, but there was no way I could stop it.

'Bitch!' Damon appeared in the doorway and lunged at me. I sidestepped, but he caught my sleeve and turned me against the wall. We cannoned together and both fell down. I kicked at him, and he seized my ankle, twisting it so that I squealed with pain and rolled over. He grasped my hair as he had done earlier and tugged on it, and I kicked backwards. He gave a grunt and fell over with a crash, thankfully releasing my hair.

A door opened on the floor below. 'Hello?' a man called. 'What's happening up there?'

That would be, as I recalled, Major Phillips, a retired army officer.

'Major,' I shouted. 'Call the police!'

'Oh, no, you don't,' Damon snarled, reaching for me again. I was on my feet now, and he gained his and charged at me. I realized there was no hope of reaching the lift, and opted for the stairs, and perhaps the support of the major, whose head now appeared at the bend in the staircase.

'Help me,' I begged.

Damon was now reaching for my throat. I gasped and turned in his arms, hitting him in the stomach with the flat of my hand, and then ducking and throwing him again, over my shoulder.

And straight down the stairwell.

The Court

'Now, Mrs Ogilvie,' Sir Barton said, in as soothing a tone as he could command. 'I know this is extremely distressing for you, but it is necessary, as I am sure you understand.'

'Yes,' Ma said, looking grimly determined.

'Let me begin by asking you how well you knew Sir Roderick Webster.'

'I never met him.'

'But you knew of him?'

'Well, of course. He employed Frankie— Frances. He was also her friend. They shared a house.'

'Was he, to your knowledge, ever her lover?'

'Not to my knowledge. And I shouldn't think he was.'

'Why do you hold that opinion?'

'From what Frances said, I understand that he was . . . well . . .'

'Gay?'

'I believe that is the word used nowadays, yes.'

'Very good. Now, as you have just said, Sir Roderick shared a house with Frances, and therefore also with her husband, Mr Damon Smith, who so tragically died at the beginning of this year.'

'Yes, he did.'

'Were he and Mr Smith good friends?'

'You could call them bosom buddies, again going by what Frances has told me.'

'You mean they were lovers?'

'I don't know about that. But they had been friends long before Damon met Frances.'

'What sort of opinion did you form of your son-in-law?'
'He was a thug.'
'Yet Frances was married to him for four years.'
'He dominated her.'
'How?'
Mummy shrugged. 'Just . . . dominated. He had a very forceful personality.'
'A very forceful personality. Now, I am sure you are aware, Mrs Ogilvie, that there has been a lot of talk in this case of Sir Roderick being murdered by means of some occult or hypnotic spell. Did the late Mr Smith ever give any indication or suggestion that he possessed occult or hypnotic powers?'
'Not to me.'
'Are you sure, Mrs Ogilvie?'
'Of course I'm sure. Don't you think I'd know?'
'Don't you think it's possible that he might have possessed such powers and used them to dominate Frances?'
'She never suggested that to me.'
'Again I know this must be painful for you, Mrs Ogilvie, but I would like you to take us through the events on the day Mr Smith died so tragically.'
'Well . . .' Ma licked her lips. 'Damon came to see us.'
'By himself?'
'Yes. Frances arrived later.'
'Did he often visit you alone?'
'This was the first time.'
'Were you surprised by this?'
'Not entirely.'
'Why not entirely?'
'I had expected him to come to see my husband and I at some stage. Frances was planning to leave him and obtain a legal separation preparatory to a divorce. I knew he did not wish this.'
'You mean, Frances had become tired of being dominated. Or was there another reason for her to seek a divorce?'
'I don't know the exact reasons behind her decision. She

did not confide in me, other than to tell me what she planned and to ask me to secure for her a pied-à-terre to which she could retire. I assumed that Damon had come to enlist my help in talking her out of her decision.'

'And had he?'

'I don't know.'

'I'm sorry. I don't understand that.'

'Well, we never actually got round to it. He came down, and . . .' She frowned, as if trying to remember.

'I know it must be traumatic for you, Mrs Ogilvie. But please try.'

'Well . . . we had lunch. He was at his very best. And when he was like that he could be very charming. Then, after the meal, he said he wanted to talk with me, and suggested that Harry – that's my husband – go out to the pub for an hour.' She frowned again, as Sir Barton spotted.

'Yes, Mrs Ogilvie?'

'It's just that . . . my husband never went to the pub. Certainly not on his own.'

'But he went on this occasion.'

'Yes. Yes, he did.'

'Leaving you and Mr Smith alone. What happened then? Did you quarrel?'

'Oh, no. As I said, he was most charming.'

'But he suggested that, instead of talking with him, you went out.'

'Just for a few minutes. He told me he wanted to have a very serious discussion with me about Frances, and that he felt, before we did, I should have an absolutely clear head, and that the best thing would be for me to take a brisk walk up and down the promenade and then return.'

'And you agreed to take this instruction from a man young enough to be your son, who was also your son-in-law?'

'Well . . . it seemed quite reasonable. At the time.'

'At the time. This was on an afternoon in January. Wasn't it very cold?'

'Oh, it was.'

'But you did not even wear a coat.'

'Damon said it would not be necessary.'

'Can you recall exactly what he told you to do? First of all, am I correct when I say that your apartment building was separated from the promenade by the main street of the town?'

'You could say that, yes.'

'This is a very busy street? But to reach the promenade you had to cross it. But Mr Smith no doubt suggested you exercise great care, because of the traffic and the slippery road.'

'No, he didn't,' Ma said, frowning again. 'He said to go downstairs and go straight across the road to the promenade.'

'Regardless of the traffic? With respect, Mrs Ogilvie, may I ask your age?'

'I am sixty-one years old.'

'I would say that is not really the ideal age to start dodging traffic on an icy road. But surely there were pedestrian crossings?'

'Oh, yes. There is one about a hundred yards away from the house.'

'And Mr Smith no doubt told you to be sure to use it.'

'No. He said not to use it, but to cross immediately in front of the house.'

'Did you not find this instruction somewhat odd?'

'I . . . I didn't at the time. I suppose I was preoccupied.'

'Just as your husband was so preoccupied that he went to the pub when it was not his custom to do so. Did it not occur to you that in obeying Mr Smith you might be risking serious injury or even death?'

'I . . . No, it didn't at the time.'

'And of course it did not occur to you that Mr Smith may have hypnotized you, and your husband, without your being aware of it.'

'Hypnotized? Why, good lord, no. How did he do that? How *could* he do that?'

'That is something we are going to have to find out. Now tell us what happened when you went downstairs. But first, before you went downstairs, Frances arrived. Is that correct?'

'Yes.'

'Was she pleased to find her husband there?'

'I don't think so. But he was pleased to see her. Until...'

'Yes? Until you told her you were going out for a few minutes? What was her reaction?'

'She told me I mustn't. She tried to stop me.'

'And what happened then?'

'Damon restrained her.'

'How did you feel about that? Did you interfere?'

'Well, no. They were husband and wife. And I...'

'You knew you needed to go out. Because Mr Smith had told you you had to. So you went out, and left them doing... what?'

'Well, sort of wrestling.'

'I see. Then you went down the stairs, and...?'

'I went on to the pavement...' Another frown.

'But you did not attempt to cross the road,' Sir Barton prompted.

'Why, no. There was too much traffic.'

'Yet when you went downstairs you were fully determined to cross the road, regardless of the traffic. But you suddenly realized that it was too dangerous.'

'Yes. Yes I did.'

'Do you think that might have been the precise moment that Mr Smith fell to his death?'

'I never thought of that,' Ma said.

'Are you now prepared to accept that you might have been hypnotized, without realizing it?'

'Well... I suppose it is possible.'

'And that your husband had also been hypnotized, without realizing it? Would you also be prepared to consider the possibility that your daughter may also have been hypnotized by this man? Perhaps even into marrying him?'

'Good lord!' Ma said, obviously considering it for the first time.

'Thank you, Mrs Ogilvie.'

Sir Barton sat down, and Mr Buckston stood up. Mr Buckston was clearly totally confused. Sir Barton had spent the entire first part of the trial deriding the idea that hypnosis could have had anything to do with Roddy's death; now suddenly he was acknowledging the possibility. He did not realize that this change of approach had been recommended by me to the Defence Counsel.

At the same time, incredibly, he seemed to be handing the Prosecution weapon after weapon. Knowing Sir Barton, Mr Buckston was properly suspicious of this. But he had to take his opportunity. 'Mrs Ogilvie, my learned friend has suggested that you and your husband, and your daughter, were from time to time hypnotized by this man Smith. You are prepared to accept that?'

'I suppose I am,' Ma said.

'Then you will also accept that this man made you do something that you would not normally have considered doing?'

'I suppose he did.'

'Then no doubt you would agree that in his ability to hypnotize your daughter, he would have been able to make her *do* something, or things, she would not normally do. Things which she might not even remember doing.'

'Perhaps.'

'Thank you, Mrs Ogilvie. I have no further questions.'

Buckston sat down. Everyone in the courtroom understood the point he had tried to make, but he had, in fact, fallen into Sir Barton's trap.

Sir Barton stood up. 'Just to recapitulate the last part of your evidence, Mrs Ogilvie, you have said that it never crossed your mind to disobey what Smith had told you to do until you were actually standing on the edge of the pavement, intending to cross the road. Only then did you realize the folly of what you were about to do.'

'Yes.'

'And you are agreed that this sudden realization happened at precisely the moment, or just after, that Smith fell down the stairwell to his death.'

'Yes. I hadn't realized that before.'

'Therefore it is fair to assume that any instructions given to you by Smith were cancelled by his death.'

'It seems so.'

'Now let us consider Mr Ogilvie. When did he return from the pub?'

'About ten minutes later.'

'Did he have any idea what had happened? Either that you had so nearly wandered on to a busy street to be knocked down, or that Smith was dead?'

'No. He told me he suddenly found himself in the pub, not really knowing how he had got there, or wanting to be there, and decided to come home.'

'Therefore, in his case as well, would you agree that his hypnosis ended with Smith's death?'

'It seems likely.'

'Therefore, would you agree that any other hypnotic commands given by Smith, or hypnotic trances induced by him, would also have, shall we say, been cancelled by his death?'

'I would say so.'

'Including any he may have given to your daughter, or any power he may have exercised over her?'

'Undoubtedly,' Ma said.

'Thank you, Mrs Ogilvie.'

Thirteen

The Lover

I knew from the sound of Damon's body striking the ground floor that he was dead. For a moment my brain went entirely blank.

'My God!' Major Phillips exclaimed. 'The fellow was attacking you!'

Precious words. 'The fellow was my husband, Major.'

'Your . . . My God!' He ran down the stairs. I followed. It would have been quicker to take the lift, but I was not thinking clearly. My brain was repeating, over and over again, I am free. It is over. I am free.

Major Phillips reached Damon's body first. 'My God!' he said a third time. 'Don't come any closer, Mrs Smith.'

I hesitated, but at last coherence was re-entering my brain. Ma! I didn't know what Damon had commanded her to do, but I didn't doubt it would have been something dangerous, if not fatal.

I ran out of the front door, across the small front yard and on to the pavement, and saw her standing, looking dazed, only feet from a bus which was just rumbling by. 'Mummy!' I shouted, and ran forward to grab her arm.

'Whatever is the matter?' she asked me.

'Damon! He's dead. He fell down the stairs.'

'Oh, dear,' she said. 'How sad.'

As I had immediately surmised, the presence of Major Phillips was an inestimable asset. He called the police, and virtually took charge of the proceedings, explaining that my husband had attacked me, that I had tried to fight him off, and that in the course of the struggle he had tumbled over the bannisters.

The police naturally wanted to know what the fight was about, and I had the satisfaction of telling them the simple truth: that I had been seeking a divorce and that when Damon realized he was not going to change my mind he had lost his temper and attacked me. This fitted perfectly well with events with which they were familiar in other marriages, and after taking a statement they departed behind the ambulance that conveyed Damon's body to the morgue.

And I could breathe again. And think again.

There was an awful lot to be thought about. In the short term, there were Ma and Pa. But they were actually no problem. Neither had the slightest idea that they might have been hypnotized, and I didn't press the point. They were desperate to be sympathetic to me in my bereavement, and I let them get on with it.

I still needed to think. I was a widow. I could not pretend to any grief. Damon had, on occasion, been a tremendous companion, and he had always been tremendous in bed. But I had never loved him: I had simply been his slave. Now I could not escape the feeling that, however inadvertently, I had rid the world of a serial killer. If I felt this was an occasion for celebration rather than mourning, I do not think I can be blamed.

The question I needed to resolve was, what exactly did Damon's death mean? Both Ma and Pa had awakened, as it were, from their hypnosis, the moment he had died. Did that mean that all the various hypnoses he had induced had also lost their power with his death? Addamms had said that this would not happen, that anyone hypnotized by Damon at the time of his death would remain like that for ever. That had to be rubbish, by the evidence of my own eyes. I wasn't thinking of myself, because I felt I had already broken the spell before his death. But what of Roddy? Did this mean he would be able to go out and get himself some handsome guy?

And what *of* Roddy, anyway? I had left him lying on the floor drugged to the eyeballs. He would be awake by now, and at the very least he'd be hopping mad.

What I had to discover was my own situation as Damon's widow; he had always kept me entirely in the dark as regards his financial affairs. I had not been required to do or sign anything regarding the house; therefore I had to assume that it was owned in Damon's name alone. However, the mortgage, which was still a considerable sum so far as I knew, had been arranged and was being paid off by Roddy. So my immediate future almost certainly depended on restoring and maintaining good relations with him.

I also needed to find out where I stood in day-to-day financial matters. I had that nest egg I had been able to save since our marriage, but that wasn't going to carry me very far without a job. Did I still have one?

Then there was Little Damon. But he at least should not be a problem. As a father Damon had been very much in the pat-on-the-head-at-bedtime class; I doubted Little Damon was even sure who he was.

But he was still alone in the house with Roddy and the servants. I needed to be there. So as soon as I could unload the police I took the train back to town. Ma and Pa would have preferred me to stay. They were both suffering from shock, the entire apartment block and its immediate neighbours were a buzz of rumour and speculation, and their lives in general had been turned on their heads. But they did understand that I felt that my first duty was to Little Damon. I promised to be in touch as soon as I could.

I approached the house with some anxiety. The taxi dropped me at the foot of the steps, and I went up them and let myself in with my own key, but naturally the merest sound at the door alerted Butterpaws, who began to bark, and this in turn alerted Horace, who came bustling into the hall. 'Madam?!' He seemed to suppose he was addressing a ghost, which indicated that Roddy was indeed up and about.

'The very person,' I said, and went up the stairs. 'Sir Roderick in?' I asked over my shoulder.

'Ah . . . yes, madam. I don't think he is feeling very well.'

'Oh, poor fellow. I must try to cheer him up.'

But I went first of all to the nursery, where Damon was being fed his supper by an anxious-looking Clara. 'Madam?' She was equally in the ghost-seeing mode.

'I told you I'd be back in a couple of hours,' I said.

'Yes, madam. Sir Roderick—'

'Isn't feeling very well. Horace told me.'

'Ah . . . yes,' she agreed, somewhat doubtfully.

'I'm afraid I have some rather sad news,' I said. 'Mr Smith is dead.'

'Madam?!!' Now she was flabbergasted.

'He fell down a flight of stairs.'

'Oh, madam!'

'Yes. Very sad.'

'But . . . the boy . . .' Little Damon was happily eating away.

'I'll explain it to him in due course,' I said. 'Now I'd better tell Sir Roderick.'

She stared at me, for the first time realizing that I was not exactly grief-stricken. I smiled at her, and went up the stairs to Roddy's apartment. I opened the door without knocking and went in. He was sitting in front of his television set, which happened to be switched on to international news. At the sound of my entry he turned his head and then leapt to his feet. 'If you come near me . . .'

'Relax.'

'You bitch. You—'

'Just simmer down, and sit down,' I advised. 'How do you feel?'

'Like shit. You—'

'You call me a bitch again, and I probably will hit you again,' I warned. 'I've something to tell you.' Slowly he lowered himself into his chair. I pulled up another to sit facing him. 'Damon is dead.' He stared at me, clearly not comprehending. 'Did you hear what I said? He's dead.'

'You killed him!'

'Of course I did not kill him. I'm not saying I didn't feel like it. But he attacked me, missed, and fell down the stairs. There was a witness.'

'He attacked you? Why?'

'I had asked him for a divorce. You saw how angry he was.'

Roddy scratched his head. 'Damon, dead! Jesus!' He looked at me. 'What are we going to do?'

'I would have supposed we should try to pick up what's left of our lives. That's why I asked, how do you feel?'

'How am I supposed to feel? Shattered.'

'I meant, do you think you are still hypnotized.'

'Well . . . I don't know. Do you think I'm not?'

'How should I know? What were Damon's instructions to you?'

'Ah . . .' He licked his lips.

'You can tell me,' I said. 'You weren't to have any boyfriends, right?'

'No,' he muttered. 'That didn't bother him. He knew I wasn't really gay.'

'Then what was it?' I was totally surprised.

He looked even more embarrassed. 'He said I wasn't ever to lay a finger on you.'

'Good God!' I could not stop myself from laughing. 'That explains an awful lot. What would happen to you if you did?'

'He never said. Just told me I wouldn't be able to.'

'Did you want to?'

'Well . . . shit. I've lain in bed wanking while I thought of you.'

I wasn't sure whether that was an answer or not. But I was lost for words. Here was a complete turn-up. The problem was that Roddy did nothing for me at all. But the situation had to be used for my advantage.

225

'Well,' I said. 'This is something that needs thinking about.'

'I don't suppose—'

'No,' I said. 'Not right now. For God's sake, I've just seen my husband turned into jam.'

'Ugh!'

'Absolutely. And we have a great deal to talk about.'

'Listen!' He leaned forward and held my hands. 'There's not going to be any problem. I'm going to give you shares in the firm. And you and Little Damon will go on living here. And everything is going to be all right.' His fingers squeezed mine. 'And then, well, maybe . . .'

'Maybe,' I promised him.

So I really had everything I wanted. As Damon had always kept a very low profile, his death was not widely known or cared about, except in the office, where I received a great deal of sympathy. Roddy and I attended the reading of the will, in which everything Damon had possessed was left to Little Damon. Mr Wright was a little upset about this, but I assured him it was all right by me, and as a matter of fact Damon had left only a few thousand pounds; this money was, with Wright's assent, placed in a savings account in Little Damon's name. Technically he now also owned the house, but Wright offered no objection to Roddy and I becoming his guardians, even if we had not been named in the will, especially as Roddy could prove that he was paying the mortgage.

Damon was cremated the next day. As he had never, to my knowledge, been inside a church in his life, I had a bit of a problem to persuade any parson to carry out the service, but eventually I succeeded, and I watched the coffin disappearing behind the curtain with a great deal of satisfaction. When I was presented with the urn I poured the ashes down the toilet and flushed it several times.

Then I had to go back down to Hastings to attend the inquest. This gave me the opportunity to visit Ma and Pa and reassure them that everything was under control. The inquest itself did not present a problem. Major Phillips was there to corroborate everything I had to say, and everyone was most sympathetic.

I spent the night with Ma and Pa and returned to town the next morning. I think it was on the train that I began to realize that I really was free. Up to then I kept expecting Damon suddenly to reappear. If he really was a creature of the occult this did not seem the least unlikely. But now it was all over.

So what was I going to do? Why, I thought, whatever turns me on. I was twenty-seven years old, I was good-looking and healthy, if I wasn't rich I was quite comfortably well off, and I was a widow. I didn't really want to do anything right then, especially something like getting married again, or even accumulating a partner. I was just realizing what a trauma I had been through over the past five years, the crimes to which I had been a party, the understanding that for those five years I had been virtually a zombie.

But the future, the freedom to which I felt I could now aspire, was blocked by Roddy. I might not wish any emotional entanglements at the moment, but I also knew that he would not allow me to have any, except with him. Equally I could not brush him aside; I was too closely bound to him. To break with him would not only mean starting my life again from scratch, with no home and no job, and a son to care for, it would also expose me to a counter-attack, as it were, if he were so disposed, and I did not doubt that he would be so disposed – he had a very mean streak. And he knew all about Damon's crimes, crimes to which I had apparently raised no objection. I did not suppose that for me to stand up in court and claim that I had been hypnotized into not doing anything about them would go down very well.

So, Roddy had to be accepted, in every way. Oddly enough, however, he did not press the point at all, although I had expected him to. I really didn't know whether to be relieved or piqued. But I was definitely piqued, at least in the first instance, when he started working late at the office; then I realized that if he was using his new-found freedom to have it off with somebody else, that had to be good news.

I was human enough to be curious, however, and asked Louise if she knew anything about it; I half suspected it might be herself, although she was no beauty. But she disclaimed any knowledge of what the boss might be doing at night; he had never required her to stay after hours.

For what I did next, I can only put forward my own feelings of insecurity; I was terribly aware that, for the immediate future at least, my home and my prosperity, and that of my son, depended upon Roddy's goodwill, and if he were to take up with any other woman on a permanent basis it could be very difficult. Certainly I felt I needed to know who my rival was, especially as he seemed so determined to keep her identity a secret that he had never brought her home.

I checked with Hatch, the night porter, but he had no record of anyone entering or leaving the building after hours, save for the boss himself, who, on the nights he worked late, usually departed about midnight, as I could confirm, for although I was always in bed by then, I often heard his feet on the stairs.

I found this even more sinister, as it meant he was letting whoever it was into the building by the private entrance. Supposing there was anyone.

I was becoming quite obsessed by the situation. There was, of course, a simple way of discovering the truth of the matter. That I did not immediately take this course was because I knew it would almost certainly involve a quarrel with Roddy. But at last I could stand it no longer, and an evening having arrived when Roddy did not come in to dinner, I saw Damon to bed, said goodnight to Clara, and told Horace I was going to bed, waited for him to do likewise, and then let myself out.

It was a warm summer night, so I did not need a coat; I wore black pants and blouse, black crêpe-soled shoes, and tied up my hair in a black headscarf. Feeling very much a femme fatale I walked for two blocks before picking up a taxi, which I had drop me two blocks away from Randell &

Company. Then I watched it go out of sight before turning down the side street that led to the back of the property. I had my key, of course, but the door was unlocked, which clearly indicated that someone else was using it tonight. I stepped into the darkness at the foot of the stairs, and waited for several seconds to get my breathing under control. Then I went up, very slowly and carefully.

There was a light on at the top, illuminating the rest of the gallery. From where I was I could see Hatch, seated at his desk in the outer office and reading a newspaper; his back was to me. I tiptoed along the gallery, past my office and Louise's — both were in darkness, naturally. The door to Roddy's office was also closed, but the lights were on inside — I could see the glimmer under the door. I took a deep breath and knocked, very gently. 'It's open,' he said.

I turned the handle and pushed it in.

'You're early,' he said.

I gazed at him in amazement, because he was standing in front of his desk, stark naked save for his medallion.

He gazed at me in equal consternation. 'What the . . .'

'Just passing by. I think I should leave again.'

'Come in, and shut the door.'

I hesitated, then obeyed. I was intrigued to see how he proposed to handle this.

'You are spying on me,' he said.

'I'd like to know who your friend is.'

He smiled. His expression made me think of a wolf. 'At the moment, you are.'

'Yes. Well, I don't want to interrupt anything, so . . .'

I turned back to the door, and had my shoulders seized. He was right against me, his arms round my waist and his hands grasping my breasts. 'Everything comes to he who waits,' he whispered into my ear as he kissed it.

'Get off,' I said, hitting behind me with my elbows. But his arms were outside mine, and as I had always suspected, he was far stronger than he looked. As I tried to hit backwards, he moved backwards himself, carrying me with him, so that my feet slipped and before I knew what was happening, I was stretched on the carpet, with him kneeling above me. He was actually astride my thighs, which meant he could get at my belt to release my pants. This also meant I could sit up, however, which I did, swinging my hand. But again he reacted first, swinging his own hand to strike me on the side of the head with such force that for a few seconds I was senseless. I must have fallen back on to the carpet, because when I came to I was again flat on my back, and Roddy had pulled my pants right off and was tugging down my thong. He was panting with passion, red in the face, and hugely erected. Now he had the thong off, and was pulling my legs apart, while I was still too dazed to do anything about it.

Then he gave a great sigh, and fell on me.

Fourteen

The Arrest

I knew instantly that he was dead. To say that I was scared stiff would be to put it mildly. Because I also knew how he had died.

I had to force myself to do it, but I touched the medallion. Roddy's body was already cold, but the medallion felt warm, at least to my touch.

I found I was panting; this might have been a result of his dropping on to my stomach, but it was really a mixture of fear and apprehension. Slowly I pushed him off me. He rolled on to his side.

I sat up, then stood up, and dressed myself. I looked around the office. There was no sign of any struggle, or disturbance, save for the naked body on the floor. I thought of taking off the medallion, but decided against it. For one thing, I didn't want to touch him, and for another, I didn't want to touch the medallion. Damon had done his work from beyond the grave; I wanted that to be the end of it.

Very carefully I opened the door and stepped on to the gallery. Hatch continued to read his newspaper, his back to me. Even more carefully I closed the door behind me. I considered switching off the light, but decided against that too. I wanted it to be as if I had never been there, because as far as I was concerned, I had never been there.

I tiptoed along the gallery and down the private staircase. I opened the private door and stepped into the night. Again I thought of changing the scenario by locking this door, and again I decided against it.

I remained standing there for several moments, trying to get my thoughts under control, and heard the tapping of heels, loud in the silence of the night. I moved away from the doorway, silently in my crêpe soles, rounded the corner of the building, and waited, confident that I was invisible in my black gear.

I watched Jane Randell come down the alleyway.

It was as if a thousand light bulbs were suddenly illuminated inside my brain. Jane and her brothers, so utterly unrelated to any of us, so far as we had imagined, had somehow known the very day that Damon was leaving for his trip to the Bahamas. I had gone missing for several hours, and Roddy had not even made any effort to discover whether there might have been an accident. And the ransom had been the return of Randell's to its rightful owners. Roddy had wanted to do that, but he had not dared go against Damon's plans, save by being able to say, 'I had to do it to save Frances's life.'

The bastard!

And now the door was open, and Jane was stepping inside, pausing only to take off her shoes. I waited while she closed the door behind herself, waited again to give her time to go up the stairs, then darted forward and opened the door. As I had suspected, she had left the shoes on the mat. I picked one up, stepped back into the night, closed the door, and hurried into the darkness.

As far as I was concerned, she deserved everything that might be coming to her.

In taking Jane's shoe I was acting entirely on instinct; I had no clear idea what I was going to use it for. Obviously she was innocent of Roddy's death, but I knew even then that it might be useful, or even essential, for me to be able to prove that she had been there. Much might depend on how she handled the situation.

In the event, she handled it very well, and apparently, on not receiving a reply to her knock on Roddy's door, although she must have been able to see the line of light, had simply left again. I could not imagine what she felt about her missing shoe; presumably she had concluded she had misplaced it in the dark and had not been prepared to risk the time in searching for it.

The first I officially knew of what had happened was a frantic telephone call from Hatch at seven the next morning. I was already up; although I had regained the house and my bed without awaking anyone, I had not slept very well. Now I simply finished dressing and hurried down to the office, where I found a crowd of people . . . but not Jane.

Brumby had been called, of course, and I was more amused than concerned to see his friend Prendergast arrive a few minutes later. The police had immediately sealed off Roddy's office, and indeed the whole upstairs floor, which made it quite impossible to conduct any business – I sent all the staff home and closed the firm for the rest of the week.

'When will I be able to open up again?' I asked the inspector in charge.

'Just the moment we have completed our investigations, Mrs Smith,' he assured me.

'You mean you are treating Sir Roderick's death as murder?'

'Suspicious circumstances, ma'am. Suspicious circumstances.'

I tried to find out from Brumby what these suspicious circumstances were, as it seemed clear that Roddy had died of a heart attack, but he merely mumbled that the matter was *sub judice* and could not be discussed.

I let them get on with it, as I did not see how the most ambitious policeman could possibly turn Roddy's death into a case of murder, and even if someone could do that, there was no way I could be involved.

I was more interested in the reading of Roddy's will. This took place in Wright's chambers as usual, and I was interested to discover that apart from myself, the only people present were Jane Randell and Mitchell, her solicitor.

I immediately understood what had happened, and thanked my lucky stars that I had had the foresight to snaffle that shoe.

Wright, needless to say, was in a state of some agitation at what he had to say. 'I'm afraid this is a very straightforward document,' he explained. 'Apart from some money in a bank account, Sir Roderick's sole assets consisted of his shares in Randell & Company. These have been valued at fourteen million pounds. And the entire portfolio has been bequeathed to Miss Jane Randell.'

He paused, and there was silence for a few seconds. Then Jane smiled. 'Thank you, Mr Wright. May I ask how soon I take control of the firm?'

'Ah . . . well . . .' He gave me an anxious glance. 'There are formalities to be undertaken regarding the transfer, but, well, I suppose you control the firm as of this moment.'

'Thank you,' she said again. 'Then I shall go down to the office this afternoon. I should like you to be there, Mrs Smith, so that you may formally hand over the business.'

'I think there are certain aspects of the situation that we need to discuss,' I said.

'I can't think of any,' Jane said. 'As of this moment, you are sacked. It is simply a matter of handing over your office.'

'I still think we need to have a meeting, in private,' I said.

She gazed at me for several seconds. Up to that minute she had felt perfectly secure, in that it was now getting on for a year since the kidnap, and she had to assume that had I any proof to bring against them I would already have done so. Now she was beginning to wonder. 'Very well,' she agreed.

'I'm sure you gentlemen will excuse us,' I said, and led her from the office.

'There is a coffee shop just round the corner,' she suggested.

'I'd prefer it if you came home.'

'To your place?' She was suspicious.

'Yes.' We had reached the pavement, and I signalled a taxi. 'I've something to show you.'

We drove in silence for a little while, then she said, 'I think you should know that I have a supported alibi for that night.'

'Which night?' I asked.

She glared at me, and the taxi stopped. Horace opened the door for us, and Butterpaws gave us his usual exuberant greeting.

'Ugh!' Jane commented. 'I have dog hairs all over me.'

'Better than being bitten,' I pointed out. 'We'll have coffee in the lounge, Horace. But you'll want to come upstairs first, Jane.'

'Will I?' But curiosity got the better of her, and she followed me up the stairs. 'I may buy this house off you,' she remarked. 'It's rather grand.'

'I intend to go on living here,' I told her, opening the door to my suite.

'What on? Isn't there rather a large mortgage outstanding?' She followed me into the room.

'I'm sure you'll continue to pay that for me.'

'You really do have an inflamed imagination.'

'I prefer to think that I have a grasp on reality.' I opened my wardrobe, stooped, and took out the shoe. 'How did you manage that night on one shoe?'

She stared at me. 'You bitch! You were there! You killed him!'

'Be real. Nobody killed him. He died of a heart attack.'

'But you were there!'

'There is nobody in the world that can prove that. But I can prove that *you* were there.'

Another glare. 'You have just said he wasn't murdered.'

'Well,' I said, 'not so that anyone will ever be able to prove it. But still, if the police discover that you were there that night, they are going to have to ask a lot of questions, some of which you might find a little tricky to answer.'

'You can't go to the police with that shoe without admitting you were there yourself.'

'So we'll be in the dock together.'

'Look, I never even got in to him. The door was locked.'

'You could have a problem proving that too.'

'You . . . What do you want?'

'Very little. I wish to retain my job and my position in the firm. And I wish you to continue paying the mortgage.'

'And if I agree to those terms, you will give me back my shoe?'

'No,' I said.

As far as I was concerned, my victory was complete. It was a fortnight later that the blow fell, entirely without warning.

I was seated at my desk when Louise tapped on the door. 'Excuse me, Mrs Smith, but there are two gentlemen here to see you.'

'Me? Clients? Can't they be taken care of downstairs?'

Louise looked even more flustered than usual. 'They aren't clients, Mrs Smith. They're police officers.'

I couldn't imagine what they could possibly want. 'Well, then, you'd better show them in.'

She did so, and I felt my first pang of uneasiness.

'Good morning, Mrs Smith. My name is Detective-Inspector Roberts. And this is Detective-Sergeant Borrow. I believe you have met.'

'Yes,' I said, hoping my feelings weren't showing. 'We have met. Do sit down.'

The two detectives seated themselves before the desk. As the office door remained open, I could hear Louise's buzzer; Jane wanted to find out what was going on.

'Now,' I said. 'What can I do for you?'

'We are here regarding the death of Sir Roderick Webster,' Roberts said.

I waited.

'We were wondering if you would care to add anything to what we already know.'

'I'm afraid that I know absolutely nothing about his death,' I said. 'Other than it happened.'

'It has been determined, by forensic and, er, other evidence, that he may well have been murdered.'

'Good lord! But . . . how?'

'We were hoping that perhaps you might be able to assist us in reaching a conclusion on that.'

'Me? Why me?'

'Simply that, amongst Sir Roderick's effects, in his safe deposit box at his bank, as a matter of fact, we found this letter.'

Sergeant Borrow took the sheet of paper from his briefcase and held it up.

'I'm sorry,' I said. 'I can't read it from there.' I held out my hand.

'The sergeant will read it to you,' Roberts said. 'It is very brief.'

'To whom it may concern,' Borrow read. 'In the event of anything untoward happening to me, and particularly with regard to my sudden death from apparently natural causes, I wish it to be known that I have been murdered by means of an occult spell placed upon me by Damon Smith and his wife, Frances Smith. So help me God. Roderick Webster.'

The sergeant raised his head to look at me, as the inspector was also doing.

'Oh, come now,' I protested, refusing to give way to the fear that was building within me. 'Surely you can see that is the purest nonsense? Sir Roderick and my husband were the closest of friends. They had been friends all of their lives. We shared the same house.'

'My first reaction was to treat the letter as immaterial,' Roberts said. 'Until I began to study the facts. Which are that Sir Roderick died in a totally inexplicable fashion, as had Mr James Randell before him, virtually in the same spot. Then I was approached by Dr Brumby and his associate, Dr Prendergast, with the suggestion that there was something, shall I say, uncanny about Sir Roderick's death. Even then

I was reluctant to proceed, until Sergeant Borrow here came to me and told me how, five years ago, a woman psychiatrist had died in peculiar circumstances, committing suicide when there was no reason for her to do so, after behaving in a very odd fashion . . . and after spending the evening with you.'

I opened my mouth, and then closed it again. My instincts were warning me that to attempt to involve Damon at this stage, and without being able to produce a shred of proof, might well be counter-productive, to say the least. In any event, I did not see how they could possibly make such a charge stick.

'Would you care to comment, Mrs Smith?' Roberts asked.

'No,' I said. 'Save to say your speculations are the height of absurdity. I think I need to speak with my solicitor.'

'I am sure that would be very wise,' he agreed. 'In the meantime, I have applied for and obtained a warrant for your arrest on a charge of murder. You do not have to say anything in response to this charge, but . . .'

The Court

'The accused will take the stand.'

I walked the short distance from the dock to the witness box, without actually looking at anyone. I was wearing a black dress and shoes, and had my hair dressed as demurely as possible. This was the crunch of the trial, and I at least had no doubt as to the outcome.

I took the oath, stated my name and age and address, and faced Sir Barton, who was beaming at me most benevolently. 'Mrs Smith, you have already, at the commencement of this trial, pleaded not guilty to the charge that you caused the death of Sir Roderick Webster. I will now ask you again, were you in any way responsible for his death?'

'Not to my knowledge.'

'Were you and Sir Roderick friends?'

'We lived in the same house.'

'And you were friends,' he insisted.

'Of course. He had been best man at my wedding, and he was godfather to my son.'

'There were also some financial matters?'

'Well, yes. He was a wealthy man, and although the house was registered in my husband's name, it was Roddy— Sir Roderick who was paying the mortgage.'

'So, now that he is dead, who will take on this responsibility?'

I glanced over the crowded courtroom. I knew that Jane was somewhere there, but I couldn't spot her. Not that I had any fear she would let me down.

'*I shall have to make other arrangements,*' I said. '*If I can.*'

'*Quite. Now, am I right in saying that Sir Roderick was also your employer?*'

'*Sir Roderick owned the firm in which I am a partner.*'

'*Will you continue as a partner?*'

'*I really don't know. That will be up to the new owner.*'

'*This must all be very difficult for you. Would I be right in assuming that the very last thing you wanted to happen was the death of this man, who was both your friend and benefactor?*'

'*I would prefer him to be alive, yes.*'

'*Now, I must ask you this, Mrs Smith, because if I don't, someone else will.*' He glanced at Buckston. '*How long did you know Sir Roderick?*'

'*About five years.*'

'*Where did you meet?*'

'*In the Bahamas. I was on holiday there.*'

'*Was this the same time as you met your late husband?*'

'*Yes.*'

'*They were close friends, so would I be right in assuming that you met them together?*'

'*Yes.*'

'*But you married Mr Smith, and not Sir Roderick. Yet you remained close friends, even to sharing your house. Now, Mrs Smith, the question I have to ask you is this: during these five years of considerable intimacy between yourself and Sir Roderick, were you ever lovers?*'

'*Certainly not.*'

'*He never attempted to make advances to you? Not even after your husband died and you continued to live under the same roof?*'

'*No.*'

'*Can you account for this? You are a very beautiful woman.*'

'*I have never considered the matter.*' I allowed myself a smile. '*Either my beauty, if it exists, or Sir Roderick's reaction to it.*'

'Or his non-reaction,' Sir Barton commented. 'Is it possible that Sir Roderick's failure to, ah, react to your charms was because, as has been suggested, he was homosexual?'

'I know absolutely nothing about Sir Roderick's sexual mores, Sir Barton. It is at least equally possible that Sir Roderick never made advances to me because he is – was – an entirely honourable man.'

'Oh, quite. Well, Mrs Smith, it remains only for me to ask you to account for your movements on the night Sir Roderick died.'

'I'm afraid I did very little. I remember being somewhat tired, so I had an early dinner, said goodnight to my son and the servants, and went to bed.'

'This has been attested to by your butler and your child's nanny. And when did you awake?'

'I was awakened by a telephone call from Mr Hatch to tell me that Sir Roderick had been found dead.'

'Very good. Now, Mrs Smith, it is necessary for us to consider this business of hypnotism. Were you, at any time during your relationship, hypnotized by your husband?'

'Yes.'

That caused a stir, and Lord Mahaig had to use his gavel.

'Can you tell us how this happened, and what were the consequences?'

'I think Damon hypnotized me on the very day we met, and kept me in a state of at least semi-hypnosis for the rest of our married life.'

More sensation.

Sir Barton waited for the noise to subside. Then he said, 'That is a remarkable admission, Mrs Smith. Were you aware of being in this state?'

'Yes.'

'And did you not resent it?'

'From time to time.'

'But you continued to live with him.'

'I didn't have much choice,' I pointed out, 'as I was

hypnotized. But actually, Damon was a marvellous husband, loving and caring. He was also the father of my son. I really had no wish to leave him, for a long time.'

'But eventually you did, as your mother has testified.'

'Yes.'

'How did you manage to do that, if you were hypnotized?'

'The hypnosis had worn off.'

'You knew this?'

'I had slowly become aware of it.'

'And you realized how much you had resented it all of those years.'

'Yes.'

'So you made plans to leave your husband, and he found out about it, and you had that quarrel in your parents' flat in Hastings, which resulted in your husband falling down the stairwell. How did you feel about that?'

'I was very upset.'

'Quite. Now, Mrs Smith, I must ask you this final question: during those years when you feel you were hypnotized, you say you were aware of being in that state.'

'Yes.'

'How did this awareness manifest itself?'

'I couldn't bring myself to leave him. I thought of it several times, but I could never do it. I tried to, but he would simply tell me to forget it, and I did.'

'In other words, thanks to this hypnosis, your husband completely dominated you.'

'Yes, he did.'

'He made you do whatever he told you to.'

'Not really. He merely did not allow me to do anything he did not wish me to do.'

'I see. You mean, during this most unusual relationship, Mr Smith never actually commanded you to do anything?'

'Nothing out of the ordinary.'

'He never gave you a command and then told you to forget it when you woke?'

'No. He never hypnotized me again after the first time.'
'Thank you, Mrs Smith.'
Sir Barton gave me an encouraging smile as he sat down. Mr Buckston stood up.
'Mrs Smith, you have testified that your husband kept you in a state of permanent hypnosis over a period of five years. However remarkable this may be, you have admitted this.'
'Yes.'
'But you also claim that throughout those five years he never actually gave you a command. Surely that is not realistic.'
'I never said he did not give me a command,' I countered. 'He gave me two commands. One was that I should always be his woman, and the other was that I should never have an affair with another man.'
'I see.' Mr Buckston looked around the court as if wondering how many of the women present would have accepted such a situation. 'And that was the sole basis of your relationship until just before his death.'
'It was.'
'But you have also stated that this hypnosis' – he looked down at his notes – '"wore off" just before his death. How were you aware of this? Was there a sudden click in your brain, or' – his turn to beam at the jury – 'a sudden blinding flash of light?'
'I knew it had worn off,' I replied calmly, 'because when I made one of my attempts to defy him, something I had tried several times in the past without success, I suddenly found I could do it.'
'Then no doubt you are to be congratulated, if what you say is true. However, I very much doubt that it is true. Mrs Smith, I put it to you that everything you have told this court is a pack of lies, and that you have been, and are, withholding the true facts of this case.'
I could only wait while he stared at me for several seconds.
'I put it to you, Mrs Smith, that while you may be telling

the truth when you say that your husband hypnotized you in the first instance, far from keeping you in that state, he made you into his willing accomplice by teaching you, shall we say, the tricks of the trade, so that you became quite as adept as himself at controlling people.'

'That is not true,' I said.

'Tell me this: does the name Jetta Smith-Lucas mean anything to you?'

Sir Barton stirred. 'Objection. Irrelevant.'

'Is this person relevant, Mr Buckston?' Lord Mahaig inquired.

'She is, m'lud.'

'Perhaps you will tell us why. But first . . .' He looked at me. 'Is the name familiar to you, Mrs Smith?'

'Mrs Smith-Lucas was my psychiatrist, briefly, five years ago, m'lud.'

'I see. Well, perhaps she may be relevant. Overruled, Sir Barton. Continue, Mr Buckston.'

'You have acknowledged knowing Mrs Smith-Lucas,' Buckston said. 'Indeed, if she was your psychiatrist, it could be said that you knew her intimately. Or certainly, that she knew you intimately.'

'I wouldn't say so,' I said. 'I had one psychiatric session with her, and that was all.'

'Why was there only one session?'

I shrugged. 'We realized we weren't on the same wavelength.'

'But you saw her again.'

'Yes. She came to my flat about three weeks later.'

'Why?'

'She said it was to give me my bill.'

'But that wasn't the reason?'

'It didn't seem like a reason to me. She could have mailed the account.'

'Then why did she come to see you?'

I had already made up my mind how I was going to have to handle this. To give even an inkling of the truth, to mention

Damon in connection with Jetta in any way, could involve me in becoming an accessory to her death, and would certainly involve me in a perjury charge, as I had lied under oath at the coroner's inquest. So I merely smiled at the jury, and said, 'I think she fancied me.'

More stir.

'You'll forgive me, Mr Buckston,' Lord Mahaig remarked, 'but I have yet to hear anything about this woman' – he glanced at his notes – 'Smith-Lucas to indicate that she has any relevance to this case.'

'I am coming to that now, m'lud. The night that Mrs Smith-Lucas visited Mrs Smith was the night that she died.'

Everyone perked up at that, including Lord Mahaig.

'Am I not right, Mrs Smith?' Mr Buckston asked.

'Yes,' I agreed.

'Can you recall for the court what happened?'

'Mrs Smith-Lucas called at my flat, we had a conversation, and she left again.'

'Just like that. Whereupon she went home, apparently undressing herself as she did so, and on reaching her home, after walking for five miles in the pouring rain, she committed suicide.'

'So I believe, yes.'

'What were your reactions to this?'

'When I heard about it the next day, I was terribly shocked.'

'But you felt no responsibility.'

'Only in that, by spurning her advances, I may have contributed to her mood of despair.'

'This worried you. In fact, you telephoned her on more than one occasion before you were informed of her death.'

'Well, she was acting very oddly before she left my flat. Such as insisting on walking home five miles through the rain. I was worried for her. I wanted to be sure she had reached home safely.'

'And had she?'

'I don't know. I only got the ansaphone.'

'Mrs Smith, I put it to you that, for some reason you have not disclosed, whether it was a lovers' quarrel or some other cause, you hypnotized Mrs Smith-Lucas into taking off all of her clothes and then committing suicide when she returned home.'

'That is absolute nonsense.'

'I also put it to you that, again using the occult powers taught to you by your husband, you hypnotized Sir Roderick Webster into taking off all his clothes, and dying, again for some reason you have not disclosed.'

'That also is absolute nonsense,' I said.

Afterwards

It took the jury only half an hour to acquit me of the charge against me. Lord Mahaig's summing-up was very much in my favour, and Sir Barton made an impressive closing speech. Mr Buckston could only point out the obvious: that I had been closely connected to several inexplicable deaths – thank heavens no one brought up Anthony Taggart or appeared to know anything about Clermont in the Bahamas – but as Lord Mahaig pointed out, nothing had been produced to prove that I had had anything to do with those deaths, save proximity.

In any event, by now the media was far more interested in my story, and I received, and eventually accepted, an offer from a tabloid for a series of articles on living under hypnosis for five years; this not only took care of Sir Barton's fee, but added a substantial sum to my nest egg.

Then it was celebrations all round. For this last day of the trial, Randell & Company had closed, and nearly all the staff were there to shake my hand and hug and kiss me. Even Jane joined in the congratulations, apparently as willing as everyone else to believe that everything I had said or done over the past five years was a result of my hypnosis, and was thus to be forgiven.

I was in seventh heaven. I was free. My life was mine to do with as I chose, regardless of any other consideration. And the first thing I wanted, after so long, was a man, on sexual terms – or better yet, on my terms.

Jeremy was in the throng, as enthusiastically congratulating me as everyone else. So when he hugged me I said, 'Why don't you take me home. As soon as we can get away.'

'You bet,' he murmured. He might not know how, or why, my being hypnotized might have interfered with our earlier encounter, but he was certainly willing to have another go.

We took a taxi. Horace opened the door for us; it was the first time I had been home in six months.

'Madam,' he said. 'Oh, madam! You're—'

'Acquitted, Horace,' I said, and stooped to give Butterpaws a hug. 'I bet you've forgotten me.'

But he hadn't.

'Master Damon is out with Clara, madam,' Horace said.

Damon had of course come to visit me twice a week while I had been on remand; he really wasn't old enough yet to fully understand what was going on. My task was to make him forget it had ever happened.

But first . . . 'This is Mr Nichols, Horace,' I said. 'He has come home to help me celebrate. We'll have a bottle of champagne.'

'Of course, madam.'

I led Jeremy into the lounge.

'Some place you have here,' he said admiringly.

'I'll show you upstairs after we've had a drink.'

He licked his lips, turned towards me, and checked. I realized that Horace had come into the room behind us.

'Yes, Horace?' He was carrying a tray, but without any champagne on it.

'I thought you might like this, madam. I found it in Sir Roderick's room when I was going through it. While you were . . . away.'

I stared at him in consternation, and then at the locket lying on the tray. I looked at Jeremy, who of course had no idea that anything was wrong. But everything was wrong. I no longer wanted to have sex with him – or with anyone. My set-to with Damon had been only a set-to, such as we had had often in the past, and from which he would, as always in the past, have emerged the victor, had he not fallen down the stairs. He would continue to control me from beyond the grave. I would never be free, to the end of my days.

Then I thought, like hell. 'I don't want this anymore, Horace. It reminds me too much of Mr Smith. What I would like you to do is place it in the incinerator, turn the heat up to maximum, and leave it there until it has melted to a liquid, then pour the liquid away.'

'But madam . . . this is solid gold.'

I smiled at Jeremy; I knew it was only going to be a matter of time – until the incinerator had done its stuff. 'There are some things that are worth more than money, Horace,' I said.